January Dreams

CARRIGAN RICHARDS

January Dreams
By Carrigan Richards

Copyright © 2021 Carrigan Richards
ISBN: 979-8-9858225-4-0
First Edition published 2016
Second Edition

Published by Carrigan Richards Publishing, LLC

Cover design by Nick Taylor.
Edited by Lindsey Alexander.
www.readinglisteditorial.com

To learn more about author Carrigan Richards, visit her website at www.carriganrichards.com

ACKNOWLEDGMENTS

Thank you to all of my readers and fans. You are truly amazing. Thank you for your support and love!

Angie – thank you for your unconditional love and friendship. Laura, you are incredible, and I don't know what I'd do without your friendship. Nicole, thank you for always being my friend, no matter what. Jennifer, thank you.

Sarah – thanks for being a great friend, a fan, and your kindness. Nick Taylor – this cover is beautiful! Thank you! Lindsey Alexander – thank you for your valuable advice and editing. You're amazing.

To my mom and Rob; my dad; Patrick, Morgan, and Alison. Thank you for your support and for cheering me on. I love all of you.

To my dad, for believing in me every step of the way.

All that we see or seem
Is but a dream within a dream.
—Edgar Allan Poe, A Dream Within a
Dream

One

Through the thick fog, I see a silhouette of a man, sauntering toward me. He is tall, lanky. I can't see his face. I'm on my knees, in the middle of a forest, breathing hard as if I ran for miles. The leafless trees sway from the building wind. The cold is almost paralytic over my body, and I do my best to stay alert of the mysterious man's approach. He doesn't seem to be in a rush as he keeps walking a steady pace.

"Well, hello traitor," he speaks in a deep voice.

He found us and he's going to kill me. "Please, don't," I beg.

"You knew this would happen when you ran away with him."

"I never meant to hurt you. Please!"

Clouds drift across the moon as rain starts pouring heavily, pounding into the ground. Stumbling to my feet, I start running.

Faster.

Fear grips me.

"You can't run from me," the man screams.

I pick up my speed, letting branches and wet leaves slap my face.

He found us. It was stupid to run away. I know Casper is my enemy, but I love him.

"Megan!" I hear Casper's voice.

With a sharp intake of breath, I come to a halt looking for him. My heart knocks against my ribs and an unusual excitement rushes through me.

"Casper." I whisper once I see him running toward me.

"You won't take her away." He runs past me clashing with the dangerous man. The two of them wrestle until a gunshot echoes in the night. I jump losing my breath.

Neither of them moves.

No.

"Casper?" I warily move toward them.

"Megan, are you okay?" I relax when I hear his voice.

Pushing the man off him, he gets to his feet and rushes up to me.

His beautiful, brown eyes are intense as he checks me for injuries. Rain drips from his bleach blonde hair that stops right above his eyes.

Placing my hands on either side of his angular face, I rub the slight stubble of his cheeks. "Casper," I say. I'm shaking, not only from the cold. "He was going to kill us."

"Are you sure this is what you want? Being with me is dangerous."

"I'm not leaving you. I love you. I don't care that we're enemies."

His soft hand touches my face, and I close my eyes loving his warmth. "I will protect you with my life."

What a foolish mess I've gotten us both into.

"We'll go back for the Nuummite Jewel when it's safer. It's too dangerous right now. We have to find another way."

"But without it, you're not immortal."

"It doesn't matter."

How can he say this? The Jewel is the only thing protecting him and we don't have it. I can't bear the thought of Casper dying.

"Everything will be okay, Megan."

I wake with a start, sitting upright with my hand to my chest, trying to calm my pounding heart. What was that?

It was a dream. That's all.

Savannah, my mini-Jack Russell, burrows out from under the covers and sneezes. She yawns and stretches while looking at me sleepily.

I settle back against my pillow, calmer now. The fear of someone trying to kill me still grips my insides. And the intense feeling I got when Casper looked at me. Why on earth did I dream about *Casper*? Ugh. It's not like I've been thinking about him or anything.

I hate Casper Truitt. Actually, hate is such a nice word for the way I feel about him. He has no regard for anyone but himself and isn't afraid to let anyone know. He hails from a stupid rich family and probably bathes in hundred dollar bills every night, at least that's what Cherry and I joke about.

My room is dark, and I relax a little thinking I have a couple more hours before I have to get up. When I check my clock, I curse, realizing I forgot to set the antiquated alarm. One hour late. I'm used to my phone where I program it and not have to worry about it, but Mom took it away.

I kick off the covers and rush through my morning routine. Great way to start the week.

Grabbing my backpack, keys, purse, coat, I breeze by my goodbyes to my dogs, all five of them, and run out the door. Luckily, my old as dirt car starts without too much issue and I carefully speed through the neighborhood to get to school. I hope I can get there before the bottom falls out. A storm is coming, and it doesn't look like it'll be brief.

I scramble out of my car and rush to the front office. When I open the door, I see Mrs. McCarthy dressed in a pumpkin outfit. *Crap*. It's Halloween and Cherry is going to kill me. I completely forgot.

Mrs. McCarthy looks up, removes her glasses revealing her brown eyes and smiles. Her short brown hair makes her look like most of the female teachers around here, something I have always wondered about. Is it a requirement to have such short hair when you become a school administrator? Her makeup always looks like it's permanently stained on her face.

"Can I help you?" she asks in her Southern drawl.

"I need to sign in for a late pass," I say, panting.

A tall boy with cropped dark, brown hair fumbles through the door almost tripping. He's wearing a long-sleeved shirt and jeans on his lean, muscular body. He is hot. Is he new? This school is huge, but how could I have missed him? He's not part of the popular crowd, though.

"I'm so sorry I'm late," he tells Mrs. McCarthy as he makes his way behind the counter.

"It's okay, Vincent." She smiles as she stands. "I've got some errands to run so you'll be at the front desk for the remainder of the block. Oh, and this young lady needs to sign in." She winks.

Vincent turns around and seems to do a double take. His face turns pale as if he's seen a ghost. Mrs. McCarthy grabs her purse and is out the door. He drops his backpack on the floor and when he looks up, our eyes lock. His eyes are beautiful. They are the color of the deepest part of the ocean. So blue they almost look black. He looks at me like he's enamored or something and it makes my heart pound. My stomach starts fluttering like there are butterflies or freaking penguins flapping their wings in there.

He breaks our gaze and his eyes dart from mine to the sign-out sheet to the door and so on.

I smile. "Hi, Vincent."

He blushes and mumbles a hello. I bite my lip and notice his hands are gripping the desk like it's the only thing holding him up.

"I'm Megan. Can I sign in?"

"S-sure." He clears his throat.

I hope he isn't going to choke on his own saliva since it's obvious how uncomfortable I make him. I don't ever get this reaction from anyone, but I guess there's a first time for everything.

"Fill this out." He points to a sheet of paper on a clipboard.

My hands are frozen so I try to fill out the form as best I can.

He urgently scribbles on a pink pad of paper and rips it from its base, handing it to me. "They don't ever read these things."

"Thanks," I tell him.

Blood flushes his cheek and he looks away. "You're welcome."

I give a small smile. "You're a junior, right?"

"Yeah."

"Have we ever had a class together?"

He shakes his head.

"Well. Um. It was cool meeting you."

As his seductive lips stretch into a warm, sexy smile, he meets my eyes and my body warms. "You too."

I walk to class smiling to myself and thinking about what it would be like to kiss Vincent. His lips looked soft, and I bet he's a gentle kisser. Not that anything will come of Vincent and me, because nothing ever does, but it's still nice to fantasize.

Two

O nce the adrenaline wears off, grogginess sets in. I am not a morning person by any means, so I constantly yawn and grumble until about lunch.

I can't believe I forgot my costume. I love Halloween. I'm probably one of the five people not dressed up and it bums me out. Cherry and I got costumes. A bee for her and a ladybug for me. The bell rings and I make my way to my locker.

"Where is your costume?" Cherry demands as she props her hands on her hips. She's adorable in her bee costume.

I give her an innocent smile. "I'm sorry. I forgot."

Cherry Stimm is my best friend since the fourth grade. And yes, she catches all kinds of grief over her name. We are by no means popular, but we're not at the bottom of the pole either. So, I guess we're doing pretty well in high school, even though we both hate it. We are not what they call 'emo' kids and dress in black and talk about how life sucks all the time. We're pretty happy kids, or average I guess, even though our parents cause enough stress to last a lifetime. Both of us come from divorced families, both sets of parents have remarried, we each have a sibling who used to taunt us constantly, we work at the grocery store together, we don't have time for extracurricular activities at school, and we both love the arts. She's the artist. I'm the writer, obviously, since I'm writing this.

"Where were you this morning? I thought you were going to start coming to school earlier so we could chat before class."

"I overslept."

Her soft brown hair falls in loose curls past her small shoulders. A soft yellow ring circles the iris of her blue eyes—very rare but I think it's cool. It makes her unique. I am not so unique with long jet-black hair and Caribbean blue almond-shaped eyes. I have an oval face and when I smile dimples appear, which Cherry always tells me it's cute. We are both average heights, about 5'6" which we both prefer, and slender. Well, I'm not slender like the cheerleaders or dance team and I don't have a ridiculously flat stomach. I could probably lose a few pounds.

As we make our way to junior history, I tell Cherry about my dream. The damn thing is still haunting me.

"Casper? Gross." She scrunches her face in disgust and takes her seat next to me in class.

"I know." Sure, he's gorgeous. Every girl wants to be with him, but he's only after one thing. I'll never forget Trinity Taylor crying because as soon as he got what he wanted, he dumped her. And he wooed her for a good month. That still doesn't stop ninety percent of the girls to swoon over him. I guess swooning is healthy.

"Well, at least it was a dream," Cherry says. "Could make for good story material. You haven't written anything in a while."

I nod. Nothing's come to me in a long time, but this could be something. "By the way, I had to get a late pass and I met someone."

She lifts her eyebrows and grips my arm. "Vincent Young?"

"How'd you know?"

"He's the hot office assistant. He's got blue eyes that you could seriously get lost in. *Everyone* knows who he is."

Except me, apparently. The school is fairly large. I don't know everyone in my class, but somehow Cherry keeps tabs on who's who. I'm not sure how she finds the time.

"Did he ask for your number? Did he ask you out?"

"Whoa, slow your roll. I just met the guy. Besides, I'm still grounded. Not like I can go anywhere or talk to anyone."

Cherry lets out an annoyed groan. "When does this current grounding session end?"

"I think Mom said the eighth."

"Of what year?" she jokes.

"November. One more week."

"Yeah, until you sneeze the wrong way and then it'll be another stupid month."

"Probably."

Something I forgot to mention. My parents love to ground me. At least, that's how I see it. I am grounded for the dumbest things. Like one time my mom thought I was being a bitch, which I was stressed out, and so she grounded me for two weeks.

My jerk of a stepdad thinks I'm a crazy teenager. How crazy can I be when I get good grades in school, I work, I don't drink, I don't do drugs, I'm still a virgin, I don't sneak out—I could be the poster child of the century. None of these things ever interest me. I haven't been curious to try any of it probably because

I don't like losing control of myself. I don't want to end up with consequences or things like that. However, my mother is adamant that I will have the same life as her because it happened to her. She doesn't believe me when I say I will not lose my virginity at sixteen or get married at eighteen or have a baby at nineteen. I know that's why they keep me under lock and key.

"Ugh, I wish you could go trick or treating," Cherry says. She has no idea how much I wish I could go. Halloween is my favorite holiday.

"Even if I wasn't grounded, you know my mom wouldn't allow it. She thinks it's rude for people to go around to houses asking for candy."

She lets out a frustrated groan. "Your mom seriously deflates any kind of fun."

"You're telling me?"

"Why don't we go to Sloss for the haunted house?"

"You know I want to."

"Then do it. Come on. You're always grounded. Your parents will never find out. Tell them you're working."

I mull it over. I'm tired of being stuck at home all the time and never having any sort of fun. I deserve it. I've been too stressed out from school, parents. Mom and Ron will never know.

Screw it. "Okay."

She squeals.

After class, I make my way to precal. When I look up, my heart skips a beat as I see Casper by his locker. The dream comes back to me. Usually, when I dream, they are very vivid, but they tend to go away, and I forget about them. But this one with Casper is *still* there, which bugs me. It was so dramatic, like something straight out of a Cure song.

He normally pays no attention to me but today his beautiful brown eyes are fixed on me for some reason. Heat pricks the back of my neck and fills my cheeks. His ragged bleach blonde hair sweeps across his eyebrows. Okay, yes, he's good-looking. He has abs like Jason Mamoa for crying out loud beneath that simple white T-shirt. I only know this because I caught him one day after school without his shirt. His tanned skin would probably make me look even pastier if we stood next to each other. Not that I ever want to stand next to him.

But I can't tear my eyes away from him, almost as if they're magnets to his. Why is he looking at me? I can't explain it, but I feel something inside me as we gaze at each other, like I did in my dream.

Three

've always wanted to go to the haunted house at Sloss Furnace. As one of the famous landmarks in downtown Birmingham, it's now used for concerts, haunted houses, and any kind of social gathering now. It's haunted. I've lived in Birmingham my whole life and haven't experienced much of the city. My parents love doing things without Jonathan and me. I want to go places. See the history. See the landmarks. Live life. I guess I'm too young.

After rushing home to change into my ladybug costume, I meet up with Cherry in the parking lot.

Cherry squeals when she sees me, her bee headband flapping back and forth.

"I'm so excited that you're here." She smiles.

"Me too."

The storm cleared, for now, but the cool breeze moving the wispy clouds above creeps me out. It feels like an Edgar Allan Poe story. It doesn't help that there is some weird slasher movie music playing. I try to ignore the chill that comes over me as we wait in line to enter the haunted house. I can't remember the last time I went to one. Mom's not big on letting me experience much if anything. She says a lot of things are a waste of time and there's no point. Didn't she ever want to do things like this when she was a kid?

We slowly enter the tunnels of Sloss furnace and of course one lone orange light shines. Weaving our way through the creaking iron tunnels, we're surrounded by iron towers and boilers that was once the reason for the city's nickname the iron city.

We walk down the stairs to enter the underground tunnel. It's dark. I can't see my hand in front of my face, but there are black lights every few feet. Flashing strobe lights. Every so often, we hear someone screaming. Male and female. Cherry and I hold on to each other as we wait for something to grab us or someone to jump out. Adrenaline courses through my veins.

A skeleton falls from the ceiling. Cherry screams.

I giggle.

"You just wait," she whispers.

Chills reach my neck.

We reach a room where a corpse lies on a table and a woman dissects him with a knife. She looks up, blood running down her chin and eyes that glow. "Are you next pretty girl?"

Cherry rushes me along.

I know it's a haunted house, but I can't get over the feeling that someone is following me. Glancing behind me, I see a shadow and gasp.

"What?" Cherry asks.

I look again and see nothing. "Nothing," I tell her, but I speed her along.

People jump out. Blood splatters the walls. I'm ready to get out. Every time I glance back, I see him. It feels like the same man who tried to chase me down in my dreams. My pulse edges higher. I hate this feeling and I hate how much the dream keeps flashing in my head.

"Stop pushing me," Cherry says.

"I don't like this."

"It's okay, Megan. It's all fake."

I take a deep breath and keep going.

A man jumps out with a knife and both Cherry and I scream. He moves toward us; his dark eyes send an uneasy feeling over me. Then I recognize him.

"Vincent?"

He relaxes his face. "Megan, right?"

Cherry playfully punches him. "Omigod, you scared us."

"I should be sorry but I'm not. Means I'm doing a good job."

"You should get a raise," Cherry says. "How'd you get this gig?"

He shrugs. "Signed up."

"Can you take a break?"

"I'm not supposed to, but I can. Why?"

"This one's freaking out." She jerks her thumb at me.

I throw her a glare. *Way to make me look good.*

Vincent gives a soft laugh. He seems more relaxed here than when I first met him. I like that. "I could walk with you." His smile sends my stomach to do flips.

Cherry ends up walking ahead of us and I feel completely awkward and nervous. I wasn't prepared for this.

"You look cute by the way," he says.

"Oh, thanks. It was Cherry's idea."

"I like it."

We're quiet for a little bit as we continue through the tunnels. Something crashes down in front of Vincent and me and I scream clutching onto his arm. He's patient and doesn't let it deter him.

Once my heart returns to normal, I thank him.

"It's okay. This isn't your thing, is it?"

"No, I love Halloween. I've…" I shake my head, not wanting to bore him with my problems.

"What is it?"

"I've been having scary dreams lately."

"That sucks."

I shrug. "Cherry says I should write them down for a story."

"You write?"

"Yeah sometimes."

"That's cool."

I see something glint in the light around his neck. "What's that?"

"It's a nuummite crystal. My mom gave it to me."

I can barely make out the gold specks inside the black, round crystal. It's unique and I've never seen anything like it. The name nuummite sounds familiar, but I can't remember where I've heard it.

He walks me to a certain point in the tunnel and stops. "I should head back but you're at the end." He grips the back of his neck.

"What? What is it?"

"There's a scary guy in chains who will chase you." As he says this, I can hear Cherry's blood curdling scream. Vincent laughs. "You'll be fine."

"Yeah." I nod. "Guess I should get this over with."

"Gary's cool. He scares the crap out of people though."

"Good to know."

"See ya Megan."

I take a deep breath and use the adrenaline of talking to Vincent to propel me out of the haunted house. Gary doesn't fail. Covered in chains with a bloody disfigured face, he chases after me until I run into Cherry's arms.

We laugh and it's just what I needed.

"Thanks for convincing me to come out tonight," I tell her.

"Anytime. And you got to see Vincent."

My lips stretch into a huge grin until I realize where I've heard about the nuummite. In my dreams.

Four

constant beep sounds in my head. It's so annoying and I can't end it. It grates on my nerves. I can't shut it off.

"Megan."

"Hmmm."

"Megan, turn off the alarm."

My eyes jolt open, and I try to adjust. Mom hovers over me, her eyes staring into mine with a heated glare. She's seething and her arms are crossed.

I reach over onto my nightstand and shut off the irritating beep. My heart slows down after almost jumping out of my chest.

"I wish you wouldn't let that go off for thirty minutes straight." Her voice is loud, especially in the morning.

"Sorry. I didn't hear it."

Mom sighs and leaves the room. Like me, she's also very cranky in the mornings.

At least I remembered to set it this time.

The grey morning light bleeds through my blinds. Savannah slowly worms her way out from under the covers, looking as sleepy as I feel.

I had another dream about Casper. Madly in love and on the run. What is going on? I don't like the guy. Yeah, he looks good, but that doesn't mean I have to dream about him like I'm in love with him. Maybe my mind is giving me a story to write. I rub my face and slip out from under the warm covers. Okay, I know it was only a dream, but it felt real. Too real. Or maybe I'm delusional and unaware of how much.

I arrive at school still stupefied.

"Good morning." Cherry smiles. She usually greets me the same way every morning—very cheerful and way too energetic. This is where we are opposites. Cherry can wake up before her alarm, whereas for me, sometimes it takes my mother yelling and screaming at me to wake up to turn the damn thing off. I can't help that I'm a deep sleeper.

"Morning."

She raises an eyebrow. "Are you okay?"

I shrug, not looking at her.

"Did your parents find out about last night?"

I shake my head. I look up to answer, but my eyes catch Casper's who watches me as he walks by. He furrows his eyebrows like he's frustrated. Why is he looking at me like that? Why the hell is my heart pounding like a freaking animal stampede?

"Is there something I don't know?" Cherry raises her eyebrows and puts a hand on her hip.

"Eww, no."

"Are you sure? Because it got hot in here." She fans herself.

I roll my eyes. "I had another dream, Cher. We're *in love*. It's so bizarre and it feels real."

"Okay. I think your secret crush has seriously gone into a full overdrive."

I give her a pointed look. "I don't have a secret crush on him."

"Tell that to your subconscious." She says, scrolling on her phone. "It's okay. It was a dream. It's not like you're going to actually fall in love with the Douchebag."

She's right. I'm overreacting, but it's a strange coincidence that I've had two dreams about him and he's staring at me like he's in love.

When the final bell of the day rings, I flee to my locker, as fast as the thick crowd allows me. I pull out my backpack and a folded piece of paper falls out.

Probably a note from Cherry. I shove it in my pocket, grab the books I need, and close my locker. Walking out to my car, I open the note.

I can't explain it, but I can't stop thinking about you. Call me. Casper.

I roll my eyes and sigh. *Oh, clever girl, Cherry. Clever.* I'll get her back somehow.

I get home and release my dogs into the wooded backyard so they can play. They rush past me almost knocking me over like I'm nothing but a vase. I watch them wrestle with each other, knowing the dropping temperatures make them frisky. Except Savannah. Little delicate Savannah. It's like in the high fifties and she holds up her tiny paw like the ground is too cold. I pick her up and she snuggles close to me, shaking.

I'm off from work tonight, thankfully, but I have to cook dinner before I start my homework. I'm not supposed to talk on the phone as a stipulation of the grounding, but I have time before my parents come home so I call Cherry.

"Very funny."

"What?" she answers as innocently as she can.

"You did a good job with the crappy handwriting so that it looks like Casper wrote it. Good job. Just wait for payback."

"What are you talking about?"

"You can stop. It was funny, but come on, don't drag it out like you usually do."

"Meg, seriously, what are you talking about?"

"The note you left in my locker."

"I didn't leave a note."

"Then who did? Did you get someone to drop it in?"

"No. It wasn't me, geez. What does it say?"

I read her the note.

She gasps. "Omigod. He left his number. Is it really his?"

"He overheard us talking about those stupid dreams and he's playing a cruel joke." I pause a minute. "You didn't tell anyone about my dream, did you?"

"Yeah, I told the entire school. What do you think?" she asks, sarcastically and obviously a bit offended.

"Sorry. What if he overheard me and now, he's messing with me?"

"I doubt anyone listens to us. Maybe he's finally realized what a fox you are and can't keep his eyes off you."

I roll my eyes. "Yeah, I don't think guys like him would go for this pastiness," I joke, and she laughs. "Besides, I'm not going to be one of his conquests. He'd be the *last* person I'd date."

"Good. You can do so much better. Like Vincent."

Hearing his name does funny things to me. "I never see him. How can I get to know him?"

"Maybe you need to visit the office more. Get his number..." her voice trails off.

"Oh, like you have with Luke?"

"Love takes time," she laments.

"What should I do about this note?"

"Ignore it. Or call the number and see who answers."

"No. I'm not going to call and relive humiliation. Remember in fifth grade when Maggie wrote all those letters and cards saying they were from Casper? Casper pretended to like me and asked me out only as a joke."

"I know. Throw it away. If it is from Casper, you know it's not good."

"True."

I hear the hum of the garage door opening.

"I gotta go. See ya tomorrow." I hang up, let my dogs in, and run down the hall to my room. I open my backpack, pull out whatever book I grab first and pretend to be studying. Seeing as it's only 4:30, I assume it's my stepdad. I cringe when I hear his stupid stomping on the hardwood floors, and he stops in my doorway and greets me happily.

"Hello," I nonchalantly answer without looking up.

"What are you so mopey about?"

Certainly not the fact that I'm grounded. "Nothing."

A few seconds pass.

"Aren't you going to ask about my day?"

I sigh internally. "How was your day?"

"It was good. I made some sales and picked up a few new clients."

"Good."

I relax once he leaves.

Ron has been my stepdad for five years, but it's felt like an eternity. I honestly try to get along with him, but it's so difficult. He forces us to have a civil chat every day or small talk. It's all fake, at least from my side. I have no respect for the guy since he treats Jonathan, my brother, and me like crap and Mom like a queen.

I hear Ron's loud footsteps as he approaches my room again. "You know you're cooking dinner tonight, don't you?"

"Yes," I groan and finally look at him. I hate the way his brown eyes bug out, like any second, they're going to fall out of their sockets. He's short with a beer gut and swears to my mom he doesn't drink anymore, but you can't hide the smell of alcohol. He lies to her about smoking. When my mom caught him smoking, he told her it wasn't his cigarette. He had picked it up from someone who threw it out from a passing car.

He repulses me which only fuels my hatred for him more. I'm not a hateful person, but Ron makes my life a living hell.

"Don't you think you need to get started?" he asks.

"I'm going to finish this chapter and start."

"Your mom will be home soon so you should get started on it now."

I clench my teeth trying my best to hold in the anger. I don't want another month added to my grounding. "Okay," I finally say, and he stomps to the living room at the front of the house.

I hate the way he walks. I don't get why he has to walk so hard that it sometimes rattles the windows. Then again, I'm sure his chunky body doesn't help.

I slam my book shut and go to the kitchen. I drag out a pot and ingredients for chili. I'm surprised they aren't going out to eat and leave Jonathan and me to fend for ourselves. I started cooking when I was eleven and I hate it. Probably because anytime I try to experiment my parents won't eat it. That and I hate cooking in this ancient kitchen. Only two eyes work on the stove and of course they are the two small ones. The sink is the size of a Dutch oven and there isn't a dishwasher. But according to Ron, Jonathan and I are the dishwashers. God forbid he lift a finger. And there is a random bathroom that Ron uses as a storage closet.

The house belongs to Ron's parents, but they let us live in it. It's a dated house, built in the early 1900s, and while I like old things it does have several disadvantages. Like how cold it gets in the winter.

Before Mom, Jonathan, and I moved in, the place looked like a bachelor pad. Mom arranged the millions of antiques they both had, repainted, and decorated the place. Yes, Jonathan and I had a hand in those repairs. We don't mind doing chores so much; it's the way our parents make us. I'll never forget Ron actually referring to us as their slaves.

That's why I have to get out of here and the only way I can is to focus on school. So far, I'm right on track with grades. I'm counting down: a year and a half.

I finish cooking the chili and everyone grabs a bowl. We sit at the table tonight. Mom must have read something that convinced her we'll be a closer family if we eat at the table and talk about our days. They don't want to hear about mine or Jonathan's days though. We're teenagers. What struggles can we possibly have? We're lazy, moody people who don't do anything but stay glued to our phones or computers. She puts on classical music in the background, and no one talks. Just the sounds of spoons hitting bowls.

Jonathan's cell phone rings and he quickly silences it.

Mom clears her throat.

"Sorry," Jonathan says. "It was Dad."

Mom makes a disappointed sound. If it were me with the cell phone at the table, she'd have grounded me. But Jonathan is her baby. He even got her looks. Same brown eyes and same shade of reddish-brown hair.

"Probably calling to make fun of your mother?" Ron says, and I clench my teeth. Dad doesn't say a word about Mom, but they always talk about Dad. It's infuriating. Jonathan tolerates Ron more than I do. Ron wanted us to start calling him "Dad," shortly after he and Mom married, but I refused. Jonathan did for a while which upset me, but he doesn't anymore.

"I hope he sends that child support check," Mom says. "If he doesn't, I'm going to call my lawyer."

"Mom."

"Megan, if he can afford a new family, he can afford to pay for you and Jonathan."

You mean pay for your car. I know that's what she uses the money for.

Once dinner's over, I flee to my room to do homework and grumble at the silence. I always listen to music, but Mom took all my music away like always when I'm grounded. She knows how much I love music and I guess she loves torturing me.

Savannah shifts under the blanket on my bed and lets out a long sigh.

"I hear ya," I tell her.

My door opens and Jonathan slips inside, closing it. He hands me his phone. "It's Dad."

"Hey Dad," I whisper. Jonathan acts like a lookout by the door, listening for footsteps. The things we do for each other.

"Hey," Dad says. "Why are you grounded this time?"

"I can't even remember."

"They shouldn't have taken your phone away or ground you from talking to me."

"You know how ridiculous they are."

"That's not right. Let me talk to your mother."

"No, it's okay." We talk for a few minutes. He tells me about work and Kimberly, my stepmom, and Olivia, my half-sister. She is three and cute as a button. I hardly see them since they are in Atlanta, and I'm not allowed to drive there alone at my age. It's only three hours away. I'm pretty capable of driving the distance. I don't text and drive. I know I've only had my license for about six months, but I miss them like crazy. My dad always treats me like I'm a person. I can't remember the last time Mom and I actually sat down and had a conversation. He tells me Olivia keeps asking about me, which makes me feel guilty.

Jonathan waves his hand for the phone.

"I gotta go, Dad, love you," I quickly say and give Jonathan the phone.

My door opens and it's Ron. He never knocks. "There are still dishes to be washed," he tells Jonathan, not caring that he's on the phone.

Jonathan nods and says goodbye to our dad.

Ron looks at me. "Were you on the phone?"

"No."

"Remember you aren't supposed to."

"I know. He was relaying messages."

Ron walks out and I'm sure he'll tattle to mom that I was on the phone. He's such a kid.

"Thanks," I tell Jonathan. Even though we've had our fair share of fights, we are close. People say we look alike, but I don't see it. He's taller than me by quite a bit. He's lanky and not very athletic. He prefers to play video games over actual football any day. He kinda keeps to himself, but with work and being a freshman in college keeps him busy. He's saving enough money to move out by May. I don't want him to leave me here alone though.

"No problem. I was thinking about going up Thanksgiving weekend actually."

"Yeah, sounds good."

"Cool. Don't do anything stupid to get you grounded."

I roll my eyes.

He smirks and leaves.

After doing homework all night in the boring silence, I feel as if my eyes are going to pop out of my head. I take my shower and curl up under the blankets. Savannah gets comfortable and I close my eyes. The dreams with Casper come back to me. I still remember every little detail. I groan and roll onto my side. Why can't I get him out of my head? He teased me constantly when we were kids and spread rumors about me. The last (and only) guy I dated, Matt, dumped me because he thought I cheated on him. He told me Casper found me with some other guy. Douchebag Casper. Why would I have a dream about being in love with him?

I turn on the lamp beside my bed, pull out my journal from underneath my mattress, and grab a pen. Writing has always helped me cope with my stressful life. I constantly change the location of my journal because my parents have read it before.

Even though it's been a while, I'm excited to write out a new story idea. I can't wait to see where it'll take me.

Maybe if I write down my dreams, it'll help me not focus on them so much. I don't get my mind's current obsession and why all of a sudden Casper Truitt is paying attention to me. Why can't it be Vincent?

Maybe I should try to talk to him more. Take risks. Isn't that what being a teenager is all about? Challenging yourself and learning who you are? I don't even know the guy, but I felt a connection. My heart pounds at the thought. Will he think I'm weird? A freak? I've asked guys out before, but they always only want to be my friend, which means they never want to talk to me again.

Vincent seems different. I set aside my journal and turn off the light. I'm going to talk to him tomorrow.

Five

tanding on a cliff, darkness shrouds me except for the full moon hiding behind the tall trees. I hold myself as if it will make me warmer, but the strong gale pushes against me, almost knocking me over. I look over the cliff and gasp when I see several feet below, waves crashing against sharp pointed rocks, trying to reach me. I take a step back but collide with something hard. I try turning around. It's no use. Hands force me to stay straight.

"Don't scream," a dark gruff voice demands in my ear. He presses something hard into my back and leads me back toward the cliff.

"Please don't do this," I beg.

The waves continue to rumble below, and I have no way out. I close my eyes and cold tears trail down my face.

"It's finally your time to die, traitor."

"No, please!" I wail and push against him but like a statue, he doesn't budge.

The man whirls me around to face him, but all I can see are dark eyes under a hood. "He doesn't love you, Megan. He used his magic to make you fall in love with him. He's an Elf. That's what they do."

I narrow my eyes. "No. You're wrong."

The man laughs. A deep throaty laugh. "You are a fool. A sad, pathetic fool if you ever believed he loved you. He only wants the Jewel. He's only using you as leverage."

A gunshot sounds and the man releases me. I lose my balance. My heart jumps to my throat as I fall. Grasping the edge of the cliff, small rocks break and fall past me. They always say don't look down, so I look straight up into the indigo starry night, holding on tight.

"Megan." Casper calls and grabs my wrists. His beautiful face takes the place of the stars, and he hoists me up until I am safely in his arms. Holding me close, he kisses me fervently. "I can't lose you. This is getting too close. We have to keep going. There could be others."

The man on the ground groans and I stiffen. We get to our feet. I cautiously walk toward the man, but Casper holds me back. I can't see the man's face.

"You think you've won," he says through a thick garbled voice. He coughs and I see a pool of liquid spreading around him under the bright moonlight. "The night of the eclipse, the war will start."

Casper takes my hand and pulls me through the thick forest, picking up his pace the further we get. It is hard though, running in such a long dress.

"He will find you, Megan," the man bellows. I gasp and look back, losing my footing. I crash to the ground.

"Megan." Casper helps me to my feet.

Is the man right? Is Casper only using me? The man wants me to go back home. He wants me to forget about Casper. But why is he grasping my wrist, holding me against him as we run away from my home?

The dreams are increasingly scary and more confusing. Trying to make sense out of it as I ready for school, but nothing comes to mind. My nerves are a on edge since I keep picturing the creepy, dark figure trying to kill me. His large body stalking toward me with a gun in his hand. I could never see his face. I always feel so incredibly safe with Casper in my dreams, but now, I feel like there isn't anything keeping me safe. I try to shake the ridiculous impending doom sensation, but I can't.

The dark morning mirrors my mood with its dreary rain. It's one of those days where I want to curl up in my blankets with my dogs and read.

"Good morning." Cherry smiles but it fades. "Geez, you look hungover or something. What did you *do* last night?"

I trade my backpack for my history book and notebook. "I dreamed that someone tried to kill me."

"Whoa. Damn, Megan. Again? Are you okay?"

I shake my head. "It scared me."

I can't help but look around at everyone like they're going to appear from the shadows with a gun pointed at me.

Cherry purses her lips to the side, and I see the concern in her blue eyes. She places a hand on my shoulder, and I jump. "Whoa, it's me. It was only a dream. It isn't real. Keep telling yourself that. I've had pretty scary dreams and that's what I gotta do to calm myself."

I close my locker and we walk to history class.

"Was...*he* in it?" she asks.

I nod. Speaking of Casper... "How can I figure out if he wrote that note? I don't want to go up and ask him."

"He probably wouldn't tell you the truth anyway. Maybe ask Vincent to get a writing sample."

I did tell myself I would speak to Vincent. Maybe this is a good excuse. I ponder it all through class, and when the bell rings, I finally decide to do it.

Once I reach the office, I catch him as he's packing up his books. When he sees me, he smiles and blushes.

"Just the girl I wanted to see."

"Me?"

He chuckles. "What's up?"

"Um, I was wondering if you could help me before you leave."

"Yeah, sure. I can walk you to class."

"Well, actually..." I hold up the note and realize that I don't want him or anyone to read such a personal note. "Is there any way you could show me a sample of Casper Truitt's handwriting?"

He crumples his face before replying. "Sure. He's always checking in late. I'm sure you can check his signature on the sign out pad here."

"He *would* check in late. How does he get away with that? Does his daddy invest in the school or something?"

Vincent smirks as I check the pad. I find Casper's signature and I mirror the note against the writing. It's a match. So now, it's obvious that Casper is playing a trick on me. Fantastic. Here I am dreaming about some douchebag, and I can't get him out of my head while he decides to mess with me. Again.

"Is something wrong?" he asks, probably because of the scowl on my face.

"Vincent, why can't they all be nice like you?"

Blood flushes his cheek. We walk together down the hall. "I was wondering if I could call you sometime," he says.

My heart jumps and I smile. "Sure. Except I'm grounded right now, so no one can call."

Vincent nods and frowns. "I see." He starts to turn away.

"Well, don't you want my number?"

He glances at me. "Sorry. I guess I thought—"

"I wasn't making that up. Give me your phone." He hands it to me, and I enter my number into his phone. "My parents are ridiculously strict. They ground me for looking at them wrong," I joke.

Vincent smiles, his eyes gazing into mine. "That sucks."

I shrug. "You start expecting it after a while."

"Don't you have a cell phone?"

"I do but they took it away."

"When can I call you?"

"Monday."

"Three more days."

"Yes. I have to be extra good this weekend. Shouldn't be too hard since I'll be at work most of the time. Anyway, I gotta go."

"Have a good day." He smiles awkwardly.

"You, too."

I head to class, excited that he asked for my number. If I keep being late to class, Mr. Landry will probably start to guess something is going on between the office aide and me. At least I hope that will be true, I smile to myself. My heart swells and I feel good.

"Casper wrote the note," I tell Cherry as we count the money in our tills inside the grocery store office. We always chat while we count before hitting the registers.

"What?"

"Yeah. Who knows what kind of sick joke he's playing?"

"Ugh. I can kick him."

I shake my head. "It's not worth it. Vincent asked me for my number, though."

Cherry's jaw drops and she playfully punches me.

"Ow!"

"Why didn't you start with that? Omigod, that is so exciting."

"I know." I smile, loving how good I feel.

"When Vincent asks you out, you must tell me every single detail."

I roll my eyes. "Aye aye captain."

"I wish Luke would ask me out. Too bad I can't dream about a hot guy and have another hot guy ask for *my* number." She teases.

"Maybe you should ask Luke out." I do not want to talk about Casper.

"If he liked me, he would ask me."

"Maybe he's shy."

"Honey, no one is shyer than Vincent and he asked you for your number."

"Maybe I'll drop hints." I grin.

"Careful. I may take you up on that."

We make our way downstairs to the slightly busy floor. Cherry goes to customer service, and I land on an empty register. As soon as I place my till into the drawer, customers flood into my line. Most of them are people rushing home from their office jobs picking up something quick for dinner, but there are the occasional ones actually grocery shopping. The later it gets, the more we tend to get the ones on welfare. I guess they come in late because they work late. My favorites are the ones who stroll in wearing slippers and pajamas, even in this cold weather.

That's what Birmingham is like. There are a mixture of classes and people. I like it here, but I'm ready to live far away from my parents. Maybe to Atlanta. I hear colleges are good there.

The night is uneventful and tiring, but I still think of the dream and Casper. I swear, I will never forgive myself if I do have a secret crush. I shudder at the thought. Every time he pops into my head, I force him out and think of Vincent. Imagining us on a date. Kissing. I want it to be good, and not the product of a prank or whatever. I want Vincent to genuinely like me.

What if Casper starts spreading rumors and Vincent hears them?

Casper and I run fast as the rain slants downward, soaking us in the cold. My body trembles and I taste something metallic in my mouth. Blood I realize. It trails down from my eyebrow to my chin, and I wipe it with the back of my hand. It doesn't stop bleeding.

"Keep running, Megan," I hear Casper's voice behind me. I don't want to run. I want this endless nightmare to end. I want to be with Casper, but I lift my long skirt and run. I jump at the sound of a gunshot and stop behind a tree. I frantically search the thick woods for any sign of Casper. My breath locks in my lungs as I clutch the tree so hard it feels as though the branch will break.

Not again. How many men did they send to find us? We don't have the Jewel. We want to be together.

I never thought my own kind would try to kill me. Florence is the only person I told the truth. She wouldn't have told anyone. I knew that once the army returned, they would come after me.

I wait in the dark, wet night then I see Casper. I dart for him and as we collide, our arms wrap around each other. He leans down and presses his lips against mine with a hard edge. I kiss back with the same lust, grazing my tongue against his. Our mouths are slick from the rain that falls between them. The heat from his kiss exudes my body. I never want to leave his arms. I never want to part from his lips. His heart. His soul.

No matter what we'll face, we'll face it together.

"You have to go back, Megan."

"No!"

He cradles my face in his hands forcing me to meet his eyes. "I won't let them kill you. I won't let them hurt you. But I refuse to let this be your life now."

My heart sinks. "I won't leave you. I chose this. It won't be like this forever."

"Yes, it will. Our kinds hate each other. We are constantly at war."

"We can save the world. You and me."

He gives a knowing look, but I refuse to part from him. "You know he will keep coming for you."

"Then we kill him."

Six

ey! Are you planning on going to school today?" I hear Ron's loud voice and when I open my eyes, I flinch.

Ron stands over me, eyes about to pop out of his sockets, a vein on the side of his head about to explode.

"What time is it?" I gasp.

"Nine-thirty," he shouts. "Are you planning on staying home all day?"

I silently curse and sit up. "No." Why is he at home? Why didn't my alarm ever go off? Didn't Mom think to wake me before she left? How long has Ron been in here while I was having such an erotic dream?

He walks out of the room. I hustle to throw on some clothes and grab my backpack all while thinking of that kiss. I can't tell if I'm trembling from having to hurry or if it's from the kiss. Or the fact that I mentioned killing someone. As I open the door, I groan at the pouring rain. Pulling the hood of my sweatshirt over my head, I jog out to my car.

When I arrive at school, I go to the office to snag a late pass. My heart does an unexpected flip once I see Vincent. God, he's cute.

"Good morning." His lips turn up into an easy smile and there's a slight redness to his cheeks.

I smile back, removing my hood. "Morning. I need to check in."

"Sure. Fill this out." He points to a sheet of paper on a clipboard. "You sure you aren't being late on purpose?"

It's my turn to blush. "Maybe I am."

"It's fine with me. It's the only time I get to see you." He tears off a sheet from a pad.

I smile. "Thanks for this." I hold up the slip of paper and turn toward the door.

"Megan."

I look back and he winks. "I can't wait to call you."

"Me either." I leave but feel weird. I can't stop thinking about that stupid dream with Casper. Why do I keep having them?

After class ends, I make my way to my locker, stopping mid-stride. A guy bumps into me and the other students grunt, annoyed that they have to go around me.

Casper's tall, lean body casually leans against my stormy gray locker. My whole body freezes, except for the insane pounding of my heart. I don't know what he wants. I don't want to talk to him, but he does look hot.

Maybe if I talk to him, he'll leave me alone.

I want to leave, but his brown eyes catch mine. I decide to play it cool and amble to my locker.

"Excuse me," I tell him with a cutting tone. "That's my locker."

"Can we talk?" Casper asks. His voice is smooth, and it reminds me of the sweet voice in my dreams. "I had a dream about you." He lowers his voice. He isn't flirting like I've seen him do with other girls. His face is grim. He is a good actor.

"Is that what you tell all your conquests?" I ask, keeping my voice strong. I don't want to dwell on the fact that he is obviously messing with me. I also don't want to think about my dream while he stands here either.

"No. I had a dream about you."

"Awesome," I say sarcastically. "You wanna move? I need to get my books. I'm running on a time limit here."

He moves and crosses his arms in front of his chest, flexing his lean muscles in the process. I'm sure it works for other girls. "Did you get my note?"

"Look, whatever this is, stop, okay?" I spin the combination lock, trying not to let him see my hand shake. He stands a little too close for comfort. I open the locker, blocking his face from my view, but he moves to the other side of me.

I take out my book and slam the door. "What do you want?" I snap. Genuine confusion and what looks like hurt flashes in his eyes, but maybe it's my mind playing tricks.

"Nothing," he finally says and walks away without looking back. I don't know why I feel guilty for how I acted toward him. Maybe it was his solemn demeanor. I've never seen him act like that or knew him to be that way. I am somehow known as an emo kid so maybe he thinks I'm into that as a way to mess with me. I shake my head. He's playing a cruel joke.

When I get home, Ron is there, feigning sickness. He annoys me. He never works. He always goes in late, leaves early, or takes two-hour lunches and anytime he needs money, he goes running to his parents for it. All while demanding my paycheck to help pay for my car, they say. With the constant battles between my mom and dad over child support, money is always a messy subject with my parents.

Unfortunately, because I'm grounded and I am off work, Friday nights are torture, and on this particular night, it worsens when Mom comes home. She opens my door and greets me with a look I know all too well that tells me I'm in trouble. Her lips are pressed tightly together, and she stares at me with a hardness that intimidates me. My mom used to be cool, but ever since she married Ron, she changed. He feeds her lies to get me in trouble and she believes every word.

"What?" I ask softly.

"Were you going to cut class all day today?" She folds her arms across her chest.

"No. I overslept. I think I forgot to turn on my alarm."

"Ron says you had planned on staying home all day."

Of course, he said that. I don't get the appeal of lying. Is he trying to make himself look good? "I didn't say that. He woke me up and I left."

"Did you go to school?"

"Yes. They would've called—"

"I saw your car at the mall," Ron interjects.

I laugh. "It wasn't mine."

"I saw a silver Volvo."

"Am I the only person who drives an ancient, silver Volvo?" I probably am, but that's beside the point.

"Megan," Mom warns.

"I know it was yours because I know your tag number."

"What were you doing at the mall? Weren't you supposed to be working?"

His face turns red, and he glares at me. "You're grounded even longer," he says in a stern voice.

"What?" I shout.

"You heard me."

"I didn't do anything."

"You lied to me," Ron says.

I feel like punching him. I never understand why he always makes this stuff up. And he wonders why I don't like him.

"I can get a copy of my late slip Monday to prove it."

"Then get one to me by Monday or you're grounded," Mom says and shuts my door.

My heart sinks. They are always angry with me, and I don't get why. Nothing I do is ever good enough for them. Sometimes I feel like my mom regrets having me or that I'm such a problem child. I want to run away. Somewhere that isn't stressful.

Pulling out my notebook, I return to a world where I can be free. Casper's face circles my mind as if thinking of him is comforting. Why is he the first one I think about?

I sigh, pushing him from my mind. I think about the two characters in my story. Living in a world where they are lovers and immortal beings. I imagine Vincent and me on a date, smiling and laughing. I picture his dark blue eyes peering into mine before he leans down and kisses me.

Will he ask me out? Will he like me? If he ever meets my parents, he'll run for the hills. I take a deep breath and continue writing. It's the only thing that brings me solace.

Seven

asper launches a punch into the man's face. The man groans then tackles Casper to the ground. They have to stop. I look around to find something to hit the man. The gunshot explodes and I freeze. I wait for Casper to move out from underneath the man but it's the man who stirs. He grasps the gun and gets to his feet. It's *him*.

I run. Fast. The man screams for me, but I keep running, past several trees. I come to a halt after I see a hole in one of them as if lightning struck it. It's small enough for me to hide in. I hold my breath, and my heart pounds inside my chest; it throbs in my ears. His footsteps approach.

I should turn myself in. I shouldn't have fallen in love with an Elf, but I did. And now I don't know if he's dead or alive. I bite my lip to keep from making a sound. The man's shoes crunch over branches and my chest burns from holding my breath. I close my eyes and a tear falls down. I can't let him see me.

He walks past and I hear his footsteps become more and more faint. I'm not sure how much time passes before I exit the tree, but when I do I dart toward Casper's body. "Casper," I whisper as I crawl toward him. My vision blurs from the tears as I shake him, but he doesn't move.

Tears slide down my cheeks as I try to take a deep breath. I sit up and reach behind me to turn off my alarm before it goes off. The dream stays with me, and I feel as if I've lost my true love.

Someone knocks on my door, and Mom comes in. "Good mor—what's wrong, Meg?"

I sniff. "Nothing. A bad dream." I quickly wipe my tears.

"What was it about?"

I shake my head. "Nothing. It was stupid."

"All right. Well, have a good day. See you tonight." She hugs me and I hold onto her a little longer. She pulls back and kisses my forehead. "Are you sure you're okay?"

I nod.

"Okay. Don't forget the copy of the late pass," she says and leaves.

Savannah burrows out from under the covers and sneezes. She yawns and stretches while looking at me sleepily. I hold all twelve pounds of her to my chest, hoping for some comfort.

Once I see Casper, I'm sure I will calm down. It's the strangest thing. I feel like the dream really happened which is why I have to see him.

I get to school rather impatiently and meet Cherry at my locker. She's talking, but I only half-listen because my eyes are peeled on the vast group of people walking down the hall. I chew the inside of my cheek. I fidget with the strap on my backpack. My eyes dart back and forth looking at every single face that passes by. None of them is Casper.

"Okay, seriously, Megan, what is with you?" Cherry asks.

"Nothing," I mumble.

"Well, could you pay attention to me for five seconds?" She lets out an exasperated sigh. "Who are you looking for?"

I don't see him at all. Something is wrong. My heart drops to the pit of my stomach, swirling around with all of the other uneasy feelings.

"Hey." She grabs my arm, making me look at her. "Calm down. Lay off the Red Bull. Yeesh. What's the matter with you?"

I can't calm down. She doesn't understand my urgency, but it doesn't matter now. "I have to go check on him."

"Who?"

I swallow. "Casper."

Her eyebrows push together with disbelief in her eyes. "What?"

"He was shot, Cherry. I have to see if he's okay."

"What?" Her eyes enlarge.

"It was a dream," I tell her. "You don't understand." I quickly add as she gives me a disapproving look.

"Meg, it was a dream. It wasn't real. Why does he concern you all of a sudden?"

"I don't know. I gotta go."

She grabs my arm again and the bell rings. "Are you crazy? You can't go to his house."

"I need your phone."

"What?"

"Give me your phone."

When she hands it to me, I google Casper's dad's name and am able to find their address. I'm familiar with the area since it's around my work.

"I have to. Cherry, please. Let me go."

"What's gotten into you?" she shouts as the halls clears.

She searches my eyes, but I can't explain it to her. She won't understand. I need to see if Casper is hurt. "I'll call you later, I promise."

Cherry looks at me like I am seriously out of my mind, which I probably am. How am I even going to get inside Casper's house? I drive like a lunatic on the way to his house.

I arrive at, what I expected, a giant mansion with a driveway lined with tall bricks. Not my first choice in houses, but hey, to each their own. As soon as my car is in park, I yank the keys from the ignition and flee the car. I rush up to the door and pound on it, but no one answers. I'm sure there's an alarm system somewhere. Hoping that the door is unlocked, I turn the knob and like something out of a movie, the knob turns, and the door opens. Hesitantly, I cross the threshold and call out Casper's name. When I get no reply, I close the door and run upstairs, checking each of the several rooms. I get to one and find him sprawled out on the floor wearing only boxers, as if he'd fallen from the high sleigh bed.

"Casper," I yell. I shake him. "Casper!"

He finally stirs awake.

When he opens his eyes, he gazes at me with love and relief. "Megan." My heart lurches forward. For one fleeting moment, the way he says my name, I want to curl myself into his arms, breathe him in, and feel safe.

His eyes widen with fear, and I realize this isn't a dream. "What the hell are you doing here?" Casper scrambles away from me.

"I-I had to check on you." I stand, backing myself against the wall away from him.

"What?" He gets to his feet as I grip the chair rail on the wall behind me. He seems much taller than ever before, and my eyes sweep across his flawless smooth chest.

I imagine running my fingers down the center. I hope he can't hear the erratic beating of my heart. It's throbbing in my ears as my throat closes.

"Check on me for what?" he demands.

I clear my throat. "You didn't show up for school today and I panicked." Okay, now I'm sure he thinks I'm seriously crazy. I'm acting as if I have the biggest obsession over him. *Great.* "I had to come see if you were okay. I didn't mean to frighten you." My voice is barely above a whisper.

He narrows his eyes. "What are you doing to me?" His voice reverberates in the room, making me jump slightly. "What is this game you're playing?"

That brings me up short. "Game? What are you talking about? I should ask the same about you," I quip.

"Get away from me, you freak. I don't know what you've done to me. You're one of those freaky voodoo people or whatever aren't you? Putting spells on people."

My jaw literally drops and I'm not sure why there's a pain in my stomach, as if his words hurt me. "I—"

"You're the one making me think of you all the time, aren't you? Making me have these crazy dreams. Get out of my house or I'll call the police."

Shock doesn't even describe how I feel. Okay, maybe it does, but a more intensified version. Without a word, I leave the weird scene. I don't know what I expected to happen, but not that. I wonder how long it will take the rumor mill to start that I'm some voodoo witch putting spells on people. Does he believe that, though?

If he did write that letter, why did he have such a strong reaction to my coming over and waking him? Other than freaking him out, apparently. All I know is that I needed to see him. The dream felt so incredibly real. Too real.

Once I get back in my car, I feel completely humiliated. What is wrong with me? Running to some guy's house to see if he's okay after having a dream. Who does that? He mentioned having crazy dreams. Are they as insane as mine?

I need to chill out and stop focusing on these stupid dreams.

I decide to go back to school. The last thing I need is someone calling my mom telling her I skipped. I arrive meeting Vincent in the office.

"Y'know, I'm starting to feel like you're only using me for my late passes." He smiles as his cheeks redden.

His infectious, warm smile already makes me feel better I can't help but smile back. "I would never."

"Why are we late today?"

"Oh. You know. Slept late."

His eyebrows furrow. "I saw you this morning before class or I thought I did."

"Oh. That's my evil twin."

He cocks an eyebrow. "You're a very strange girl." He hands me the pink late slip.

"I know. Thanks."

"So, you're off your grounding, right?"

"Oh, about that. Can I get a copy of my late pass from the other day? If I don't show my parents, they'll ground me again."

He looks at me like he's upset or something and my cheeks warm. "Why are they like that?"

I shrug. "My stepdad doesn't like me."

He writes something on a pad, tears it off, and hands it to me. "Use that. If they call, we have the records here in the system."

"Thanks."

"Can I ask you something?"

"Sure."

"Why were you looking for a writing sample of Casper's the other day?"

"Oh, that. He's playing a joke on me. Trust me, I'm available." I stop. That sounded way too needy. "I meant you don't have to worry about him. I don't like him."

"Why would he play a joke on you?"

"Because he's a jerk. He likes playing games. I don't know. The list is endless."

"That's weird." He seems surprised and I wonder if he knows something about Casper that I don't. "Want me to say something?"

"No, it's okay."

"I'm sorry he's being a dick to you."

"Don't be."

"Do you wanna go out Friday night?" he asks.

I smile. "Yes."

"Great. I'll call you." He gives a meek smile that fills me with warmth.

I make it to the tail end of my class and the bell rings signaling lunchtime. I find Cherry in the line and walk up beside her. She gags at the soggy green beans and sighs.

"You know, you could always bring your lunch," I tell her.

"Oh, hello, my crazy psychotic friend. How are you?" Her lips upturn into a wide smile. "Is your boyfriend okay?"

"He's not my boyfriend."

"If you say so. Seemed like you were making an emergency booty call."

"Seriously?" I give her an annoyed look.

Cherry shrugs and carries her tray to the cashier. I follow her to a table and sit across from her.

"Aren't you going to eat? I bet all that exercise—"

"Enough," I cut her off sternly.

"Then tell me what the hell had you busting out of here like the place was on fire. And for Casper."

"It's hard to explain."

"Hard to explain? You're acting so weird ever since you started having dreams about Douchebag Casper."

"Shh! Keep your voice down."

"They're dreams, Megan. They aren't real. I mean, you dream about him getting shot and suddenly you have to go check on him? There's something going on."

"Nothing is going on." I buried my face in my hands.

"Then help me understand, because honestly I feel like I'm losing you here. You're my best friend, Megan. Lately, it's like all you ever talk about is

Casper. Very little about Vincent or anything else. I'd rather hear you bitch about your parents than hear about Casper."

"These dreams are so real, Cherry. They feel like they're a part of me. Or something. I don't know what it is."

"Maybe you secretly want them to be real so you can be with Casper. I mean, I get why you'd want to hook up with him."

"Can you please stop?"

"I didn't mean that as a tease. I'm just saying, Dream Casper is all romantic and completely the opposite of the real Casper. I don't want you to forget who he is and what he's done to you and me and get involved with him so he can hurt you again. He's only messing with you. You know that."

"I'm not getting involved with him. I wish I knew why I'm having them."

"Maybe see a shrink. I don't know. Stop spending so much time dwelling over them. Seriously. It's not healthy."

"I'm trying. It's hard when they consume my mind."

She frowns. She's right, but she doesn't understand how it feels and I'm not sure I can explain it any better. "Then write about them. Get it out of your system. Maybe that'll help."

I have been. I nod, needing to change the subject because I don't want to spend our lunch hour talking about Casper. "Vincent asked me out."

"I knew it." She squeals. "When are you going out?"

"Friday."

"Omigod. I can't wait."

"You realize it's my date, right?"

She waves her hand. "That doesn't mean I can't live vicariously through you."

"You need a life."

"Well, it seems as though you have two, so let me have one." She bats her eyelashes.

She isn't going to let it go.

"I'm kidding. Trying to lighten you up is all."

"Thanks."

The rest of the day, I worry that Casper's told the entire school what I've done. But I hear nothing. I'm scared of Casper. Terrified of the fool I made of myself this morning and the rumors that are sure to follow. I want to avoid him at all costs. Maybe Cherry is right. I shouldn't focus on the dreams so much and think about Vincent instead. That is harder than it seems. Why am I running for my life in them? Imagining the dark figure walking toward me, I shudder. I can't get it out of my head.

I come home, pull out my books, and open them. My eyes sweep over Casper's note and I read it again.

I focus on the words until they blur. Why is he playing with me? We never talk. I don't understand his need to feel superior. I sigh and bury my head in my hands. What possessed me to run to Casper's house like some crazed moron? What are the kids at school gonna say about me now? Being called an easy lay is bad enough and now this? Maybe I could be sick tomorrow.

The garage door jolts me back to reality and I wait for Ron to pass by my room.

"How was your day?" he asks, stopping in the doorway.

"It was fine," I answer moodily, not looking up from pretending to do my homework. I'm not in the mood for pleasantries with him today.

"Well, aren't you going to ask how my day was?" he huffs.

I sigh. "How was your day?"

"It was good. I think I got a deal with a large company," he says and launches into some boring explanation of some account he can get, but I know it's all talk. Like all the other times, he gloats about how much money he'll make on an account, but there never is a follow-through. Suddenly, the company had issues, or whatever the excuse, and it's never his fault. I think he makes it all up for attention so that we'll be impressed.

He's a liar. This isn't the first job he's been like this with. It's his third job this year.

I nod and pretend I care. He talks only because he likes the sound of his own voice. He does this with everything. Even when he's giving Jonathan or me a lecture. He will spend a good thirty minutes to an hour discussing what we did wrong to how stressed he and Mom are with their jobs to how we need to do better jobs at life to something completely random and off topic. I hardly pay attention to him prattle on about stupid things.

"Do you have your late slip?" he asks when he's done with his annoying tangent.

I pull it out of my bag and hand it to him.

"Good," he says. "Remember you have to set your alarm every night before you go to bed so you'll wake up in the morning," he says as if I'm a five-year-old.

I bite my tongue from saying something I shouldn't and nod. When he finally leaves, I roll my eyes and relax. I place my elbows on my desk and hold my head in my hands.

A year and a half. That's all I have until I can leave.

Eight

Vincent is picking me up in about ten minutes, and my nerves are rampant. It's been a while since I've been on a date.

I settle on a cozy black sweater and dark jeans with booties. I curl the ends of my long hair, contemplating cutting it as it reaches my lower back. I like my long hair though.

For the past week, I've tried ignoring the dreams with Casper and focused on Vincent, which sometimes worked. Casper and I still run for our lives in the dreams and avoid each other in real life. He hasn't stopped staring at me in the halls, and I pretend like he isn't there. No one's called me a witch or a crazy psycho, save for Cherry, so I consider myself lucky and grateful that Casper seems to have kept Monday's incident private.

When the doorbell rings, all five of my dogs bark because of the intruder, and I start freaking out internally. I like Vincent, but my parents make it so awkward. Especially Ron.

Walking down the hall, I feel heat race up my neck to my cheeks as I see Vincent standing by the door with deep purple calla lilies. My heart swells. Those are my favorite flowers. How did he know? He must have talked to Cherry.

"Hi." I smile, taking the flowers.

"Hey." I can't stop looking at him. He looks hot in his gray long-sleeved shirt and jeans.

"Mom, Ron, this is Vincent."

Mom reaches out to shake his hand and Ron follows.

"Hi, I'm Ron. I'm not Megan's dad."

I stiffen and die of embarrassment. Can he make this worse for me? I throw a glare in his direction. What is wrong with him?

I see a flicker of confusion in Vincent's eyes.

Mom offers him a seat on the sofa in the living room, the one room we never use except for Christmas. Both of us sit on the couch, and all I want to do is run.

Vincent takes my hand, giving it a light squeeze, and I relax.

"So, Vincent, tell us about yourself," Mom says.

I hate being asked this question, but Vincent answers like it's the easiest answer in the world.

"I'm seventeen, an only child to my parents who are still married after twenty years. I'm a straight-A student and I plan to attend LSU for architecture."

Mom raises her eyebrows obviously impressed. Ron stands there staring at our clasped hands. I try to remove mine, but Vincent holds tight.

"I like your daughter and I promise to take care of her."

I bite my lip, knowing Mom hates it when a guy she barely knows promises something. She thinks it's something guys say in order to please, and she wants to see results. To a degree, I'm like her.

"Where are you taking Megan tonight?" she asks.

"To Cosmo's Restaurant and to see a movie."

"What time is the movie?"

"It starts at nine and should be out around eleven."

Mom looks to me. "Be home by eleven thirty no later."

I nod, and she turns back into cheerful Mom and smiles. "Have fun."

Vincent and I walk out to his car and when we're strapped in, he lets out a breath. "That was intense."

I release a nervous laugh. "Sorry."

He starts the engine and backs out of the driveway. "No worries."

"You get an A."

"For?"

"Well, for showing up on time and for impressing my parents."

He smiles showing his dimple, which I think is adorable. "That's good. Are they the only ones I've impressed?"

"Hmmm, don't push your luck, now."

He takes my hand in his again and my heart goes crazy.

"So, architecture?" I ask.

"Yeah, my dad was an architect. Designed a lot of buildings."

"Wow. Is he retired now?"

"Yeah."

"What about your mom?"

He loses his smile and tenses. "I'd rather not talk about her right now." When he glances at me, I don't miss the sad look in his eyes.

"Sure. Sorry."

"Don't be."

The rest of the drive is a little awkward only because I feel like I brought up something bad and ruined the night. I don't want to screw things up with Vincent.

He pulls into a parking space at the restaurant. I reach for the door handle, Vincent stops me. I bite my lip seeing the torment on his face and all I want to do is hold him. Comfort him from whatever hurts. He intertwines his fingers with mine and my heart does its crazy dancing. The way his thumb strokes my hand makes my body warm.

Vincent sighs. "Megan, my mom...my mom has cancer." He looks up and meets my eyes. "It's not good. I don't tell people about it. Aside from my friend, you're the only one who knows."

"I'm so sorry." My heart aches for him. I know my mom can be a pain in my butt, but I never want her to get cancer. "Why would you tell me so soon?"

"I trust you, Megan. I wanted you to know."

"I'm here for you if you ever need to talk."

"That's what this necklace is." He pulls a necklace out from his shirt. It's the same one I saw at the haunted house. Round, polished black stone with specks of gold. It looks a little variegated, too. "It's a nuummite. My mom gave it to me for healing."

"It's beautiful."

We go inside the restaurant, and when Vincent gives his name, they immediately seat us. It's a popular place and pricey. Makes me wonder if Vincent is rich. The celestial decorations are beautifully painted on the walls and ceilings. The soft yellow and blue lighting creates a warm and cozy atmosphere. I'm usually nervous on dates, well at least the first few I went on with Matt, or in any setting that puts me with someone I barely know, but with Vincent it's different. The more we talk and get to know each other the more I feel like we've known each other for years. He makes me comfortable and at ease. I feel like I can tell him anything.

"What do you like to do? Other than design things."

"If I tell you, will you promise not to laugh?"

I press my lips together and nod.

"Play the guitar. I know it's a silly notion but I kinda hope to become a musician someday." He blushes.

"Do you play it well?"

"Yeah, I guess. I mean, I think so."

"Then you're a musician."

He chuckles. "I wish it were that easy."

"Why not? If you want to become famous and all that you gotta try. Have you got a demo tape?"

"Not yet."

"Are you in a band or is this a solo gig?"

"Right now, it's solo but I wouldn't mind having a band."

"We should do tryouts. I'm sure there are lots of people at school that would like to join."

"Are you going to be our singer?"

"No, I don't sing. Besides, I'd get all the attention and the band would resent me and we'd eventually fall apart or something."

He raises his eyebrows. "Why would you get all the attention?"

"Come on that's music 101. Female lead singers always get the attention."

"Yeah, that happens for every band though. Lead singers always gets the most attention."

"Still. I can't sing to save my life. My dog cringes when I sing in the shower."

He laughs and I join him. "You could lip-sync or use auto-tune."

"If I'm going to do something, I'm going to do it right. Lip-syncing is lazy and if you have to use auto-tune, you shouldn't be singing."

"Fair enough. My dad's not a big fan of this path, though. It's probably all a pipe dream."

"Which do you enjoy more?"

"Both. I don't know. Everything is kinda all up in the air right now."

"I'm sorry." I hate apologizing so much but I don't know what to say. I wish I knew the right words.

"What about you? What about your writing?"

I shrug, feeling self-conscious. "I scribble some words down."

He cocks an eyebrow. "Like what? Tell me."

Playing with my napkin, I stare at my hands. "I sometimes write poetry and stories. I'm actually working on a crazy idea right now."

He leans forward. "What's it about?"

"I'm not sure." I give a soft laugh. "I had a weird dream," I begin leaving Casper out of this conversation. "About two people who are in love but they're enemies. Kinda like Romeo & Juliet. One's a Sprite and one is an Elf. They're searching for this Jewel that helps them stay alive from a bad guy who wants to kill them. It's weird because it takes place in some other time period."

"Like when?"

I shrug. "I don't know. Like the Rococo time period. Early 1700s France."

"That's specific."

"It seems to work. The dream I had was in that time."

"That's amazing that you can come up with such a story from a dream."

"Stephenie Meyer did it with *Twilight*."

"Maybe you'll be the next Stephenie Meyer." He winks. "That's amazing though. I love history, so if you ever need any ideas, I can help."

We continue our music conversation and talk about how we both enjoy writing. He says he writes songs all the time and I mention wanting to read them or hear him play. I've always been a sucker for poetry and lyrics. It's like my Achilles' Heel. Learning this about Vincent makes me like him even more. I love his passion and the way he describes wanting to help people with his music and wanting his art to matter. It's such a shame that his dad seems to reign that part of him back to focus on architecture.

We talk all the way to the movies and there is never an awkward silence. I love how simple it is with Vincent. Sometimes our words seem to overlap each other's, and we joke around matching each other's jabs. He can dish it and I can take it and vice versa. I've never had this connection with a guy before, something that feels right.

We choose to see a comedy and while I stand in line for popcorn and drinks, Vincent gives me money to pay and goes to the restroom.

Bored standing in line I look at my nails.

"We need to talk," a voice says from behind me. Before I turn around, my heart stops. Its beating races as I peer up into Casper's brown eyes. "I'll be waiting," he says and nods toward the counter. "Your turn."

I turn back and order awkwardly. My words are jumbled, and it takes me a second to get out what I'm trying to tell the cashier. I don't understand my reaction at all. Except that I'm scared about what he wants to talk about. I don't want to rehash Monday at all.

Vincent reappears and I catch Casper standing down the hall before we walk into the theatre. I hope Vincent doesn't see him. We take our seats and watch people trickle in until about five minutes into the previews. I try to think of an excuse to leave for a minute to see what Casper wants.

"I'll be right back," I whisper to Vincent. "Do you need anything?"

"No, I'm good. Is everything okay?"

"Yeah, they gave me diet Coke instead of regular. I won't be gone long. Promise."

He nods. I follow the orange stair lights to the exit door and as I exit the theatre, I look for Casper. Immediately, I think this is a trick. He grabs my hand and pulls me against the wall behind a giant movie display. It's like our private little bubble filled with this weird tension.

"What are you doing?" I ask, searching his eyes. His hands splay out on the wall as if keeping me from leaving. It makes me feel a little uneasy, but I don't let it show. I wonder why his eyes are so intense.

"Why did you come over that day?"

"I'm sorry. I shouldn't have. Are we done?"

"I've been dreaming of you for two weeks straight now."

At this, my back straightens, and tightness clutches my stomach. This is not what I wanted or expected to hear.

"I wrote you a note so we could talk. You never called so I thought it was useless and tried to ignore it. Then you came over to wake me up. Which was strange because I swear, I thought I died. This man shot me—"

"He was trying to shoot me, wasn't he?" I tense and my stomach continues endless somersaults.

His eyebrows furrow. "Yeah. And we're on the run. I was looking for this jewel—"

I shake my head. "Why are you messing with me?"

"I'm not."

"Yeah, your word is as good as O.J. Simpson's." I cross my arms in front of my chest.

"Megan, please. I'm not messing with you. I can't explain what it is. But I'm so." He pauses. "I'm so in love with you in my dreams. And the dreams are so intimate."

Heat rises on the back of my neck, and it angers me. Someone overheard Cherry and me talking about my dream and he decided to play. People are so cruel. I can't believe he would use my own dreams against me. I want to throw my full cup of soda on him, but I don't want to cause a scene.

I take a breath. "I have nothing but contempt for you. So, if you would please let me get back to my date." I push him, he drops his hands and I start toward the entrance to the theatre.

"You have to stay away from him," he blurts, and I halt. "I don't know why, but I don't feel good about him."

I scoff and shake my head. "You've got some nerve." I take a step, but he grabs my arm. I can't stop myself as I turn back to him, I chuck the Coke all over him. The brown liquid drips from his chin and soaks his shirt. I immediately want to apologize—this isn't me, but maybe he will get the hint and leave me alone. He releases my arm.

"What have I done to you for you to hate me so much?" he shouts wiping his face with his sleeve. I'm sure people are staring now.

I raise my eyebrows. "Wow. Would you like me to write it all down and hand in my 20-page research paper by next week?"

"What are you talking about?"

"Right now, is an example. Stop harassing me because I'm tired of this little game." I leave him standing there dripping with Coke and ignore his calls for me. I find my way back to my seat and feel tears surfacing, but I hold them in. That's what hot showers are for.

"Are you okay?" Vincent whispers.

"Yeah." I give a fake smile.

I can't decide if the movie isn't that funny or if my mind is set on what Casper said or didn't say. Something he said doesn't sit well with me. I haven't told Cherry about how intimate the dreams are or about the mysterious jewel. Is he embellishing or can he see into my head or something? How does he know about the jewel? Maybe I did tell Cherry about it.

I know all this is another one of his tricks. Why would he tease me so cruelly over my dreams? Like I can help what I dream about. Why go through so much trouble? We are in high school. Doesn't he have other things to take up his time?

And why would he tell me to stay away from Vincent? Who does he think he is acting protective over me?

"Are you sure you're okay?" Vincent pulls into my driveway, and I feel guilty for the silent car ride.

"Yeah, sorry."

"What did he say to you?"

I meet his eyes. "What?"

"I saw him talking to you in line. Kinda figured he wanted to talk to you."

He saw Casper talking to me? Did he even go to the restroom? Was he watching us? Maybe my brain is overthinking. "Nothing. It's no big deal. He brought up bad memories is all."

"I'm sorry."

"It's okay. I had a good time tonight." I try to put on my best smile.

He lifts an eyebrow. "You did?"

"Yes." I wonder if he thinks my night was ruined by Casper. "Did you?"

"Yes."

We get out of the car, and he walks me to my front door. It isn't that cold outside, but I know the cold weather will come back. Weather in Alabama is like playing the lottery. No one ever knows what's going to happen from one day to the next. One December it snowed the day after a tornado raged through.

"Do you want to do something tomorrow night?" Vincent asks.

"No dice. I have to work."

"Do you always work?"

I let out a small laugh. "Yeah. Sorry. You can thank my parents for that."

"How late do you work?"

"Midnight."

"Ouch. Well, maybe this will give you something to think about." He takes a step closer, and his lips touch mine. His hands entangle through my hair, and he presses harder. My heart is frantic, and I love the softness of his lips. Suddenly, in my mind I see a man in a black pinstripe suit smiling at a woman in a long navy dress. Their faces are blurry though. Vincent abruptly pulls away.

"I'm sorry," he says breathlessly. "A little eager." Blood rushes to his cheeks under the porch light and he looks away.

"It's okay." I wonder who on earth I saw in my mind or what I was thinking.

He brushes my hair from my face and pulls me closer with his hand cupping my neck and tilting my head toward his. He kisses me again, softly, and I see the man in the suit kiss the woman in a navy dress with raven hair. Vincent draws me closer against him and my pulse quickens. Once his lips are on mine there is desire and passion and hunger. The immense feelings jolt me. He pulls away and searches my eyes. I'm so wound up from the intense kiss that I think my knees are actually weak.

"I gotta go," he says, winded. "But I'll call you." He clumsily walks toward his car. He doesn't look back. Something has him rattled. Like he's scared. Is he embarrassed by how passionate that kiss was?

Thanks for making me incredibly insecure, I want to tell him. Before I can say anything, he's already in his car and speeds away like he has a plane to catch.

My heart sinks. I don't know what I did. Either I'm that good of a kisser that it made him so awkward and nervous or he's suddenly afraid of me. Maybe I can't kiss at all.

What was I thinking about when Vincent kissed me? It was more of a vision or something. Am I hallucinating now? Dreaming of one boy while seeing things when I kiss another? *Great.* So now I enter the world of absolute craziness.

Nine

s I hold Casper, waiting and hoping for him to wake from the gunshot wound, I'm reminded of when we first met. We spent every single day with each other. We took walks in the rose garden. Lie in the lazy wheat field. Or under a cover of trees that gave us our own private space. Danced with each other at the balls. We talked endlessly and I could not get enough of this strange man. I had always known Vincent, so maybe this attraction was because Casper was new and exciting. But it felt stronger than that.

Days turned to weeks, and I fell in love with him. I was with another man, and while it was so wrong, my feelings for Casper were stronger than anything I had ever felt. We gazed at each other and I placed my hands on his chest. He reached up and tucked a few strands of hair behind my ear and I felt his fingertips trace along my shoulder, sending the hair at the nape to stand on end. I slid my hands up and around his neck, running my hands through his soft hair.

Casper leaned down ever so slightly, and our foreheads touched. Briefly, our lips touched sending a current to my heart. He nibbled on my bottom lip and drew me closer in, his mouth locked onto mine. I couldn't tell if it was the summer heat filling me or if it was from his kiss. I had never felt such passion and I knew I could never say goodbye to him. I wanted him forever. And I would do anything to make it happen.

Casper abruptly pulled away, breathless. "Megan, we can't—this can't happen." His voice was low but hearing the ache in his voice I knew he didn't want it to be true.

"I would end it with Vincent. For you," I whispered.

He sighed. "Once I fall for someone, I'm in it for life."

At his words, I froze. I realized what he'd been trying to tell me all along. Why it would torture him for the rest of his existence. Why we shouldn't have even been talking to each other. It had nothing to do with my being with someone else. He wasn't a Fairy Sprite.

He was an Elf. My enemy.

I didn't run from him that night. Instead, I promised him I would help find the Jewel, a mysterious Jewel to keep his kind alive. For days and weeks, we searched and came up empty. I told Florence about Casper and myself. I convinced him to run away with me. It was the only way we could be together. And now I'm not sure what I've done.

Casper's eyes flutter open, and relief washes over me. I kiss him. "He can't keep doing this to us. We have to end this."

"We will. We will survive this."

Cherry stares at me, wide-eyed, eager for details like a Labrador waiting for a treat or something. We made plans to eat lunch before work. Hopefully, lunch and work will keep my mind off Casper and the dreams and not make me fret about Vincent's weird reaction last night. I'm tired of waking up and feeling an urge to see Casper. To be in his arms. To feel his lips on mine.

Ugh. Why does it have to be Casper? Can't I dream about Vincent?

"We have any dreams last night?" She waggles her eyebrows and nudges me.

I swallow hard. "Of Casper?"

She recoils. "No, Vincent. Tell me what happened." She props her elbows on the table.

"We went out."

"And," she presses.

"Then he took me home."

Cherry's smile immediately fades. "What happened? You don't seem as happy as I expected. Was he a jerk?"

The waitress returns with our drinks, and we order sandwiches and fries.

"No. We had an amazing time, and he kissed me." Cherry squeals at this. "Then he left in a hurry. Just left. I don't know what I did."

"What? Was it a good kiss?"

"I thought so. What if it's me? What if I'm a terrible kisser?"

Cherry presses her lips together and thinks for a moment. "I don't think he'd flee like that if you were a bad kisser. What happened the rest of the night? Was there something that happened that made him run like that?"

I hesitate not wanting to tell her. "Casper."

She looks at me confused. "What?"

I tell her what happened, and she laughs.

"You threw your coke on him? That is priceless."

"He keeps messing with me. Vincent saw us talking. If that bothered him, why would he kiss me in the first place?"

"Hmm, true."

Maybe he had to check on his mom. But that doesn't seem right because his phone never went off. "I don't know."

"He's a very shy guy. I wouldn't worry. Maybe send him a text telling him what a great time you had."

"Maybe. Oh, you'll be happy to know I've started writing."

"Yay!" She smiles. "I wanna hear all about it."

"It's about a couple running from the bad guys in search of a Jewel that will save their lives."

"I can't wait to read it." Cherry smiles and the waitress brings our food. I'm starving, but my stomach is still wound up from last night and everything else.

"Luke works tonight."

"You gonna ask him out?"

"I thought you were gonna drop hints?" She gives me a puppy-dog look.

I roll my eyes. "Wimp."

"It should be the guy's job anyway."

"I'll tell him you said that."

"Yes. Wait-no. Don't say that. He'll think I'm demanding."

"You are a little."

"But he doesn't have to know that."

"He will if you two start dating."

"Not in the beginning. You gotta release small bits of crazy at a time." She smiles innocently.

I laugh, shaking my head.

Afterward, we head to work where we count our tills still trying to come up with a good enough reason why Vincent left. But neither one of us do.

We finish counting our tills and walk out of the office. I hear something hard and plastic crash to the floor and coins scatter. I look behind me and Cherry stands mortified that she had bumped into Luke, sending her entire till and its contents across the floor.

Luke smiles and his dimples show on his slightly chubby cheeks. He is thin and attractive in that cute-boyish way. I like my men to be a little manlier, but I think about Vincent. He kinda has both looks going for him. Cherry talks endlessly about Luke's green eyes and how much she wants to run her hands through his thick brown hair. Any time he looks at her, she tells me about it. Which is a lot, apparently. He goes to a different school, so she only sees him at work, but that doesn't stop her from switching shifts to work with him all the time.

We help her pick up her money and he smiles widely at her. "I'll see you down there."

Her face turns so red. It's cute.

Working Saturday nights suck. I'm at work and all these other kids are out with their friends or boyfriends and girlfriends. They never have to work because their parents pay for everything. They all have to come into Bailey's for gum or a Coke before walking around the strip mall. I finish bagging this lady's groceries and turn to greet my next customer with a smile, but it turns into an annoyed frown. Casper stands with a bunch of gum and drinks. His friends wait for him by the door.

"Hi," I say, only because I'm required to greet customers. I scan his items without meeting his eyes.

"Not gonna dump the coke on me, are you?"

I sigh.

"I didn't know you worked here."

"There's a lot you don't know about me." I feel his heated gaze on me, and I try so hard not to look up. "Twenty-four ten," I say, meeting his eyes.

"How was your date last night?" he asks, and I suspect a hint of jealousy.

"None of your business."

He hands me money and I take it without touching him. I give him the change and receipt.

"Will you call me tonight?"

"Nope. You'd better go before they start making fun of you for talking to me."

"I don't care what they think. Please call me."

"Sorry. I didn't need your number, so I threw it away." That isn't true. I haven't gotten around to throwing it away.

He seems hurt, which makes me feel guilty. "Why are you being like this?"

"Why are *you* being like this? I don't like you."

"Sorry I bothered you," he snaps and walks away.

I exhale and I feel bad. I don't like being mean to people. Does he expect me to be like all the other girls and fawn all over him?

"What's his problem?" Luke asks from behind me as he mops the aisle.

"He's a jerk," I say.

"Yeah, sounded like it. Reminds me of some of the guys at my school."

"Reminds me of all guys."

"I resent that," he teases.

"Sorry. Most guys. Anyway, when are you going to ask Cherry out?"

"What?" His eyes widen and he stops mopping.

"You heard me." I'm not being subtle at all and I'm sure Cherry would kick me if she heard me, but I don't want it to drag out since she's putting me in the middle. Of course, I could have said no but I want Cherry to be happy.

He sighs. "Does she even like me? Sometimes I wonder."

I laugh. "Are you kidding me? I think you need a lesson in what it means when a girl acts like this."

"She doesn't talk to me."

"She's shy. Around you."

"Oh. I wasn't sure. Sometimes she seems mad at me."

"Yeah, she's masking her feelings."

"Oh. She likes me?"

I roll my eyes and nod. "Yeah. You should ask her out tonight."

He smirks and continues mopping past me.

Our shift finally ends and the three of us walk out together, but I tell them goodnight and leave them. I see a piece of paper under my wiper on my windshield. I yank it out and read it:

I'm sorry, but please call me. We need to talk. Casper. He left his number again. I sigh, wad the paper up and toss it in the backseat. Can't he get a clue? I slam my door shut and run my fingers through my hair. What is wrong with me? I repel the nice guys and yet attract the jerks.

I won't call Casper and Vincent never called or texted me which worries me. Whatever happened, he doesn't seem to like me as much as I thought. This is another reason I hate having my parents meet my date before we go out. Now they will constantly ask about him and wonder what happened to him.

Dejected, I drive home, and when Savannah sees me, she frantically runs around in excitement. Hopping on her hind legs, she begs me like a child to be picked up. I toss my purse and keys on my bed, and pick her up, wherein she licks my face dry and gets her black and white hair all over my shirt. But I don't mind. I love the little goober. And she makes me feel better. I set her down on the ground, round up my pajamas and head for the shower, in which she follows.

She patiently waits for me on the rug in front of the bathtub until I finish my shower. Our nightly ritual. I climb into the bed, and she burrows under the covers, until she's comfortable. Which can take anywhere from five seconds to five minutes with her turning around in circles, moving the blanket, and burrowing some more. Crazy dog.

Same as always. I need a life. And not the messed up weird, crazy life that my dreams are.

Why am I even still thinking about these stupid dreams? Because they feel so real? Because Casper is in them and it's like a little fantasy?

I shake my head. There is no way that Casper is remotely a fantasy. I'm still left with a cruel desire deep down like I'm missing something in my life, but I don't understand how I can when I don't even know what it is.

Dreading to sleep, I take out my notebook and write. So much comes to my mind. If anything, it will ease the stress. I hope.

Ten

fter running through the forest with Casper, I dress for school. Is that the only time a boy is ever going to like me? In my dreams? I shake my head. I shouldn't be so focused on boys anyway. I should focus on school so I can get out of here.

When I arrive at school, I close my car door on my backpack strap which spills out my books. Anger fills me. I want to sleep. Without dreams. I want to know what happened to Vincent and why I deter him so much. I want Casper to leave me alone with his stupid pranks.

As I pick up my last book and free the strap from my car door, I start walking toward the school, but stop when Vincent approaches me.

Rolling my eyes, I walk around him. He didn't have the decency to tell me he doesn't like me in private. Has to wait until we're at school so he can make me cry.

"Megan—"

I spin around. "You never called. If you don't like me, at least tell me. I mean what was that Friday night? I thought we hit it off, I mean, you kissed me. Then ran."

"Something happened. I didn't know what to do. I freaked out."

"Wow. I never heard that excuse before. Thanks for helping my self-esteem."

"Come on, Megan. What do you expect me to say when something like that happens?"

Has he never kissed a girl before? "We kissed. What's the big deal?"

"It was more than that. It was intense."

"Yeah, it was. Does that scare you?"

"A little. I don't know how to explain it. I...I saw something."

That brings me up short. "What?"

He drags his hands down his face. "When we kissed, I saw us, I guess. Like we've known each other forever."

What is seriously going on? I'm dreaming about one guy and sharing *visions* with another? What am I? A freak? Am I a witch?

"I knew you wouldn't understand." Vincent shakes his head and starts to walk away.

"No, wait," I call out. "I-I saw it, too."

He stops abruptly and turns around. "What?"

"I saw it, too. When you kissed me, I saw two people kissing like they'd been in love."

His eyes widen. "What does this mean?"

"I don't know." I'm not sure I want to know. I think I'm seriously going to have a panic attack. Whatever happened to normal teenage life? You know, boy meets girl, they like each other, they date, they have a great time. Maybe I need to see a shrink. If I'm seeing these things, and Casper and Vincent are seeing these things, I'm obviously the common thread. Does this happen with every guy I encounter? I briefly think about pulling the next guy that passes by and kissing him to see what happens.

"Can I try something?" Vincent asks.

"What?"

He closes the distance between us, and my breath hitches. He reaches his hand around the nape of my neck pulling my mouth to his. His soft lips brush mine. My heart rattles against my chest as my knees wobble. If anyone is watching, I don't care. As his lips dance with mine, the kiss awakens something inside me that I never knew existed. Except when I kiss Casper in my dreams.

Vincent slowly pulls away resting his forehead on mine. We stand there catching our breath. "I've never felt anything like that," he breathes.

"Me neither." Unless the kisses in my dreams count. *Ugh*. Why am I thinking of Casper? "I didn't see anything, did you?"

"No."

"That's very bizarre."

"What could it mean?"

"I don't know."

"Do you forgive me for not calling?" he asks, his eyes filled with sadness. "I was freaked out and I spent the weekend at the hospital with my mom. I'm sorry. I should've called."

"Vincent." I take his hand squeezing it. "I'm so sorry. I didn't know. Is she okay?"

"She's fine. They were administering tests. Do you forgive me?"

"Of course. I wish you would've called or texted though. This whole time I thought you hated me or something."

He shakes his head, and his eyes are fixed on me with an intense look. "I could never hate you." He gives a crooked smile. "Besides, if you didn't see the same thing as me, you would think I was some freak."

"Maybe we both are."

He smiles wider. "I like that."

"Promise me something?"

"Anything."

"Don't keep me on edge like that. If you need to talk or whatever don't be afraid of me. I'm here for you."

"You got it." He kisses my forehead and takes my hand. His thumb caresses my hand sending warmth all over me. We walk inside the school, and he escorts me to my locker.

He gazes into my eyes, and I almost melt. I love the dark blue color of his irises. It's my favorite color. "You are beautiful, Megan. You shouldn't hide such beauty." He kisses me with enough heat to set my insides on fire and in my mind, I see myself running into Vincent's arms as if I haven't seen him in ages. He wraps his arms around me and holds me tight.

We pull apart, panting. "What was that?" I whisper.

"What?"

"It felt like I hadn't seen you in forever."

"I know." He plants one more kiss on my lips.

"We should get to class."

He grins. "I'll see you later." I make my way to history class in a complete daze and sit next to Cherry.

"Are you okay?" she asks. "I mean, I take it from the huge grin on your face that you're fine. Where were you this morning?"

I giggle. "Vincent."

She laughs and playfully punches me on the shoulder. "You two are good then?"

"Yeah. It was all a misunderstanding."

"Good. When are we double dating?"

"Whenever you want."

I finally found a distraction from the dreams.

Eleven

"Let's skip today," Vincent says, his blue eyes pinning mine.

"What? Why?"

"You're leaving me for three days."

It's the last week of school before Christmas break, and we're standing by my car in the school parking lot. Jonathan and I are going to see our dad for the weekend, and while I'm excited, part of me is sad because I have to leave Vincent. Maybe the whole distance makes the heart grow fonder is true. Things have been amazing with him. I'm falling head over heels for Vincent. We spend many nights on the phone or hanging out writing out my story. It's weird but I like it.

My dreams still continue, but Casper and I haven't said a word to each other in weeks. Just the way I like it.

I squeeze his hand. "It'll be okay."

"We should have today then. I want to hang out with you before you leave."

"We have school though."

He shrugs. "Come on." He kisses my neck, warming my body.

"You know I'll get in trouble."

Vincent lets out a sigh. "You don't want to spend time with me?"

"That's not it at all. We have school. And my parents."

He rolls his eyes. "No one's going to care if we miss today. You have work tonight, so I'm not even going to see you before you leave. Please? One day? I need to get away for a while and I want to be with you."

Biting my lip, I agree.

Smiling, he leads me to his car, and soon we're driving on the interstate going north.

"Where are we going?"

"It's a surprise."

Nerves hit my stomach. "I can't be too far from home. I still have to work tonight."

"Would you relax? I promise it'll be worth it."

Taking risks. That's what being a teenager is all

about, I remind myself. "Okay."

An hour later, we arrive at Noccalula Falls. I haven't been here since I was a kid. I don't wonder why he brought me here, because once I see the water, I'm eager to get out of the car. The falls are at the start of the park. We get out of the car and walk across the wooden bridge over the falls. There's an iron statue of Noccalula attempting to fall.

As we round the fence, we find a spot and with him holding me from behind, we gaze at the beautiful, flowing water as it cascades down into the creek. A little rainbow forms at the bottom.

"You know the story, right?" he asks.

"Vaguely. It's been a while."

"Legend has it she was a Cherokee princess. Her father arranged a marriage between her and another man from a neighboring tribe. But she was in love with someone else. Her lover was driven away, and her father demanded she marry the other man. Distraught, she jumped into the falls killing herself. Her father remorseful, named the falls after her."

"Oh yeah. It's so sad."

"Mm-hmm." He holds me tight, and I feel like something's wrong. "Please don't leave me," he whispers in my ear.

I twist around to face him. "Why would I leave you?"

His eyes are serious yet sad. I lean back against

the fence, loving the sound of the waterfall.

"It's…" He tilts his head back and closes his eyes.

"What? What is it?"

He opens his eyes and looks at me as if he's afraid to tell me. "I feel very strongly toward you. And I've got demons from my past that I'm afraid will come back to haunt me."

"Demons like what?" I ask slowly.

He watches me as he speaks, I guess watching my reaction. "Megan, I used to do cocaine. And heroin."

"I know a lot of people who have tried drugs." I shrug.

Vincent hesitates. "I used to be addicted."

I'm not sure what my face looks like, but inside I'm shocked. He's only sixteen. How can someone so young have already been addicted? "D-do you still do them?"

"No. I was in rehab for a while. Which is probably why you don't know me. I started at this school in ninth grade, but I hardly went and in tenth grade I was even more messed up and my dad forced me into rehab. I've been clean since June. I don't want you to worry that I would involve myself in that again. I've got a new addiction." He meets my eyes.

I'm not sure that's healthy either, but I don't think about it too much.

"Sorry. That was bad. I was trying to lighten the mood." He lets out a short laugh.

"I'm not here to judge you. You've decided to make your life better. You're a good person," I tell him. His eyes are fixed on me for a moment, and he crushes his mouth to mine. I love the feel of his lips and I love the passionate way he kisses me.

"Thank you," he whispers. "You're so amazing, mon trésor. I got you something for Christmas." He hands me a black, velvet box.

I open it and gasp. It's a silver necklace with a snowflake pendant made of crystals. "It's beautiful. Thank you." I kiss him.

"Merry Christmas." He clasps it around my neck, and I smile.

By the time we get back to my car, lonely in the parking lot at school, it's almost time for my shift at work.

"Are you sure you have to work?" he asks.

I smile. "Yes."

"Can't you call in?"

"I wish."

"What time do you get off?"

"Midnight."

He groans. "What am I going to do?"

I give a wicked grin. "I'll give you something to think about." I unhook my seatbelt and climb over the console and into his lap, straddling him. I press my mouth to his, hard, and find his tongue. He softly moans and I smile on the inside. His hands are all over me and I move to his neck and nibble on his ear. He grips my thighs and tenses up. His breathing picks up and inches his hand up my skirt.

I stop his hand and kiss his forehead.

"I'm definitely going to need to take a cold shower tonight."

"Vincent." I playfully slap him on the shoulder.

He brushes his lips against mine and wraps his arms around me tight and lets out a relaxing sigh. "Thank you for today. I needed it."

"Of course."

His lips travel down my jawline to my neck and my heart responds quickly. "You're mine." His hand moves up my sweater and traces beneath my bra sending heat to spread throughout me.

When his mouth is on mine, a vision hits me and I see Vincent above me, naked and panting, as we make love in the glow of the candlelight. He lowers his mouth to my ear. *I love you, Megan. Don't leave me.*

"I will never leave you. My love is only yours."

I pull away from Vincent, breaking the vision, and we're both out of breath. I'm so hot and worked up from the vision of us actually...making love. These visions are too much. If I'm not careful, I'll let it consume me and I won't have any control over my actions.

But they're so addicting.

I press my lips to his and he responds with the same urgency as me. I have never thought about wanting to lose my virginity, but I do now. I want Vincent. I slip my hands under his shirt and feel his smooth stomach. Hands are everywhere. Our kisses turn messy. We both moan at each other's touch and things are starting to escalate. I want him, but not like this and he seems to sense that.

I pull back slightly, resting my forehead against his. "I gotta go."

"Call in tomorrow."

"I can't."

He kisses my neck. "Please. I miss you, mon trésor."

"What does that mean?"

He kisses my cheek. "It's French for my treasure. Sorry. Do you not like it?"

"I love it. Do you know French?"

"A little. My family originates from France."

"How am I now learning this?"

He shrugs.

"It's kinda hot when you speak French."

He smiles. "Je veux être avec toi pour toujours," he whispers in my ear sending chills down my spine. "Call in tomorrow. I want more time with you."

I can't resist. "Okay."

Vincent widens his smile and kisses me once more. I slide off his lap and get out of the car.

"Hey, Megan?"

I turn back as he hangs his head out the window. His eyes rove up and down and he looks at me with desire. "You're sexy as hell."

I blush, rolling my eyes and reluctantly get inside my car completely drunk on happiness. I laugh at how much I'm smiling, but I can't help it. Now if only I can dream about Vincent instead of Casper.

I'm supposed to work a few hours before Jonathan and I leave for my dad's, but instead I meet Vincent at IHOP. He doesn't ever seem to want me to go to his house. We've been together for two months now. I wonder if he's afraid of letting me see his mom or vice versa. Do his parents even know about me? It's a mystery.

When I arrive, I give him a hug, but he seems distant. He looks exhausted, almost like he's hungover or something. "What's wrong?" I ask.

"Kinda left me high and dry last night and now you're leaving town."

I'm taken aback. "What?"

"Nothing. Let's eat."

I hate that he's upset with me, and I want to make it right. When we get to our table, he stares at the menu. My heart is pounding.

"I'm sorry." I reach for his hand across the table.

"Where's your necklace?"

I absently touch my neck. *Dammit.* "I left it at home."

"You don't like it?"

"No, that's not it. I'm not used to wearing jewelry and I forgot to put it on."

He gives me a pointed look. "When a guy gives you a necklace, you wear it, Megan. If you don't like it, I'll take it back."

"I love it. Why are you being like this? I didn't mean to leave you high and dry last night. I had to go to work."

"Like always."

"But it's true."

"Was there someone at work that you'd rather spend time with?"

Where is this coming from? Why is he being like this? What have I done? "No. Why would you think that?"

"Well, you were in a hurry to get to work and now you're not wearing your necklace."

Damn my forgetful memory. "I'm sorry."

"Just order."

I swallow hard and the rest of breakfast is awkward and tense. I shouldn't have forgotten the necklace. I don't want to bring it to my dad's, and something happen to it. Last time Vincent acted like this I was going to my dad's. Does he hate it that much when I leave? He gives me a one-armed hug and tells me goodbye leaving me completely mystified.

All weekend at my dad's, the only thing I can think about is Vincent and how I upset him. I haven't heard from him at all. I don't know what to do. I can't even enjoy myself, and it makes me sad and guilty. I love spending time with my dad, Kim, and Olivia, but now I want to go home so I can see Vincent and hash this out.

"Men and their secrets," Kim says to me in the car. We're on our way back from the store and I've told her everything that happened. She's a lot younger than my dad and maybe that's why she and I get along so well. She's only seven years older than me. "They never tell you the whole truth." I can't help but wonder if she's talking about my dad. I don't ask to elaborate.

"I trust Vincent, though. He's been very truthful to me." I left out the part where he was addicted to drugs, but who would come out and tell someone that if they didn't want to be completely honest?

"Well, maybe he has a lot on his mind with his mom."

"That's true." I know it's probably on his mind constantly and I don't think about it because it isn't happening to me. Guilt falls over me. I haven't been fair to him. It's Christmas and I can't imagine what it must be like to have a sick mother not knowing if she's going to survive. I send a text wishing him a Merry Christmas and letting him know I'm here.

He never responds.

Twelve

asper and I laugh and play and chase each other until we collapse breathless in the tall grass. He smiles and leans over me, holding himself up on one elbow. The desired look lingers in his brown eyes. I grab his shirt, pulling him to me, and kiss him. He slides my white top down, exposing my shoulder, and his lips graze against my shoulder to my collarbone. He travels to my neck and the spot behind my ear, his touch hot against my skin.

"I love you," I whisper. "I'm yours, forever."

Casper crushes his mouth to mine with an edge to his kiss. His tongue licks my upper lip, and he tugs on it with his lips. He kisses my cheek and nibbles my ear. I feel his hand touch my side through my navy dress and it sends a rush of passion throughout me. My fingers curl around the front of his shirt, finding the buttons. I unbutton them and graze my hand across his smooth chest. I feel him shudder. His mouth is all over me. My lips. My neck. My jaw.

"I love you so much, Megan. I will keep you safe," he says.

When I open my eyes, I gasp at the moon. A shadow slowly passes over it.

An eclipse. Except, it's not.

Casper and I untangle ourselves.

"Is that a..."

"Dragon."

I hold Casper tight refusing to let go. The Sprites have declared war and sent dragons. I want it to end. For them to stop chasing us so we can be together. I know it will never stop. Not unless I do something about it. I will do anything to be with Casper. He is my heart and my soul. He is what home feels like.

"We have to go," he whispers, pulling me to my feet.

A screech echoes in the night causing us to cover our ears. Fire erupts from the mysterious flying beast above. We hear a loud explosion off in the distance and both turn our heads in the direction. The same direction as Casper's home.

I gasp at the dragon above us with wisps of dark smoke. In the distance, I hear more cannons and guns and orange illuminates the sky. A war started by our love.

I want to skip school today, but the way my parents are, I know better. Plus, it's the first day back after Christmas break. It's been two weeks and I still haven't heard from Vincent. It makes me sad.

Dragging myself out of bed, I reluctantly slip a maroon sweater over my head and slide on some jeans. I brush through the thick, long tangled mess that is my hair and put on makeup. My eyes are bloodshot like I have been awake all night or cried all night. Or like I spent the entirety of my dream running through a forest. Every time a cannon fired, I woke up. And when I fell back asleep, I returned to the dream like I never left. Needless to say, I'm exhausted.

When I meet Cherry at school, I put on a brave face, but every time someone slams a locker, I jump. I keep looking around thinking I'm going to see an orange sky in the distance or a dragon.

"Are you okay? Why are you so jumpy?"

"Dreams."

"Ugh. You're still having them? Have you written down the story at all?"

"Yes. I've written everything. Even Vincent and I came up with ideas and created this elaborate world but I'm still having the dreams."

"I take it Vincent doesn't know you're dreaming about Casper."

I give her a pointed look.

She throws up her hands. "Hey, just asking."

"It doesn't matter. Still haven't heard from Vincent."

"Ugh. What is up with him?"

I shrug.

"Least you remembered to wear the necklace today. Maybe he's going through a lot and isn't used to having anyone to talk to about it."

"Maybe." A small part of me wonders if he's using drugs again or is there someone else? My stomach twists at the thought. Did something happen to his mom? I have to trust him.

All day is a blur and I'm so sleepy, but I'm scared to pass out in class for fear I'll dream again. I don't want to say something in the middle of class or scream if a cannon goes off in my dream world.

On my way to third period science, I feel someone tenderly take my hand and pull me off to the side. I jump ready to attack, but when I turn, I'm shocked to see Casper. He looks exhausted. My heart launches into rapid-fire mode, not because he scared the crap out of me. We haven't spoken in weeks, and I thought for sure the dreams would have stopped by now, but they've only worsened.

"What?" I ask.

"Will you please talk to me?" Casper pleads. "This is driving me crazy."

I sigh and try not to focus on all the people staring at us as they pass. Like they're shocked that Casper's speaking to someone like me. I meet his eyes. "Fine. I'll call you tonight when I get off work, okay?"

"Can I have your number in case you decide to throw mine away?"

I stare at him, and he raises his eyebrows. I reluctantly agree. If this is what it takes to get rid of him, fine. He can call all he wants, but I don't have to answer. "Do you have a pen?"

He holds one out but the end of it looks as though a dog chewed on it. He clears his throat and reaches for another one. "Sorry," he says. "Little on edge lately."

I take the non-chewed pen and he holds out his hand. I disregard the tingling sensation I get when I touch his hand. I write my number, hand him back his pen and walk away. I can't believe I gave Casper Truitt my number. I am stupid. I totally set myself up for endless prank calls and who knows what. My number could be posted all over town if someone wanted to have a good time. I wouldn't put it past him or his friends to do that. What have I done? What on earth possessed me to give Casper my number? *Stupid. Stupid. Stupid.* Am I that lonely now that Vincent and I aren't together or whatever we are? Casper wants to talk. It isn't like I'm going to fall in love with him.

Thirteen

hy are you talking to Casper?" Amber McLachlan demands as she shuts my locker door narrowly missing my hand. I jump. Her blue eyes cut into me. Her long bleach blonde hair is full of thick waves. She stands my height and inches forward, making me step back. Her vanilla scent engulfs me, and I cough.

"Don't you think you should limit your perfume to one spray? I think five is enough."

She doesn't laugh. "Why are you talking to Casper?"

I personally don't see how it's any of her business. Her loud voice stops some students in their tracks to watch us like we're going to have a cat fight any minute.

"Get 'er, Amber!" I hear someone antagonize.

"He talked to me," I argue. "So, if you wanna be mad at someone why not him?"

"Yeah, like I believe that for one second. Why would Casper of all people want to talk to *you*? Trailer trash you are."

I'm almost positive you actually have to live in a trailer to be called that. But this is Amber McLachlan. Straight-C student. Captain of the dance team. Homecoming Queen. Boyfriend expert.

"You're right. I don't know why Casper would talk to me. Wait, maybe he got tired of your whoring." I know I shouldn't have said it. Sometimes when I get pushed that's what comes out. It's like I can't hold back.

Next thing I know, I'm lying flat on the shiny concrete floor with my face throbbing and a bunch of oh's sounding from the crowd.

She kneels beside me wafting vanilla my way. "Next time I catch you talking to him, you'd better run." She leaves taking the crowd with her like she is some hero.

I'm angry. Beyond angry. I sit up brushing my fingertips across my cheek. I know I'm going to have a bruise. What the hell? Psycho Amber punches me for talking to a guy? I sigh. These are the Days of our Lives at Spring Valley High.

"Are you okay?" a small girl with long, brown hair asks as she picks up my book.

I nod and stand up. "Thanks." I take my book.

"I'm so sorry. You might wanna put some ice on your cheek. It's starting to swell." She gives me such a pitiful look.

"Thanks."

She walks away and I'm left in the empty hallway alone. I want to skip English, but I don't want to get into trouble. Last thing I need is another grounding. As I walk in, the bell rings and the one and only empty seat is right across Casper. *Great.* Now I have a class with him? How did he manage to get into AP English?

I move my hair so it can hide the oncoming bruise though I know most everyone in the class saw what happened. Only one person stopped to help. Soon the entire school will know what a weakling I am. A weakling, an easy lay, a crazy psycho witch. My reputation is certainly growing into a strong one.

I inadvertently look up and lock eyes with Casper. His angular face holds such concern. It's so fake and I want to slap him or something. I glower at him instead. It's his fault. I can hear whispers from people talking about how Amber kicked my ass and how I'm a wimp. Heat rises inside of me, and I sink into my seat waiting for class to end.

My cheek aches and I need to find some ice soon. I'm sure it's already started swelling, since I can see my skin bulging out under my eye. My head is pounding and as sad and pathetic as it sounds, I want to curl up in a ball and cry.

As my awesome luck has it, Mr. Burress announces an assignment for the first day and teams Casper and me together. I groan internally especially when he takes his seat next to me. My heart hammers wildly in my chest.

"Hey," he says.

I cross my arms refusing to look at him. Can this day get any worse? I can't wait to hear the rumors that I somehow forced him to partner with me.

"I'll be back." He stands from his desk; tells Mr. Burress something then leaves. When he returns, he places a Styrofoam cup on the corner of my desk. His eyes hold the most apologetic look I've ever seen in his eyes—and that is a lot, coming from him. But it isn't enough to soften me.

I glare at him. "Leave me alone."

"I brought you some ice."

I want to knock the cup over or throw the ice on him. It's his fault anyway. "Thanks," I mumble, grabbing an ice cube. I press it to my cheek and although it stings at first, I'm relieved.

"I'm sorry. She shouldn't have done that."

"Do you know why she did it?" I ask coolly.

He shakes his head.

"Because she saw us talking. Were you one of the ones cheering her on?"

He sighs. His brown eyes are no longer remorseful. Instead, they are intense like in my dream. "No, Megan."

"Well can you tell your girlfriend to chill out and stop harassing me?"

"She's not my girlfriend."

"You might wanna tell her that. I can't say what will happen if she confronts me again. I'd hate to mess up her pretty face." Except I can't fight. I have never been taught.

His lips curl into a grin obviously laughing at me. "This isn't funny."

His grin fades. "No, you're right."

"Why *are* you talking to me?"

I wait and he scratches the back of his head. He either doesn't want to answer or doesn't have a reason. It only means he's playing a cruel joke.

"Well?" I urge.

"I think I like you," he finally says looking down into my eyes. I ignore that my heart skips a beat. Why do I care that he "thinks" he likes me?

"I'll make it easy for you. I don't like you so you can stop talking to me." I turn back to the blank page in front of me. I haven't even started the assignment and already half the class has passed. My cheek throbs.

Throughout class, we analyze the meaning and symbolism of some British poem. I'm mostly quiet. Casper tries to make small talk, but I don't bite.

As soon as the bell rings, I'm out of the room and outside. Dark clouds warn me that any second it will start raining. I toss my backpack into my car and climb in. It's cold and the heater doesn't work. Neither does the radio. I hate this car, but Ron is adamant that I pay them back for the car that I didn't get to pick out. I turn the ignition. It doesn't start. My stomach sinks. I try again and again, but nothing happens. This is the third time it's left me stranded.

Could this day get worse? I want to cry. I miss Vincent and I'm angry that he hasn't even bothered to talk to me. We're a couple. Aren't couples supposed to tell each other everything?

Someone knocks on the window, and I almost jump out of my skin. I turn and see Casper by the car. Of course. I open the door and get out. "What?"

"Is everything okay?"

"Why are you here? Aren't you afraid that Amber will see us?" I cross my arms.

"Are you having car problems?"

"Are you stalking me?"

"I was trying to catch you. What's wrong with your car?"

"I don't know. It won't start."

"Do you need a ride?"

"I have to work," I snap.

"I can take you. Are you sure you want to go?"

"No," I answer mildly, tired of being angry. I want to sleep, but if my parents found me asleep instead of at work they would yell or worse ground me. I learned my lesson before. Once I had given blood at school and came home feeling a little disoriented and faint, so I called into work. Big mistake. Ron was not pleased. I never call out, so I'm sure my manager won't mind. She's always been understanding with me.

A harsh wind blows, cutting through my coat. I hug myself and turn away from the wind.

"Come on. We can hang out and talk. Please?"

I need a ride. Everyone I know is working and I can't call Cherry because she has to work. Vincent...who knows what's up with him. "Fine. Where are we going?"

"Wherever you want."

"I have a weird request." I bite my lip. "Can you take me home first?" I need my work uniform to change into so that when I come home my parents will think I went to work. Sounds dumb, but a girl's gotta do what a girl's gotta do sometimes.

"Yeah, sure."

I follow him to his hideous yellow SUV he'd gotten for his birthday. He opens the passenger door for me, and I get in. Of course, he got a brand-new car. The new car smell makes me nauseous, though I usually like it. He comes around to the other side and slides on an old, faded crimson Alabama hat as he gets in.

"Ugh. As if I needed one more reason to dislike you." I look out the window.

"Why? Are you an Auburn fan?"

"Yes."

If there's one thing people don't understand about the South, or Alabama more specifically, football is intense here. You're born either an Alabama or Auburn fan. Not like you have much choice at birth.

He sucks in a breath through his teeth and puts his hand to his heart. "That stings," he teases but I'm not in the mood to laugh. I think he senses it because he turns serious. "I'm sorry about your cheek."

"You should be. She did it because you won't leave me alone."

"I'll talk to her."

"Oh really? Will you be my knight and shining armor and make her stop? I doubt it. She *punched* me. Who does that?"

"She has issues."

"Thank you, Captain Obvious."

He pulls up the driveway to my house and I glance at the clock. It's after 4:30.

"Give me a minute," I tell him as I climb out of the SUV and close the door. Inside the house, my dogs jump and happily greet me. I jog down the hall, toss my books on the bed, and grab my teal polo. I glance into the mirror. Bad idea. My cheek is purple and puffy. It's gruesome. I don't want people seeing it. I part my hair, so it covers the giant bruise.

A thrill of exhilaration courses through me. I'm about to spend time with Casper. I'm not sure I should feel this way. On my way out the door, I get a Ziploc bag and fill it with a couple of ice cubes.

I lift the handle of the passenger door and climb in, barely beating the pouring rain that dumps from the dark sky. He blasts the heat to which I'm grateful.

"Okay, let's go."

I glance at the clock and my heart stops. We have to get out of my neighborhood before my parents see us since Ron likes leaving work early.

"Don't you need to wait and tell your parents about your car?"

"No. Can you start driving? Away from here. Please?"

"Okay," he slowly replies. He shifts the car in reverse and backs out of the driveway and turns at the stop sign. "Are you afraid of being home?"

"No."

"Why do you seem freaked out? You afraid someone will see us?"

"Yeah. My parents."

"They don't like you being with guys?"

"I don't want to explain the giant bruise on my face. I also don't want them knowing I called out of work."

"I'm sure they'd understand."

I give a short laugh. "You don't know my parents."

I can feel his eyes on me briefly and I stare out the window. I call work and tell them I'm sick. They buy it, probably because of how dismal I sound. Suddenly, I don't think this is such a good idea to be alone with Casper. He is a manipulator. He uses girls. When he is done with them, he tosses them aside like they're yesterday's newspaper. But for some strange reason, I feel comfortable around him.

"What do you do when you skip work?"

"Usually hang out with Cherry."

"Why would your parents get upset that you called out of work? Wouldn't they see how it would make you uncomfortable?"

"They wouldn't care."

"But it's your job. Your money."

"Not really. They take my paychecks."

"What?" he asks, shocked.

"I don't want to talk about it."

"Okay," he relents. "Want to grab something to eat?"

I tense. It would feel too much like a date and I'm not on a date with Casper Truitt. Especially if Amber sees us.

"I don't want people to see me."

"Why?"

"I don't know. Maybe because your girlfriend mangled my face after she saw us talking."

The muscle in his jaw twitches. "She's not my girlfriend."

"Could've fooled me."

"Why do you hate me so much?"

"Why are you being nice to me so suddenly?"

He slows to a stop at a red light. "I'm so sorry for offering you a ride. But since you seem so repulsed by my presence why don't you walk?"

I turn my head to see the challenge in his eye. He doesn't think I will do it. I've been around my dramatic mother plenty of times for her to rub off on me. Although, I try so hard not to be like her. Today, apparently, isn't that day. Glaring, I open the door and hop out into the pouring, freezing rain. It's stupid, I know. Casper yells my name, but my slamming of the door cuts him off. The light turns green and the car behind him honks while I charge toward the sidewalk.

Fourteen

My clothes are soaking wet and it's cold. My black hair is sprawled all over my shoulders in a wet mass. I'm sure I look awesome.

I walk inside the Waffle House and avoid the disapproving look from the chubby woman behind the counter. Her thin, brown hair is pulled into a messy bun, and I assume it's her attempt at trying to cover some of the baldness. There is a man sitting on one of the orange stools shoveling in his food. I assume he is the proud owner of the eighteen-wheeler parked next to the building. The cook, who is a young black man sips coffee and reads a newspaper.

I slide into the hard booth and shiver. Is there ever a Waffle House that believes in heat? It is freezing outside, and I swear they still have the air on.

I pull my hair down over the right side of my face, which is facing the windows, luckily. The waitress comes over with a pot of coffee. Her short-sleeved white shirt has an orange stain in a bad spot on her chest.

"Ain't you a little young to be by yourself?" she asks with a thick Southern accent. The same one you hear whenever they need to interview the public on the Channel 13 news. Her front teeth are brown and small. The fat in her hands look as if it's constricting them. That is mean, but the look in her brown eyes clearly shows she is judging me.

"You want coffee?" she asks.

I shake my head. "I'll have water and a grilled cheese."

"You want hash browns?"

"No."

She turns back toward the counter. "Hey D. Grilled cheese."

"Comin' right up."

I hear the door behind me open and I have a sinking suspicion it's Casper.

"That must be the boyfriend." The waitress makes no effort to keep her voice low.

I hoped he wouldn't find me, but he probably saw me from his rear-view mirror. I cross my arms and peer out the window at the pouring rain. He slides in the booth across from me, drenched and his precious Bama cap is soaked. He removed his sweater. Water from the rim of his hat drips onto his shirt, which is now clinging to his chest and does not hide the hard muscles. I feel his eyes on me which makes heat tingle in my cheeks.

The waitress sighs as if we are disturbing her and sets down my water. "Do you want coffee?" she asks Casper.

"No."

"Are you eatin' anything?"

"No."

She goes back to the counter, and he glares at me. His eyes look black under his cap. He places his arms on the table and leans forward.

"You think that's funny?" His voice has a hard edge to it.

I shrug and sip my water. "I didn't do it to be funny."

The waitress comes back with a small plate holding a grilled cheese and my stomach growls. "Y'all need anything?"

"We're good," he snaps at her.

"Well, here's your check." She tosses it on the table and mumbles something under her breath as she returns to the counter.

"That wasn't a very nice thing to do, Megan."

"Yeah, I don't aim to be nice to people who treat me like dirt." I fling my words back at him and take a bite of the warm gooey sandwich. I don't care I've angered him.

"When have I treated you like dirt?"

I give a sarcastic laugh. "That's quite a loaded question. Though, I shouldn't be surprised you don't remember *everything* you've done because I'm not the only one you've treated so poorly."

"Well?"

"I don't know Casper. I don't exactly keep a log of times when people are shitty to me." Which technically I do since I keep a journal.

"So, you can't come up with anything?"

I finish one half of my sandwich and sip my water. "You've never respected me. You told all your friends I'm an easy lay."

"What? I never said that about you. I've barely talked to you."

"Let's see, in elementary school you constantly made fun of me. Asked me out after a few days before you decided to tell me it was all a joke knowing I had a crush on you. You and your little friend Hunter wouldn't let me participate in a group project because I came from a so-called poor family. You've called me names. You always act like you're better than everyone else because you have money. Oh, and you told Matt that I cheated on him. Is that enough for you or you want me list some more?"

He is taken-aback. "Most of that was when we were younger. I wasn't exactly mature as a kid. I never told Matt that. Why would you even think that?" He's offended, but I don't care. How can I possibly feel sorry for him?

"Because all you are is a liar."

I scarf down the second half of the sandwich as we sit in silence. I grab my bag and ticket and walk up to the counter. I feel him standing behind me and I have to restrain myself from touching him. *Ugh.* What is wrong with me? I pull out my wallet, but he already gives the waitress money telling her to keep the change. Annoyed, I shove my money back into my bag and leave the restaurant.

The rain has stopped, but my hair is already disarrayed. I can feel it.

"Where are you going?" he calls after me.

"Away from you." I shiver and my breath comes out in little white clouds.

"Don't you need a ride?"

"I know my way home."

"Yeah, but I thought you didn't want your parents knowing you ditched work."

"So, I won't go home until it's time."

"Fine." Out of the corner of my eye, I see him throw his hands up. He stops walking, but I keep going. I can go to the library or the park. As I cross the train tracks into the old part of town, I pass the busy Whistle Stop Café and keep walking. The wind picks up and I hug myself tighter. The temperature keeps dropping. It's dark and so cold outside.

My cheek burns and throbs. I check my phone and it isn't even seven yet. The temperature says thirty-three. I can't stay out much longer. What am I going to do for three more hours? I start typing a text to Cherry telling her what happened. I know she won't look at her phone until her break. I'm so pissed off; I need this outlet.

A shuffling sound nearby makes me snap my head up. My pulse quickens. I gasp and look around. I see nothing. I usually don't mind being alone, but the creepy feeling like I'm being watched settles over me. Hugging myself tighter, I try not to focus on a branch snapping nearby or the howling of the wind. I feel like I'm in my dream. Something or someone's after me. Fear grips me and I'm not afraid to admit what a scaredy cat I am. I turn back into the direction of the diner and run.

I'm always running or wanting to escape. Run from my dreams. Escaping reality. Escaping my parents. Running from some creep who is trying to kill me.

I'm shaking all over and I want out of these woods. The dreams. I want out of my parent's strict rules. Away from the psycho people at school. I glance behind me, and my foot catches on a root and I crash to the cold, wet ground.

"Megan, are you okay?" Casper asks. My heart skips and heat floods my body. When I sit up, I'm face-to-face with him. Our eyes meet and for a second, I feel like the girl in my dreams. Then reality hits me and I scramble to my feet.

He holds his hands up. "I didn't come to make you mad. I can't leave you here by yourself."

"How chivalrous."

He rolls his eyes. "It's cold outside, come on." He offers his hand, but I don't take it.

I follow him to the yellow boat and climb inside, closing the door.

He already has the heat blasting which feels great. I hold my icy hands close to the vents. He gets in and starts driving.

"Look, I can't have a civil conversation with you until I get answers," I say. "Why did you lie about me to Matt?"

"Megan, I swear I didn't tell Matt that."

"He said it was you."

Casper sighs. "Matt wanted out of the relationship. I told him it was a dumb thing to tell you and that he should tell you the truth. He made it up so he could get the sympathy from Erica."

Tears well in my eyes and I shake my head. "That's not true." Except he started dating Erica right after me.

"I'm sorry."

"How do I know you're telling me the truth?"

"You don't. You have my word. I have no reason to lie to you."

"I'm sorry but it might take a long time for you to gain my trust."

"If I can get Matt to admit what he did, would that help?"

"What are you going to do? Beat him up until he admits to something *you* did?"

"Megan," he says my name like a warning. I don't know what to think about him. "In case you freak out tomorrow, I had your car towed so they could fix it."

I look at his profile, stunned. "You did what? Why?"

"Because I feel bad that your car broke down and it didn't seem like anyone could help you. I didn't want to leave you stranded or have to face your parents."

I don't know what to say. I don't want to accept it. If my parents knew that someone did this for me, they'll think I coaxed them into it. "Please don't tell my parents."

"Why would I tell them? What would it matter?"

"I know how they think. They think I'm a problem child. Like I sneak out all the time or do drugs or have sex. They think I manipulate people. Like I could manipulate a dog to chase a squirrel," I mumble.

"Well, now I know where you get your trust issues."

I roll my eyes. He's probably right. My parents never trust me, even though I never give them a reason not to. "Well, thanks for the car. You didn't have to do it."

"I know. But you're welcome."

"I'll pay you—"

"Don't worry about it."

"Why are you being so nice to me?" I'm not quite sure what his angle is.

"I told you earlier. I like you."

"Suddenly. Like one day you woke up and decided, 'hey, I like Megan.' Or because I'm one of the last girls you haven't conquered."

"That's annoying."

"What? The truth?"

"You know, for someone who doesn't like gossiping you sure like to listen to the rumors."

I narrow my eyes. "They aren't rumors. I've heard from the girls themselves how you treated them."

"What exactly did you hear?"

"That if you can't get them in bed, you spread rumors they're terrible in bed."

He gives a hard laugh. "That's a good one. What else have you heard?"

"Some girls gloat they've slept with you which I'm not sure why they would. Trinity Taylor said you called her every night and even gave her gifts until she finally caved. Then the second you had your way with her, you bolted."

"I take it you trust her."

I don't know Trinity that well, but I saw the hurt on her face when she talked about it. "She has no reason to lie."

"Of course not. But I do?" He is still smiling, but it isn't exactly a friendly smile. I'm sure he's amusing himself.

"Why would she say that?"

"Probably to get attention. I couldn't tell you."

That seems like a likely excuse he'd give. He slows to a red light. And locks the doors.

"Ask me how many partners I've had."

"What?"

"Ask me."

"That seems a bit personal, and I don't feel like talking about your conquests."

"One," he tells me anyway. "And wouldn't you know it? Trinity is right about the story. But *she* was the one who bolted," he says with all seriousness. His tone is low. His eyes stay on mine, and I search them for any hint of lying but find none.

For some strange stupid reason, I wonder why Trinity would lie about that. Why would she say Casper is the bad guy? Why do I seem to buy his story? The light turns green and shines into the car. Casper looks back to the road.

"I admit," he says. "I haven't always been the best person. I have a hard time caring about a lot of people at school. Most of them are shallow and have no real meaning to me. After Trinity, I put up a front so no one can get close to me. I let them think whatever they want. I can't believe I'm telling you all this."

"So, what about Amber? You had to have had a past with her."

I see the muscle in his jaw clench. He seems to struggle with his words. "We went out a couple of times and she thought we were together. I never liked her in that way." He pauses and tightens his grip around the steering wheel. I'm not sure what he's upset or scared about. Maybe because Amber is a psycho who stalks him, but he is holding back something. He lifts his cap and scratches his head and replaces the cap. "Truth be told, I have liked you for a long time," he finally says.

He must be crazy or is still playing with me. I laugh. I'm more shocked and I don't know what to do or say.

He sighs. "I don't expect you to believe me. Especially since you think I did all those things to you. I'm no angel, but I'm also not the terror you think I am. You've always been so inaccessible. Now I know why. But if I have to prove it—"

"You don't have to prove anything. I'm not going out with you."

I see for a split second his face fall. Like *I* can actually hurt Casper.

"Are you and Vincent still together?"

"Yes, why?" Has he heard otherwise?

"Just curious why you didn't call him."

"He's going through some stuff."

"Sorry. Look, I know you're with him, but it's like you're consuming my mind. You must feel *something* for me if you rushed to my house—"

"I shouldn't have done it, okay?" Truth is I did feel something that day. Like he was in trouble, and I needed to save him. There is something more that I don't want to acknowledge. I can't let myself admit it.

"Megan, I dream about you every night." The raw emotion in his voice makes my heart dissolve into mush.

He's toying with me. Someone definitely told him about my dreams. "Give it up already, okay? Just because someone overheard me talking to Cherry and blabbed to you doesn't make it right to throw it in my face. I can't believe you. For one second I actually thought—"

"Will you listen to me?" He cuts me off. "Every night, I dream we're running away from someone trying to kill us." His severe tone tells me he isn't lying. "There was a dragon that made us stop...you know...messing around," he murmurs the last part. "There's a war and the dreams have been messing with me."

I haven't told Cherry about the war or us messing around. Are we actually *sharing* dreams? This can't happen. It isn't possible for two people to have the same dream. My heart starts vibrating against my chest. I can't seem to catch my breath. This is insane. It's not possible.

Fifteen

"These are my dreams," Casper continues but the ringing in my ears muffles his voice. "Every night, it's like a strange story. We're running from something or someone. I can't explain it, but in the dream, I'm in love with you." His voice lowers at the last part. "I knew something was up that day you came to my house. Why did you come to check on me? Of all days? How could you have known what I was dreaming?"

My body trembles and my stomach clenches. "Pull over." My breaths are short and shallow.

"What's wrong?" He pulls the car into an abandoned parking lot.

"Unlock the door." The walls are closing in, and I can't catch my breath.

"Please don't run," he says softly.

"I can't breathe. Open the door."

He unlocks it and I tumble out onto the pavement. The rush of cold air hits my face, stinging a little, but I welcome it. He runs to my side, kneeling beside me.

I scramble away from him. "What are you? How are you inside my head?" I try to stand, but my legs deceive me and won't hold my weight. Casper catches me before I hit the ground. Everything is dizzy.

"What are you talking about?" He steadies me against the car.

"You swear you aren't lying? You didn't overhear Cherry and me? No one told you?"

"I'm telling you about my dreams. Why would you and Cherry be talking about them?"

"Because those are my dreams," I whisper.

"What?"

"I have been dreaming about you every night for months now. Exactly the same dreams you described. There's a man trying to kill me. One time he pushed me off a cliff. I held on until you saved me. You always kill the man, but he always comes back. Except the past couple of nights. The day I came to your house, he shot you and I held you in my arms. When I came to school that day, you didn't show, so I worried."

"You swear this isn't some witch thing?"

I narrow my eyes at him.

"Sorry. I'm trying to figure this out. I'm so lost."

"That makes two of us."

"How is this possible?" He wonders out loud, letting me go, even though my body seems to miss his touch.

"I don't know. But this is why you think you like me, Casper. They're dreams. They don't mean anything."

"You don't think it means something when two people dream the same dream? That alone should tell you there's some inexplicable link between us."

I can't deny that. Doesn't mean I want to fully accept it either. "I don't feel that way about you. Besides, you think you wouldn't get a lot of crap if you told your friends you liked me?" I shiver.

"Again, I don't care what they think. If they can't accept you as my girlfriend, then I can't accept them as my friends."

"We aren't together."

"Sorry. I know. I meant…" He shakes his head. "Can we get back inside the car?"

I nod and climb in.

He puts the car in gear and drives off. "Why don't we go to my house? You need to put more ice on your cheek."

"Is it bad?" I pull down the visor and open the mirror. I gasp. My cheek is swollen and black. It looks terrible. Sighing, I close the visor. I don't know how I'm going to hide it from my parents.

"My mom can help. She's a nurse."

"What? I'm not going to your house."

"Why?"

Why? Because a girl like me does not belong in a house like that. Because this is Casper Truitt and I'm in no position to meet his parents. I look terrible. My hair is a messy frizz ball. My makeup came off in the rain. I'm not the type of girl someone like Casper brings home.

"My parents will be there if you're worried—"

"I'm not a charity case. If that's why you're doing all this."

"I wish you would believe me. What are you worried about?"

"Casper, I don't belong. I'm not like you. I can't have my parents find out about my black eye. It's..." Pointless since he pulls up the driveway to his drug-lord mansion.

"They won't bite," he says and gets out of the car. I stay put.

He opens the door and when I don't get out, he closes the distance, resting his arms on the top of the car. Again, a little too close for comfort. My heart seems to like it.

"Megan," he says softly. "What's wrong?"

My hair hides my face, which is a good thing since tears well in my eyes. I don't know why I'm crying. Emotional day to the extreme and it's all finally crashing on me, I guess. I have disliked Casper for so long yet one night with him seems to change it all. I want to dislike him. What if he meant what he said? I would still never go out with him. Right now, it seems like he genuinely cares. And we share dreams. That doesn't absolve my insecurities of meeting his parents who are a nurse and a doctor and who could tell my parents.

My curtain of hair is brushed behind my shoulder and my body tingles at his touch. I know he can see the long trail of a tear that rolls down my cheek in the soft light of his car.

"Why are you crying?" His voice is gentle.

"I'm a mess," I finally admit. "I can't meet your parents looking like this. And I don't want them to see this." I point to my eye. "I don't want them to tell my parents."

"You don't have to impress anyone, you know. They'll like you and won't say a word. If you feel that way, we'll go in the back door. You need to put ice on your cheek."

I consent and follow him on a path that leads to the garage. We enter the kitchen and he open a door that leads downstairs for me. "I'll be down in a minute," he says after turning on a light and closing the door. I feel awkward that he snuck me into his house. I guess that's what he did. I walk down the stairs and gawk. Okay, so his entire basement is like the size of my house. There is a loveseat and a couch that faces a large HDTV. I peer into the room on the left. And gape. It's a room with hardwood floors, a pool table, and a ping-pong table with a sink. On the other side of the room are two doors, one of which is closed, and the other that leads to a bathroom. I'm scared to see the bathroom. It's probably the size of my room.

Casper clambers down the stairs and hands me a plastic bag. "Here's some ice. Mom always says to put it on immediately. She said this will also help the swelling."

I take it. "Thanks. Did you tell her I was here?"

"No." He smirks. "I've had a few black eyes in my lifetime. Is your hair naturally curly?"

"No, it gets out of hand in the rain." I place the ice to my cheek hoping it will numb the pain.

"Have a seat." He sweeps his hand inviting me to sit on the white plush couch. I sink into it. "Do you want some ibuprofen?"

"Yes, please."

He walks into the bathroom and comes back with some medicine and a cup of water. He clicks on a couple of lamps then turns off the overhead light. He sits down on the couch and stretches his legs. I swallow the pills and drink the water.

"I can't believe how big your basement is. It's like three of my houses for your one."

"It's kinda too big for the three of us. My brother and sister moved out last year."

"Are you close to them?" I guess I'm humoring him by carrying on a conversation. I don't want to feed into his whatever he feels for me.

"Yeah."

"That must be hard not seeing them every day."

He shrugs. "It's not that bad. They're only half an hour away."

My phone beeps and I reach in my bag to answer it. It's Cherry.

OMG! Amber's a bitch! Are u ok?

Yeah. I'll be fine.

I can't believe she hit u! I'd stay far away from Casper. She's crazy!

I know. Are they upset that I called in?

No. Diane asked about you. I'll tell her ur puking. My break is almost over. I'll call u when I get off work.

It's ok. I'm kinda tired so I'm probably going to bed early but I'll c u tomorrow.

K. U 2. Love u.

Love u 2.

"So, your parents won't know you skipped work?" Casper asks.

"No. They never go out that far."

"Aren't they going to notice when I take you home or are you going to make me park down the street?"

It isn't a bad idea actually. "They'll be asleep by then. They're strict. Anything I do gets me grounded. It's better that I don't tell them anything. Where do I need to get my car tomorrow?"

"I can take you." He turns on the TV and leaves it on the sports station. I welcome the distraction.

"Will they have it ready tomorrow morning?"

"No, but I thought I could take you after school."

"Oh."

"Do you wanna watch a movie?" he asks.

I shake my head. It's strange having the man of your dreams sitting next to you. Literally. I think about how intimate and tender we are in the dreams. It's a little unnerving.

"Do you know who the mysterious guy is in the dream?" he asks.

"No." I focus on the TV instead of him. I feel his eyes on me.

"I'm trying to wrap my head around this. The dreams started a few months ago. At first, they started out with me running and searching through the woods looking for you. I'm tense and nervous but when I find you, it's like, everything's okay. Except that I have to fight with some guy. The dream where you fell off the cliff, I knew I had lost you. When I woke up, it got to me. Not to sound…whatever, but my heart literally ached for you. I can't explain any of this."

Speechless, I listen to Casper reveal his inner thoughts. Okay, if he is playing a trick on me, I'm sure he wouldn't have told me that his heart ached for me. How am I to react to that? Somewhere inside of me wants to know how he feels.

"Does your heart ache for me now?" Bug-eyed, my hand flies to my mouth but not in time to stop the words from escaping. I don't know what possessed me to even ask that. "Sorry. That was stupid. I shouldn't have-I-wow."

"I'm afraid to tell you my answer, actually."

"Yeah, no it's cool. You don't have to answer that. Pretend I never asked."

We sit in awkward silence, watching TV, though I'm pretty sure neither one of us is paying attention to it. I can't believe I asked that. What is wrong with me? I wonder if I should I tell Casper what I saw when Vincent and I kissed. What would he make of that? Are the two even connected?

"Why did you tell me to stay away from Vincent?" I wonder if he knows about Vincent's prior drug issue.

"I don't know. I don't even know him, but he gives me a bad vibe."

"Are we talking about the same Vincent?"

"Yeah. I can't explain it."

"Bad vibe like mine with Amber McLachlan?"

"It's...different. He doesn't sit well with me."

I wonder if he means how intense Vincent is sometimes.

"What are you thinking?" he asks.

"My thoughts are all over the place. Definitely weirded out yet you aren't at all what I thought."

"Is that a good thing or a bad thing?"

"I don't know." I tell him honestly. "What are you thinking?"

"You don't want me to answer that."

My heart loses its regular beat. "Might as well tell me." What is wrong with me? Why should I care what he's thinking?

Casper takes a deep breath and plays with the fringe from one of the pillows. "I can't stop thinking about kissing you. It's so intense in the dream."

I'm not sure what to make from my body's positive reaction to that. I'm so glad for the ice to help cool me down. Now if I could only control my heartbeat.

"Sorry. I don't mean to make you uncomfortable. I'm not going to make any moves. I'm not that guy."

I shrug. "I asked. If it helps, they're intense for me, too." Now I am going to kick myself. I pull out my phone and check the time. "I've gotta go."

"Yeah."

The drive back to my house is quiet, but not awkward. I guess we are both thinking the same thing but not talking about it. For some reason, I feel a little pang of sadness as he pulls into my driveway.

"Thanks for tonight," I say.

"You'll need a ride in the morning, right?"

"I can ask Cherry." But as soon as I say it, I know it's too late to call Cherry. She always likes to go to sleep early. "Actually, what time can you pick me up?"

"How early do you need me?"

"As early as possible."

He raises his eyebrows.

I feel the heat beneath my cheeks and clear my throat. "I mean seven."

"Sure."

"Goodnight." I close the door.

Inside my house, I lean against the door for a second. My heart won't stop freaking out.

My phone buzzes, and I glance at it.

Sweet dreams.

Casper's text makes me feel like I've got electricity surging through my body. I still haven't gotten any from Vincent, and that stupid ache in my chest returns.

I don't reply. I need to stop spending so much time thinking about boys. They're distracting me and if I'm not careful, I'm going to spiral out of control trying to balance everything.

Sixteen

My stomach won't settle down. Casper is giving me a ride to school. I woke with tears in my eyes after another weepy dream about Casper and me. How much more dramatic can my dreams get? It's like a romance novel for crying aloud. I'm not on drugs, but one look into my dreams, one would assume I am deep into them.

"Morning. I got us some coffee, since it's before the chickens wake up," Casper jokes. He's wearing his Bama cap and a long-sleeved blue shirt that fits snugly around his long, lean arms and muscular chest and torso. Not that I pay that much attention. He wears jeans as usual.

"Morning. Um thanks." I'm not a coffee drinker but I take it and hold it in my hands warming them. It's a nice gesture, though.

He backs out of my driveway. "I didn't drug it, if that's what you're worried about."

I steal a glance. "I don't drink coffee."

"Oh. How do you stay awake in class?"

"I've been known to fall asleep."

"You?"

"Yes. I'm not perfect."

He mumbles something under his breath, but I can't hear. The dream is still on my mind, and I wonder if he's thinking about it, too. I'm glad it wasn't one of the more intimate ones because I'm not sure I'd be able to look him in the eye if we'd been rolling around in the grass like before.

"What the hell is a Sprite?" he asks, and I exhale, grateful he broke the ice so we can talk.

"I think it's a fairy. I remember someone calling you an Elf. Why are they after us? The only thing I know is they mentioned I ran away with you. Why would they try to kill us?"

"I don't know. Are these dreams like, linked to our real lives or something? I mean, are you in some kind of danger?"

"Not that I'm aware. Unless my parents find out that some cute guy took my car to get repaired." I blush and look out the window. Cute? *Cute?* What is my problem? I peek at him out of the corner of my eye, and I swear I can see a sliver of a smile.

"How's your eye?"

"Still purple and swollen."

"I'm sorry. I am." He pauses a moment. "Not that I mind at all to take you to school, but why didn't you ask Vincent? I'm glad you didn't. I mean, I-I'm curious." He clears his throat. Is he shy around me or something?

"I didn't call him because he's...distant. I don't know. It's weird. One minute we're great, and the next...nothing." I can't believe I told him that.

"Maybe he's dealing with a lot." Casper arrives at school and parks. He keeps the heat on and both of us stare at the building. We are pretty much the only ones there so far.

"Did your parents find out anything?" He removes his hat and tosses it onto the dash.

"No." I bite my lip. "I don't want to go today."

"You and me both."

"I'm starting to feel like someone is after me. Like, I'm starting to feel paranoid. I hate it."

Casper takes my hand and squeezes it. I ignore my heartbeat. "It's like that for me, too. That's why

I've been trying to talk to you, but I let it go thinking the dreams would stop."

"But they haven't."

He shakes his head. "We could skip if you want."

"I can't. If my mom finds out, she'll ground me. I have a chemistry test." That I didn't study for. I reach into my bag and pull out my notebook opening it to the right page. I start reviewing my notes, but Casper yanks it away. "Hey!"

"I'll quiz you." How is it that I can feel so unnerved, yet comfortable by the same person at the same time? I shouldn't have spent the entire afternoon and night with Casper, let alone the morning. I need to return to my regularly scheduled program. "Come on. What is Group 16 of the Periodic Table called?"

Reluctantly, I let him quiz me. As time passes, more and more students arrive.

I'm not sure about being seen with Casper at school. I don't want another repeat of yesterday. I can't go inside yet because the school has a ridiculous policy that we aren't allowed inside until about twenty minutes before the bell. You can't even go inside to the library. We sit in the car for a few more minutes going over chemistry, but I'm antsy. I take my notebook and thank him, then open the door and get out. The wind cuts through me and I brace myself. Casper follows me for a short distance.

I turn around to face him. "I think I can handle it from here."

"Are you afraid of being seen with me?"

"I wouldn't want Amber to see us."

"She won't hurt you again."

"I can handle my own fights, thanks."

He raises his eyebrows, and his eyes point at my hidden cheek. "You sure handled it yesterday."

His comment hurts. I'm grateful he gave me something to be angry about. I don't like this weird friendliness between us. "You're such a jerk, you know? Why don't you go rejoice in Amber's victory like everyone else?"

"I didn't mean it."

"Whatever. Leave me alone."

"Oh, come on. Don't leave." He grabs my elbow whirling me around to face him. "It was a joke." Our eyes lock and for a second, I think he is going to kiss me, and I'll welcome it. At least my body wants it. Something is seriously wrong with me.

"Megan." I hear Vincent behind me, his voice sounding hurt. I stiffen, then twist around and Casper releases me. The wind blows my hair, revealing my bruise.

His blue eyes immediately grow angry. "Did you hit her?" He glares at Casper with such rage that makes me shudder. Why would he automatically assume it was Casper?

"What?" Casper straightens his stance and clenches his fists.

"What did he do to you?"

"He—"

"I didn't do anything to her. If you actually answered her calls, maybe you'd know what happened to her."

Oh crap.

"Are you threatening me?" Vincent steps closer, squeezing me in between them. Okay, so maybe he isn't so shy.

I press my hands against both of their chests. "Vincent, it wasn't him," I say, but neither one pays attention. They glare at each other sizing each other up like male gorillas. "Casper, go. I can handle it."

After a long look at me, Casper walks away and the tension eases.

"Who did that to you?" Vincent brushes aside my hair.

I back away. "I'm sure it's front-page news by now. Didn't you hear?"

"I was out yesterday."

"Yeah, you've been out for a while."

"That isn't fair. What happened?"

"Amber McLachlan hit me because she saw me talking to Casper."

"Why were you talking to *him*?"

That's what he's upset about? Shaking my head, I start walking away from him. I'm not sure how much longer of this back and forth I can take with him.

"Megan, please."

"What, Vincent? I haven't heard from you in two weeks. You were so mad at me when I went to my dad's and now you stand up for me? Either be my boyfriend or don't."

"I'm sorry you feel that way. We had to rush my mom to the hospital."

I soften, hoping he isn't about to tell me his mom died. "I'm sorry. Is she okay?"

"She's fine for now. She was having a hard time breathing."

Guilt rushes over me. I'm a terrible person. "I'm sorry."

Vincent moves closer to me. "It's okay. I'm sorry I never called or texted. I don't exactly know how to do this."

I freeze. "Are you breaking up with me?"

He takes my hands. "No, Megan. I'm a mess."

"I get it. But I'm your girlfriend. You have to let me in. I'm here for you to console or whatever you need."

He nods. "I'm not used to it."

"Try. For me."

Gazing into my eyes, he presses his lips to mine. "I love you, mon trésor. You're my everything."

Feeling my lips stretch into a grin, I return the kiss. "I love you." I've never told a boy that, but I feel it.

As we walk inside the building, people stare at me and start whispering amongst their friends. Vincent holds my hand tighter and keeps walking like he's the most confident man there. "Keep your head up. You are so much better than these people. Don't ever let them make you feel bad."

His words make me admire him and I'm grateful. When we reach my locker, I turn to him. "Thank you. It's hard sometimes."

"I know, but it won't be like this forever." He moves my hair away from my face and his thumb gently strokes my bruise. It shouldn't make me feel good, but it does. "I'll see you later."

When he walks away, Cherry approaches me. "Things okay?"

"He told me he loves me."

She gasps, but her smile fades. "Does that forgive him for not talking to you?"

"His mom was in the hospital."

Cherry frowns. "That sucks. Is she okay?"

I shrug.

"What are we going to do about these stupid rumors that Amber had your ass handed to you?"

I was on cloud nine. Discreetly, I move my hair so she can see the bruise.

With a gasp, she brings her hand to her mouth. "I could strangle that bitch." She shakes her head. "What'd your mom say?"

"She doesn't know."

Cherry cocks an eyebrow. "How's that even possible?"

"You aren't going to believe this." I relate my evening to her, except the sharing dreams part. I'm not sure I want to tell anyone that. I tell her about Vincent this morning and the near face-off between him and Casper.

"Why *is* Casper being so nice to you? I'm glad you forgave Vincent."

"I can tell he loves me. I love him. I mean, when we kiss, it's intense."

Cherry's face lights like a sparkler. "After this morning, I know he loves you a lot. So, what about Casper? Why's he suddenly paying attention to you?"

"He says he likes me," I keep my voice barely above a whisper. I don't want people to listen. Although, if they do hear us, they'll spread rumors that Casper likes me, and he'll ignore me. That isn't a bad idea. I still haven't made up my mind about him. I love Vincent and I don't want to mess it up.

"What?" she asks a little too loudly.

"Do we have a problem?" Mrs. Edwards asks with a cocked eyebrow. Her hand is poised in the air about to write on the board.

"No, ma'am," I tell her, and she turns back to writing.

"Sounds like Vincent's got some competition," Cherry whispers. "You don't believe Casper, do you?"

"No." Because the dreams are making him feel that way. He can't like me. I'm with Vincent. Even though it still bothers me that he ignored me for two weeks.

"How'd you do on your chemistry test?" Casper asks as I take my seat in English. He smiles and I can't help but notice how sexy and genuine it is. My stomach does a flip.

"Good. Thanks for your help."

The rest of the class he tries to talk and flirt with me, but I tell him we have to work on the assignment. Once the bell rings, he walks beside me to my locker like we're dating or something. It annoys me, but it doesn't.

"Have a good day?"

"Sure. You?"

He shrugs. "Yeah, I almost got into a fight."

I close my locker. "Well at least you don't have a swollen cheek."

"Touché."

"Besides, you shouldn't have antagonized him."

"Antagonize him? Please. He was looking for a fight. But if you were my girlfriend, I'd react the same way. Though if you were my girlfriend, I wouldn't keep you guessing."

Casper meets my eyes and places his hands on either side of the lockers, blocking me from going anywhere. He likes preventing me from running. I look to the ground or his chest or his arms. I can't seem to handle his heated gaze. My heart summersaults and I steady myself against the lockers. He leans closer, dangerously close, but my hands half-heartedly push against his chest stopping him. We both know he can easily ignore my pressing hands, but he doesn't. I want him to kiss me, but I don't. I can't. What is wrong with me? Are the dreams making me feel this way? Are my issues with Vincent making me feel this?

"Casper."

He drops his hands. "Sorry. That-that was weird. I-it felt..." He lets his words trail.

It felt natural. Comfortable. I shake my head as if trying to get these thoughts out. "Look, after you drop me off today, that'll be it. We can't talk anymore, okay?"

He straightens his stance. "So that's it. We can't be friends?"

"I'm tired of fighting with you."

"Then don't."

"Then stop being a jerk. Stop acting like we're together."

He nods and holds his hands up in defeat. "I know. I'm sorry. Come on, I'll take you to get your car."

The ride is rather quiet, but he keeps music playing which I like. At least he has good taste in music. He pulls up into the mechanic's place and I'm shocked to hear how well my car sounds. I actually squeal. I hug Casper. When we touch, I am content. Like before it feels natural. Like in the dreams. I have never felt anything like this in real life. I don't want to let go and the way he holds me tells me he doesn't either. We probably hold each other longer than necessary.

"Why does this feel so right?" he whispers in my ear making my body shiver with pleasure.

My heart fumbles to find a beat and I end the embrace. What would Vincent think of me? Having such thoughts about someone else. This is insane. I feel awful. How can I be Casper's friend with these thoughts looming around my mind?

He pays the mechanic and I nervously walk to my car. I fumble to get it unlocked and open the door. "Thanks, Casper. Really. I appreciate it. I don't know how I can repay you."

"You don't owe me anything. And you're welcome. Guess I'll see you tomorrow." He says and he leaves. My heart sinks. I don't know why I feel sad. What am I expecting to happen? I got my car back and I have no reason to be around him now.

But I want one.

Seventeen

When I get home after work, luckily, my parents have gone to bed. Jonathan is still awake and sees me in the kitchen rummaging through the fridge looking for something to eat. Mom and Ron suck at grocery shopping.

My hair still covers half my face annoying me, so I pull it back.

"Hey, I brought home some McDonald's for you," Jonathan says. "It's in the microwave."

"Thank god. I take it Mom and Ron went out?" I open the microwave and find a bag with a cheeseburger and fries inside.

"Yep. I wasn't invited. How was work?" He leans against the counter with a bottle of Gatorade in his hand and a rolled-up sports magazine in the other.

I shrug. "It was work."

"What happened to your eye?"

"Nothing," I mumble.

"Run into a pole again?" he teases. He will never let me forget the time when I was a kid, while reading a newspaper I ran right into a pole.

I groan. "No."

"What happened? You okay?" He lowers the magazine.

"Yeah. I bumped into a cabinet at work."

He studies me. "How are you and Vincent?"

"Fine. Why?"

He takes a long swig of his drink and starts fiddling with the corner of the magazine, which means he's going to say something that makes him uncomfortable. "You know, if something's wrong you can talk to me."

I stop mid-bite of a fry and stare at him, confused.

He cocks his eyebrow like he knows I lied about my eye. I hope he doesn't think it was Vincent. He knows I've been kinda moody. "I'm fine, Jon. Promise. Thanks."

"Since we went to Dad's. I don't know. You seem distant or something."

"Just school. Usual stress."

He nods, but I know he doesn't believe me.

I forget how perceptive he can be and how much he knows when I lie. I grab my pajamas and check my phone for messages. There is one from Casper.

You really didn't mean we couldn't be friends anymore, did you?

I sit on the edge of my bed, thinking. Savannah waits for me by the door. I see no problem in us being friends, but I still can't shake the feeling that it's all a game. No matter how comfortable I feel around him.

I bite my lip as I type my answer.

No.

Great. Sweet dreams.

I don't reply but I shower, letting the water wash away the confusion and stress. Only they congregate as soon as I go back into my room. I slide under the covers, pulling them to my chin. My phone vibrates and I reach over and grab it from my nightstand to answer it.

"Hey, you," Vincent says, and I immediately smile.

"Hey. What did you do tonight?"

"Not much. I wrote a song."

"You did? About what?"

There is a pause. "You."

"Me?"

I can hear him laugh. "Yes, you."

"Play it for me."

"It's not ready. I will when it's finished."

He releases a heavy sigh.

"What's wrong?"

"It's everything going on. Can't we be like the people in your story? Escape from everything? Live our lives without drama and pain?"

"I wish."

"Why don't we? We can be immortals never afraid of death."

"Are you okay?" I ask. He doesn't sound right. Part of me wonders if he's on something.

"Megan, I love you so much. I don't want to be here."

"Everything's going to be okay." I don't know how to comfort him, and I hope he isn't talking about suicide.

"I want to leave, and I want you to come with me."

I don't know if he's being serious. "We're almost out of school. Then we can."

"Promise?"

"Yeah."

"Let's live out our fantasy of being immortal Sprites and dragons and be happy forever."

I smile. "Okay."

When we hang up, I feel sad because there's nothing I can do to help him. I don't know how serious he is about running away or whatever. As much as I want to, I can't up and leave right now. How did we go from not talking to talking about running away?

Eighteen

It isn't unusual for me to wake up with my heart jabbing my ribs. How can I possibly dream about something that I have never done? Casper and I...made love in my dream. How can I face Casper now that we did that? Yes, it was a dream, but still. It feels *real*. I hope I didn't moan or anything for anyone to hear. I wince at that thought.

Why on earth would we do that in the middle of a war? That sounds crazy.

I get ready for school, putting makeup on my cheek, which somewhat helps but is still blatantly obvious. Luckily, my parents haven't seen it yet. My hands shake as I pick up my phone. Casper sent a message. It scares me how excited I am to read it.

Well. That happened.

haha yeah… I reply. **I don't understand what it all means. It feels so real.**

Can you meet me before school?

Why?

I don't know. This is driving me crazy. It's seriously messing me up. Like, I can't wait to see you each day yet you are with someone else. But I'd rather have you as a friend than nothing at all.

I think about it, but I don't know what to say. I feel there is no harm in talking to him before class. I can still meet with Cherry after.

Ok. Meet me by the picnic table @ the theatre entrance.

Ok. See you soon.

My stomach won't calm down. I hate the reaction I have. I have to keep reminding myself who I'm meeting which only makes me more excited. How can I feel this way toward him? It's nothing. It's the dreams getting to me. I am with Vincent, and I need to stop acting like this.

"Hey," Casper says with a sweet smile. His hat blocks the morning sun, but I can still see his brown eyes. He gazes at me like he can see into me. Like he knows everything about me. I avert my eyes.

"Hey."

"I feel awkward now."

"I know." I sit down. "I think I'm leaving though. In the dreams."

"What do you mean?"

"I kept thinking that I have to go back in order to keep you alive. I know that going back won't end the war. I want to keep you alive."

"The thought of losing you gets my stomach wound up. In my dreams," he quickly adds.

"What if there is some strange link between us? Like in another life or something? I don't know. It's bizarre enough that we actually have the same dream. You know time has passed in the dreams. I wonder how long we've been together."

"I'm not sure."

"I'm glad no one is trying to kill me. Those dreams haunt me."

"Me, too, actually. It's like my love for you in the dreams carries over and I fear losing you. But when I see you, I know it's all in the dream."

"That's how I felt when I came to your house that day. I was so scared that I lost you. I actually cried waking up that day." I fidget with my fingers, avoiding his eyes as we sit across from each other.

He places a hand on mine, softly. "You won't lose me," he says.

I tug my hand slightly toward me and he lifts his. We are quiet for a moment. Probably both thinking about how strange everything is between us. He is easy to talk to, which makes it better since Cherry doesn't understand.

"How are things going with you and Vincent?"

"They're fine. I haven't talked to him much." I want to talk to him all the time, and I know I shouldn't complain given the situation with his mom.

"I'm sorry." He genuinely seems to mean it.

"It's okay. I work all the time and we have no classes together. I think we might go out again this Friday." I'm speculating this, but I want to make sure Casper knows I'm taken or maybe I'm reminding myself.

He nods. "Your cheek isn't as swollen. Have your parents seen it?"

"No. They're usually in bed by the time I get home from work."

"Why were you so adverse to telling them what happened that day?"

I take a deep breath. "My parents are weird. I don't know. They never believe anything I say and always assume I'm lying. If I told them some psycho girl at school hit me, they'd probably think it was Vincent or something."

"What?"

"My mom would probably believe me. My stepdad wouldn't. He would think it was all my fault. I'm grounded all the time for stupid stuff. I hate it so much. It's like I have to walk on eggshells all the time because I don't know when I'll get grounded and for what. I mean, one time my mom grounded me for three months over the summer because I had an attitude. She didn't understand that I was so stressed out. When I get grounded, I can't talk to my dad or anyone. I can't even go to his house. My stepdad adds to the stress because I'm never good enough for him. Not that I'm trying to impress him, but he always assumes the worst of me. Like I'm some crazy teenager."

"Wow. So why do you have to give them your paychecks?"

"They bought me the car, but I didn't get to look at it or pick it out. It showed up in my driveway and they said 'okay, now you have to pay us back.'" I stop venting and look up. His brown eyes are apologetic. "Sorry I unloaded on you." I bite my lip, feeling weird that I told him so much about my life.

"No, don't be. I don't mind. I'm sorry. I take it there's no way you can talk to them?"

"No. I'm a child to them. Whatever I have to say doesn't matter."

"That sucks."

"It's okay. Once I go to college, I'll leave this place."

My phone vibrates and I see Vincent's name flash. "I gotta go." I walk away from the bench as fast as I can. "Hey," I answer.

"Hey. Wanna play hooky today?"

I chuckle. "You know I can't. And you shouldn't either."

"I don't know. There's this hot girl walking toward me. I might have to grab and steal her away for the day."

I look straight ahead and see Vincent leaning against his car, looking sexy in jeans and a black knit shirt that accentuates his muscles. My stomach flutters and I hang up, picking up my pace to meet him.

His lips stretch into an alluring smile that makes my stomach flip. I wrap my arms around him, breathing in his warm, spicy scent. "Steal me away, eh?"

"Yeah." He kisses me like he hasn't seen me in weeks. It almost makes me forget we're in the school parking lot and make out with him. My knees weaken when his fingers barely graze my bare stomach.

The bell rings and suddenly I hear voices from students around us. I haven't paid attention to anyone walking by us. I can't believe we made out with so many people watching us.

He groans. "Curse that bell."

We walk hand-in-hand inside until we get to my locker where Cherry waits for me.

"Hey, Cherry," Vincent says.

"H-hi," she stammers.

"I'll see you in later." He touches my elbow slightly before walking away.

I watch him then turn to Cherry whose eyebrows are raised expectantly.

"Morning?" I smile innocently.

Her lips stretch into a wide smile. "I love it."

"I'm crazy about him."

When I turn back to look at Vincent's backside, Casper is walking toward us. My throat tightens as our eyes meet.

"Hey, Megan," he says. "Cherry. It was good talking to you this morning."

"Yeah, you too," I try to say, but it doesn't come out right. Heat spreads all over my face. I don't want to face Cherry. Casper continues to walk down the hall.

Cherry raises her eyebrows, grabs my wrist, and pulls me into the bathroom. "Explain."

"I—" We hear the door open and immediately hear Amber talking to a friend. Both Cherry and I hurriedly squeeze into a stall before they come inside. She sits on the back of the toilet while I squat on the toilet seat. I don't want to face Amber again. I especially don't want her hearing me talk about Casper. That would only add fuel to her fire.

"Omigod. Have you seen Megan Devereux?" It sounds like Trinity Taylor. Cherry and I exchange a look. Did they see us? "Ever since you gave her that black eye, she's been wearing her hair like some emo kid." Trinity laughs.

"Serves her right. I mean, she *still* won't leave Casper alone," Amber complains. I hear her rummaging through her purse and spray something. It only takes seconds for the entire bathroom to smell like vanilla. "It's like she can't get the hint that we're together. You know he gave her a ride yesterday?"

"Why would he give *her* a ride?"

"He says her car broke down, but her car is fine. I saw her driving it. She is so obsessed with Casper. You know she broke into his house to wake him up one day because he didn't show up at school, right?"

I stiffen and my stomach drops. I can't believe he told them. I should've seen this coming. I knew it. I *knew* it was all a trick. After everything I told him this morning. My eyes blur but I force the tears away.

"No!" Trinity laughs. "Seriously? What a freak! Ugh. Why does Casper put up with her?"

"He's playing with her. He tells me every night all the stupid things she says to him."

Trinity laughs. "She *is* gullible."

"She'll get what's coming to her. By the way, don't be late to dance practice today. Coach was fuming yesterday."

The bell rings and they leave the bathroom. I shakily open the stall door and exhale.

"Since when are Trinity and Amber friends?" Cherry asks.

"I don't care. This is getting old."

"What did you expect would happen when you did that?" I know she's only helping, but it angers me more. "You know Casper. He's never going to change. He's still that stupid ten-year-old jerk."

"Why would he pay for my car?" And we're sharing dreams. He can't be lying about that.

"He's manipulating you to get into your pants. Why else would he suddenly start paying attention to you? Come on. Let's go to class."

It can't be true. Why would Casper manipulate me when we're having the same dream? Maybe Cherry is right. Maybe he is only wanting to get me in bed. Is he using the shared dreams to his advantage?

I shouldn't be bothered by it, but the whole thing makes my heart ache. I don't know why I'm hurt and I why I care. How could he hurt me like this?

Nineteen

All I can think of are ways to show Casper how much he hurt me. I could involve Vincent, but that won't be wise. I felt the tension between them, and I know one of them would get seriously hurt. It's ridiculous to think it would be because of me. Why did I feel such tension with them if Casper is playing with me?

Casper enters English joking with his friends. I want to lunge at him. I don't make eye contact, though I can feel his eyes on me. He strolls over to the desk next to mine and slides in it.

"Hey." He smiles.

I don't acknowledge him. I hold my pen tightly between my fingers and chew on the inside of my mouth. My hair is like a curtain hiding him from view.

"What's wrong?"

I ignore him while the teacher explains our assignment. Analyzing poetry from the Victorian era. It's going to be a lengthy assignment since we have six poems from a poet. He walks around, passes out ours, and I look over it. Elizabeth Barrett Browning. Of course, one of the poems we have to analyze is her Sonnet 43. How do I love thee? *Great.*

We work on the assignment in silence, but there is tension. Casper is nothing to me. Why do I care what he says about me? I should have known he can't be trusted. Like Trinity said, I am gullible. I fell for every word he said.

When class ends, I walk out to my locker.

"Megan, what's wrong?" I hear him behind me.

Opening my locker, I grab my history book and backpack.

"Are you ignoring me now?"

I shove the book in my backpack, close the locker, sidestepping him.

"Talk to me." He catches me by the elbow, but I push him back.

"Don't touch me." I warn and he holds up his hands. "You're such a joke. You know that? I can't believe you told people what I did. I'm sorry, okay? I can't believe you would go through so much to get into my pants."

"Whoa, what are you talking about? I haven't—"

"Stop lying. You know what? It doesn't matter anymore. We were never friends, and we never will be. You've won, okay? You fooled me. Leave me alone." I storm out the door, hoping he finally takes the hint. I know we have to see each other again for this stupid assignment.

"Megan, please. What happened?"

I spin around, the wind lifts my hair from my face exposing my bruise. "You told them about me running to your house that day. Now they all think I have this crazy obsession with you. How could you? What did I ever do to you?"

His eyes are remorseful, and I see realization washing over his face. He sighs. "The day it happened, I told Brad. At the time I was so freaked out that the only way I coped with it was laughing about it."

Tears blur my vision.

"It was wrong and stupid. I'm so sorry I upset you. But tell me honestly, if I had come to your house like that you would've laughed to Cherry about it." His voice is stern.

I hope I'm a better person than that, but I probably would have done the same. Except Cherry wouldn't have told everyone. "Even if we had no one would've believed us. Because you're you and I'm me.

Didn't you think Brad would tell everyone?" My voice wavers.

"He's been my best friend my whole life. No, I didn't think he'd tell anyone. Maybe his girlfriend. I'm sorry. I really am."

"Your friends think I'm a psycho obsessed with you."

"I don't care what they think."

"I do. I mean, have you ever set them straight? Have you ever stood up for me when they're talking about me?"

His silence is my answer.

I let out a frustrated groan. "I gotta go." I slide behind the wheel.

Work sucks and my irritable mood doesn't help. Cherry tells me to forget about it all.

Ten o'clock finally comes and Cherry and I walk out together. "You'll be okay, Megan. I'm sorry all this crap is going on, but you have me and Vincent. Don't forget that."

"Thanks, Cher. I appreciate that a lot. It sucks because I thought Casper and I could be friends."

She stops me. "I'm only telling you this because I'm your friend, but you *have* to forget him. He's bad news. Finish the project with him and move on."

I nod. She doesn't get it. I'm *sharing* dreams with him. I want to move on, but it doesn't seem like the dreams will let me.

Cherry gasps. "Is that Vincent?"

I turn and see him leaning against my car. Every time I see him, a rush of excitement burns throughout me. His sweet smile draws me closer, and he uncrosses his arms.

"Hey you. Hey, Cherry."

"Y'all have a good night," she says. "Call me."

"Good night," I tell her, and she leaves.

It's freezing outside and I fold into Vincent's arms. He smells like cigarette smoke, which almost makes me gag. He kisses me and doesn't taste like cigarettes, thankfully.

"How was your night?"

"It was busy, but okay." I shiver.

"Do you wanna sit in the car?"

I nod. He tows me toward his car, and we settle in the seats. He turns the ignition and blasts the heat. "What did you get into tonight?"

"Hung around."

Way to be specific as always. I glance at the clock, silently moaning that I can't stay too long.

"I missed you."

"I've missed you, too," I confess. "It's been a bad week."

"What's on your mind?"

"Nothing."

"Liar."

"I'm tired of people treating me like crap. Casper and his little friend Amber are spreading rumors about me." I lean back against the seat, and he takes my hand.

"What kind of rumors?" I don't miss the anger in his voice.

"It's not that big of a deal."

"Megan."

"It's nothing. How are you?"

He shrugs. "Fine." Vincent pulls me into a tight hug and kisses the top of my head. "Are you off tomorrow?"

"No."

"You should skip one day."

"I value my life," I joke.

"One night won't hurt though, will it?"

"My parents will know my check is short."

"I'll give you the money you lose."

"Paying me for my time?" I tease.

"You know it's not like that. I feel like you need a break. That's all. I know I could use one. We could work on our story."

I like that he's taken such an interest in my story, though it's odd how much he's into it and how much he wants it to be real.

"I'm off Friday."

"Let's do something."

"Got anything in mind?"

"I'm sure we can come up with something." He gives a mischievous grin. With his hands around my neck, his thumb strokes my neck, and he kisses me like he hasn't seen me in months. Vincent's arms wind around me pulling me over the console crushing me against his body. Suddenly I see us again in a vision. Dancing. He happily lifts me above him and I laugh.

I try to pull away, but he tightens his arms around me still kissing me. I see another vision. I'm sitting on a bed, and he stands before me shirtless. I smile up at him as he leans over me, rolling me on my back as we kiss.

Heat rushes throughout my body at the vision. Vincent positions me to straddle his lap. He kisses me all over. I'm not exactly keen on making out in his car in my employer's parking lot, but I can't stop.

Another vision hits me. We are lying in the bed both covered only by sheets and panting. I shiver as his fingers trace my leg. Everything about the vision seems as though it was something from our past. I can't make sense of it. We are so much in love.

His hands slide up my shirt, but I stop him. "Vincent," I pant. "We can't do this."

He lets out a sigh. "I know," he says, but pulls my mouth into another hot kiss and his fingers lightly touch my bare stomach then slides behind the waistband of my pants which drives me crazy. He slips further and I grip his shoulder then grab his hand stopping him.

"You shouldn't have gotten me so hot." He moves his hands on the outside of my shirt as we both pant.

"You're not the only one at fault." I clear my throat and straighten my hair as I return to my seat. "Did you have a vision?"

He smiles. "Did you?"

"Yeah. Of us…you know."

"I think that's what made me get carried away. That and the simple fact of when I touch you, I'm on fire."

I feel my lips stretch into a big smile. "What do you think these visions mean?"

"I don't know."

"Have you ever-I mean are you a…"

"A virgin?"

I nod.

"No."

"How can we share a vision of us you know but I'm still a virgin? I don't understand what it all means." How can I dream of being with one guy intimately and share a vision of another guy being intimate? Am I secretly a whore?

"I don't know."

"How are you not freaked out by this?"

"It helps knowing I'm not the only one sharing these things. It's okay." He leans over and kisses my forehead. "It's our little secret. I will protect you."

I let out a small laugh. "From what?"

"Uh you know. Just being sweet."

"You don't have to try too hard. You drip sweetness."

"Only when I'm around you." His lips graze my neck. "I should go so you can get home. I don't want to get you grounded."

He kisses me once more, deeply, and rests his forehead against mine. "Please say you're mine."

I pull back unsure of what he said. "What?"

His gaze is deep, but I see a hint of fear in his eyes. "Please say you're mine."

"I'm yours," I say feeling a little awkward like he owns me. There is no one for me except for him. He is mine and I am his.

Vincent kisses me as his hand tangles through my hair. He pulls away with a seductive look and I exit the car.

I need a cold shower now or drive home with the windows down.

When I get home, I check my phone. There's a message from Casper and Cherry.

Casper apologizes and asks for forgiveness while Cherry demands to know exactly every detail that happened with Vincent and me.

After my shower, I lie in bed thinking about texting Casper back, but what can I say? Did I overreact? Maybe I can play with him like Cherry suggested. Why do I even care?

Hi, I text him.

Hey. How are you?

Better.

Can I call?

Do I want to talk to him? It's getting late and I need to get to sleep. Except when I sleep, Casper is in my dreams. I can't get away from him. I want to hear what he has to say. I think. So, I tell him he can. A few seconds later, he calls me.

"I'm sorry about telling Brad."

"It's fine. I probably would have done the same. And yes, Cherry and I have joked about you, but come on. Everyone listens to what you all have to say or gossip about. I don't need rumors of me being a witch going around."

"I know. I never called you that, but I never stopped Brad from saying it."

"You say you don't care what they think, but you're afraid of what they'll say if they knew the truth. About us talking. Please tell me this isn't some game."

"I promise you; it isn't a game. We're sharing the same dreams, Megan. Whatever I feel in my dreams may or may not be the same as what I feel in real life.

It's confusing, and I'm trying not to let it cloud my judgments. I like you and I want to be friends."

"If we never had these dreams, you wouldn't even think twice about me."

"That's not true. I've thought about you a lot. When I started dreaming about you, I thought that my—" He pauses. "Crush on you lead to my dreams so I decided to finally talk to you. I never knew you hated me so much. I know I've hurt you several times and I wish there was something I could do to make it better."

"I don't know what you can do. Just know it's going to take a long time for me to trust you." That's not true. I'm giving him a hard time because I don't want to let my defenses down.

"I understand."

Wanting to change the subject, I ask if he did any of the assignment for English. We launch into a conversation that keeps us on the phone until three in the morning. He tells me about his desire to become a lawyer and how he has it all mapped out. He sounds more OCD than me about school.

I love Vincent with all my heart and I love getting to know Casper. I'm not sure how much longer I can keep both of them in my life.

Twenty

Friday after school, Casper and I go to the library to do research for our poetry analysis. I'm reminded how easy it is with him. Like in our dreams. I have a date with Vincent later on and told him to meet me in the library. Despite enjoying myself with Casper, I'm looking forward to spending time with Vincent.

"I hate poetry." Casper tosses a book aside.

"Why?"

"Because it's pointless."

"You like music, don't you?"

"Yeah."

"That's a form of poetry. Someone expressing their feelings and frustrations and worries. I mean, take Browning's Sonnet 22. She's talking about being intimately close to her lover with a burning passionate love and how their love was scorned but they stayed together no matter what. I mean, what's not to like about knowing such love exists?" I look up and see him gazing at me. I can feel my cheeks turn red.

"I like learning about poetry with you." He smiles.

I roll my eyes. "Let's get this done."

"Seriously. I've never known someone as passionate about this as you. I feel as if we're at that cabin in our dreams while I listen to you read poems."

"Do you think the library has anything on Sprites or Elves?" I ask, trying to veer away from the heated discussion or maybe it feels hot because I'm burning up. I can't get over how close that sonnet is to mine and Casper's dream story.

"I'm sure. It is a library after all."

I playfully hit his arm as we get up and search the shelves. All we can find are a couple of cartoonish kids' books.

"They also have this thing called Internet," he says.

"Don't like the old-fashioned way of researching?"

"Maybe if we were in a decent library."

"I started writing about the dreams."

He studies me. "Really?"

"Yeah, like a story. I thought maybe it would help and I'd stop having the dreams. No such luck."

"I didn't know you wrote. That's amazing. I'd like to read it sometime."

"Whatever." I laugh.

"I'm serious."

I roll my eyes.

We find some adult books and take them back to our table. Both of us thumb through trying to find anything about Sprites or Fairies or whatever. It's kind of ridiculous if you think about it. I mean, they are after all dreams. Maybe it'll help with my story research.

"Hey, look at this." Casper holds a book between us. I lean over, my shoulder touching his and follow his finger over the text. "Fairies possess great beauty and in the form of Sprites can be immortal. They have the ability to change forms, and some have wings. Their biggest enemy is the Elves…" I watch him as he reads. I watch his mouth move as he talks. He removes his finger from the book and plays with his hair. Being this close to him reminds me of the day we hugged. How incredibly safe and comfortable I felt. My heart pounds as I wonder if his lips are as soft as they are in my dreams. I want to kiss him.

Someone clears their throat and I jump. I look behind me and smile. My heart knocks into my chest. I feel like I've been caught doing something I shouldn't. "Vincent. Hi. Is it seven-thirty already?"

"It's after." His arms are folded in front of his chest. The severe look in his eyes is a little daunting.

"Oh, I'm so sorry." I get to my feet. "Let me change."

Grabbing my change of clothes, I head to the bathroom. I'm so flustered and I need to calm down. I change into a white sweater, a maroon wool skirt, and black knee boots. I touch up my makeup and glare at my discolored cheek. When I come out, I find Casper still seated at the table and Vincent a few feet away. Both of them smile approvingly which is a nice way to boost my ego.

"I'll see what else I can find and bring it on Monday," Casper tells me as I fill my backpack with my books. Vincent takes my backpack.

"Okay. Have a good night. See you Monday." I wave and walk out with Vincent.

"I called you," he says. "Didn't you hear it?" I can tell there is an undertone of envy.

"My phone is on silent. I'm sorry. I want to get the project done so I don't have to spend another minute with him," I lie. Truth is Casper is so easy to be around it scares me. And *that* makes me uncomfortable.

"You seemed to be enjoying yourself just now."

Is he getting upset with me? I don't know what I can do to make him realize I only love him. Why do I have to prove such a thing? "I'm being cordial toward him. That's all. It's easier that way."

"I don't trust him."

"Why?"

"He hurt you, Megan. He's a manipulator. He isn't good. You of all people know that."

I do know that. Recent events seem to have swayed that particular opinion. Vincent is right. Casper is probably only being nice to me for his own good. Apparently, I want to refuse to believe it now. Maybe I am a glutton for punishment.

"Look, I don't mean to come off as some overbearing jealous guy, but I saw how hurt you were the other night. I'm looking out for you."

"I know."

"See? Aren't I good boyfriend?"

"Of course, you are. The good thing is after this project we won't be partners anymore. And that leaves more time with you." I smile.

"Promise?"

"Yes." Hooking my fingers in the collar of his shirt, I pull him against me. Our lips meet and he circles his arms around me.

"Did you willingly partner with him?"

"Mr. Burress put us together," I say between kisses.

"You should've told him you didn't want to partner with Casper. And why do I keep hearing that you have an obsession with him?"

I look away. "Those are the rumors I told you about."

"Is it true?"

"What? No."

"Good."

We go see a movie and sit in the back. At some point in the movie, he leans over and kisses me. Another vision crosses my mind where we are laying in a field in love. The visions seem to intensify our kisses. We pay no attention to the movie whatsoever. My lips are raw by the time the movie ends and instead of getting up with everyone else, we stay, catching our breath, and laughing hysterically because we seriously made out for almost two hours.

When he pulls into my driveway, I don't want the date to be over. It went by too quickly.

"Working tomorrow?"

"Actually, I'm hanging out with Cherry. We could do a double date."

"I don't want to. You see her all the time. Let's have the night to ourselves."

"I made plans with her."

"I'm dealing with a lot right now and I need you. You told me you were here for me."

"I am."

"Are you? Is Cherry more important? I'm your boyfriend. I'd do the same for you. You know, anytime you need me I'm there."

I don't want to upset him. Why doesn't he understand that I made plans already?

"If you only understood what I'm dealing with. You need to spend more time with me."

"I want to. I want to talk to you more, but you're always busy."

"So, it's my fault?"

"No, I'm—."

"It's Casper, isn't it?"

"What? No." I don't want to fight with him. I can't resist the pitiful look in his eyes, but I feel like I need to prove to him that I'd do anything for him. "I'll cancel with Cherry."

"Good." He smiles.

Twenty-One

alentine's Day, Vincent wows me with calla lilies and we spend the day at the Railroad Park ice skating. I have never been ice skating and any time I almost fall, he catches me. We eat at one of the upscale restaurants downtown and he takes me to the overlook of the city. He holds me from behind as we peer out over the beautiful city lights.

"You sure you want to leave all this behind?" he whispers in my ear.

"I love Birmingham, but I gotta get away from my parents."

"Why don't we leave together?"

"What?"

"You and me. We'll take on the world and leave all this behind. Like the characters in our story. Nothing could stop them."

"It sounds nice."

"So, let's do it."

When I turn around to face him, his eyes are serious. "We will next year."

He shakes his head. "No, I mean now. We don't need school. We don't need any of this."

"Vincent...your mom."

"She won't make it."

His abrupt words shock me. "Vincent?"

His eyes hold mine, and after a few moments he shakes his head. "Sorry. Random thoughts going through my mind. I'm okay." He kisses me. "You won't be stuck here forever. Things will get better for you, and you will have an amazing life. I promise you that. Come on. There's one last thing I want to do."

A few minutes later, we end up at the rainbow color tunnel. It's an abandoned underpass that has multicolored LED lights. What was once a dark, uninviting place is now a beautiful, bright area that makes me smile.

It was such a beautiful date that I'm still thinking about it two weeks later. I'm so in love with this man. I'm so crazy about him and I want him to be my first. Because we hardly see each other, I've skipped work a few times. When he's with me it's like he sees no one else. It's almost scary how intense he is. I still wonder how serious he was about leaving. He's talked about it a few times.

While my dreams aren't plagued with war anymore, they're of Casper and me falling deeper in love—a love I've never experienced before. It's intense like always, but it feels that with each dream it deepens.

I'm still trying to keep the two lives separate. Concentrating on school, work, and family is harder. Casper and I remain friends, secretly, and he visits me every Saturday while I'm at work. I feel myself drawing to him more and more and I'm tired of struggling with the balance. I'm scared that during one of my make out sessions with Vincent I'm going to slip and say Casper's name. How would I ever explain that?

"You are ridiculous," Cherry says. I haven't told her about the intimate parts of my Casper dreams, but I explain how much in love we are. "I can't believe you're still thinking about those stupid dreams."

"It's hard not to when I have them every single night." I toss one of her pink fluffy pillows up in the air. I'm at her house which is a nice reprieve from my house. After weeks of us spending time with our boys, we force a girl's night. "Do you think people can have the same dream?"

She looks up from writing the names of songs for her next playlist. She's always making playlists for herself or for me. I assume she's started doing that for Luke. "I'm sure people have similar dreams all the time. Why?"

I shrug. "I wonder why mine are a continuation. It's like a story or something."

"Because it's your subconscious giving you a story to write."

I pick at the pink fuzz from the pillow. "I wrote a lot, but I stopped. I've had a lot going on."

She fakes a cough. "Vincent."

I throw the pillow at her. "I've never felt like this with a guy." Or two guys.

"Omigod. I know what you mean. I am seriously in love with Luke. Did you know he's liked me for a long time but was afraid to ask me out? Me. Of all people."

"Because you're a catch."

I briefly think of Casper. If he did like me for a long time like he said, wouldn't he have asked me out or at least told me how he felt before I had a boyfriend? I roll my eyes. It doesn't matter. I'm with Vincent and I feel myself falling for him, too.

"By the way, Luke's birthday party is at eight tomorrow night."

"I told you I can't go. I have to work until midnight."

"Call out."

"I've been calling out so much lately."

"Yeah, you have. Ugh. I'll find someone to cover for you. You and Vincent have to come." She smiles and raises her eyebrows twice.

I roll my eyes. I hate parties, and it's weird that Cherry is throwing one for Luke. She never likes that scene. "Since when are you such a party girl?"

"It's like a few of his friends, their girlfriends, and me. Ten people, tops. Please? I don't know any of them except Luke and his best friend. I want my bestie there to help and to keep me company. Please?"

"Okay. Only if someone covers for me." I doubt they will, but if I know Cherry, her determination will win. I text Vincent about the party, and he replies with a yes.

"Vincent's in."

"Awesome," she sings. "So, have you and Vincent ...you know?"

"No. Why? Have you and Luke?"

She bites her lip and blushes.

I'm surprised. "Cherry!"

"I know. It was perfect, Meg. He had candles and roses."

"So soon?"

"Hey, when you know you love someone, you know. Besides, we've liked and known each other for years. It felt natural. Which is strange."

"When did this happen?"

"Valentine's."

"Why am I now learning this?"

"I've barely seen you. I love him, Meg."

I smile and squeeze her hand. "I'm happy for you."

"Thanks."

"What...what was it like?"

"It hurt a little at first, but he was so romantic and gentle. It's been amazing ever since."

I bite my lip. "I don't know if I'm ready."

"Is Vincent pressuring you?" she asks, alarmed.

"No. Not at all. I've been thinking about it."

"Do you love Vincent?"

"Yes," I answer honestly. There isn't a doubt in my mind.

"The way I see you two together, it's like you were meant for each other. I'm not saying that to stroke your ego, I mean it. You move together. You both joke with each other and can take it. You might have found your one, Megan."

I feel myself smile. She's right. I may have found my one.

Twenty-Two

herry squeals as she comes to my register. "I got someone to cover you after seven."

"Already?"

"Never underestimate my magic powers. I'm covering Sherry's shift tomorrow."

I'm a little bummed because I don't want to go to this party. I don't let it show since Cherry's excited. After convincing Mom to let me stay another night at Cherry's, I call Vincent but as usual, it goes to voicemail. I send him a text with the plans. What's he doing and why can't he ever pick up his phone? I curse myself. He's probably with his mom. Maybe one day he'll let me meet her. I understand if he doesn't. Cancer's a nasty thing.

By the end of my shift, I'm tired, my feet hurt, I'm irritated Vincent hasn't called, texted back, or shown up. I'm ready to go home. I don't know how many times I have to tell him to talk to me. But he expects me to call in whenever he wants me to.

I shake my head hoping to shake the negative thoughts from my mind.

"Hey," someone says behind me. I turn around to ring them up and stop. It's Casper purchasing a coke and a candy bar. He's wearing his Alabama hat and a long-sleeved thermal type of shirt and jeans.

"Hey." Seeing him excites me and I'm not the least bit guilty. Even though I promised Vincent that Casper and I would only be classmates. He pissed me off tonight. But I'm not being truthful. Casper's a friend, though. "You can't keep doing this. You know I have a boyfriend."

Casper arches his dark eyebrows. "Buying a coke and a candy bar? What does that have to do with you having a boyfriend?" He chuckles and I feel myself smile.

I close the till drawer and give him his change. "Are you going to see a movie?"

"Yeah. Thought about it. Wanna come or do you have to work all night."

"Yeah. Gotta be here till midnight," I lie. I feel awful but if Vincent finds out I saw a movie with Casper, it won't be good.

He nods and as he starts to walk away, Cherry comes up, turning off my light.

"Time to party," she says exuberantly.

I want to hurt her.

Casper raises his eyebrows and I close my eyes, embarrassed.

"Oh hi." Cherry turns to him. "Come to terrorize Megan again?"

"No. You girls enjoy your party." He walks away.

I sigh. "Casper." I catch him as the sliding glass doors open. He turns with an amusing grin on his face. "I'm sorry. I—"

"Nah, it's cool." He shrugs. "I get it. Have a good night."

"Yeah. You, too."

"Why are you apologizing to *him*?" Cherry asks. "And why is he in here all the time?"

"It's nothing."

"There may be more people coming than I thought. I'm gonna go change."

"Like how many more?"

"I don't know. Here, I brought you some clothes." She hands me a bag.

"I have my own."

"Yeah, but you should wear my halter. Vincent won't know what hit him." She smiles. "I sorta stole your so-called party clothes and put them in my car."

"I should go home. It's obvious Vincent isn't coming, and I don't wanna be a third wheel."

"Oh, come on. It won't be bad. Please come. You promised."

I don't remember promising to go and I'm not sure why she wants me to go so much. I know what will happen. She and Luke will be hanging out and I'll have to fend for myself.

"Please?"

"Fine," I say feeling the dread.

"Yay! I'll meet you out front." She practically skips toward the bathroom. I've never seen her so excited to go to a high school party. Especially one where she doesn't know anyone. I'm feeling ornery and anxious.

I grab the till out of the drawer and walk toward the office, stopping in front of the sliding doors. I see Casper walking to his car. Checking to make sure there isn't a manager nearby, I slip through the doors. Cold air blasts me. I hope they don't think I'm stealing this till full of money.

"Casper," I call. I feel guilty for lying to him and I don't want to go to this party alone.

He looks back and makes his way toward me. "Yeah."

"Do you wanna come to this party tonight?"

"Do you want me to come or are you being nice?"

"No. You should come."

He thinks for a minute. "Sure."

Butterflies multiply in my stomach as I count my till. I'm so nervous that I have to recount. When I'm finally done, I grab the plastic bag that Cherry brought me and pull out a deep red cotton halter dress which is clearly for summer and black tights. It's like twenty degrees outside and she wants me to wear this? I brought my black boots so at least my legs will be warm. The dress barely comes to my knees. Thankfully, my coat is long enough to cover it. My hair is still straight from this morning and doesn't look bad. After shoving my work clothes into the plastic bag, my phone rings.

My heart skips when I see Vincent's name. Maybe he can join me at the party. Except I invited Casper. *Crap.* "Hey."

"Hey baby."

"Is everything okay?"

He sighs. "No. But it will soon."

"Is it your mom?"

He doesn't answer for a moment. "Yeah. Look, I'm sorry, I can't come tonight. Can I make it up to you?"

"Of course. Do you want me to come over or something?"

"I would love that, but tonight's not good."

"I hope your mom gets better."

"Me too. I miss you."

"I miss you too."

"Call me later. I love hearing your voice."

"I will." Guilt lands on me. Vincent's with his mom and I've been upset over him not responding over some stupid party. A party that I invited Casper. I hate that Vincent's mom is sick. He's had to deal with so much in his short lifetime. It's not fair. I wish I could be there for him more. I'm not sure about attending the party with Casper now. I know for a fact Vincent will hate it if he finds out. I don't want to go to the party solo and for some reason I kinda want to spend time with Casper. Which is wrong on so many levels. I should go home.

I walk downstairs to cancel on Casper but the words I need to say don't come out.

"Wow." He raises his eyebrows and smiles. It's such a sexy smile and I have to reign myself in. "You look beautiful."

I blush. "Thanks." I clear my throat. "I'm gonna ride with Cherry. You can follow us. All I know is it's at the Meadows subdivision in Vestavia."

"I know where that is. Are you sure you don't wanna ride with me?"

"Yeah. I promised Cherry I'd ride with her."

"Okay. See you there."

I put on my coat and meet up with Cherry. She didn't seem to notice Casper and me walking out together or if she did, she doesn't say anything.

The whole way there, I laugh at Cherry's off-key singing to whatever pop song plays on the radio. She has a way of making me feel less anxious. I can see how much Luke's influence has on her. She's more outgoing and seems so much more experienced than me now. I feel like she's living her life, whereas I'm along for the ride. Waiting.

Twenty minutes later, Cherry pulls up alongside the curb of a massive house with music blaring. I wonder if any minute the cops will get a call for noise disturbance, but I figure everyone in the neighborhood is probably here. My stomach drops. This isn't some small get together.

"Well, the party certainly grew," she says.

"Cherry," I hesitate.

"It'll be fine, Meg. I promise. Come on."

We make our way toward the house that's shaking from the music. The driveway is empty of cars for the skateboarders, something I don't expect. Both of the garage doors are open, and people are sitting around in chairs with red plastic cups and beer bottles. As we walk inside where it's warmer, Luke greets Cherry with a big kiss and spins her around. He introduces her to everyone and tells them that I'm Cherry's friend. I look at Cherry wondering if he forgot my name. We work together for crying out loud.

Luke leads us to a room that's filled with gyrating bodies and a *thump* from the bass.

"I'll take your coats," he yells over the music.

I clutch onto mine, but Cherry makes me take it off. Luke leaves and Cherry sort of dances in place but stops.

"You invited *him*?" She gives an appalling look.

"Look, it was a last-minute thing."

"So? This is going to make him think you're gonna give it up to him. You're giving into his game."

"Nothing will happen, okay?"

"What about Vincent?"

"Casper and I are friends. That's all."

"Yeah."

Luke comes back and wraps his arms around Cherry. I think he whispers in her ear, and she giggles. Now I feel awkward.

"We're gonna dance," Luke says. "Be right back." Cherry laughs as he steals her away to the makeshift dance floor in what I guess is the dining room and sitting room. It all has hardwood floors.

"Hey," Casper says.

"Hi."

"No offense, but this doesn't seem like your scene."

"Like you know what my scene is." It isn't my scene, but I don't like how much he seems to know me.

"I didn't mean it like that."

"Sorry. Cherry wanted me to come. I'm not sure why though since she has Luke." I hug myself feeling completely self-conscious in this dress. I can't help but notice some of the people staring at us as they walk by. I think my paranoia from my dreams is returning. I feel like a little girl standing in the corner. "Why are they staring?" I yell over the loud music.

"Ignore them."

"Do they know you?"

"Some of them."

I cringe. I hope us attending a party together isn't going to get back to Amber. I don't need another bruised cheek or worse.

"Wanna dance?"

I look at the sea of couples molded together or grinding against each other and suddenly my stomach feels heavy. "No."

"Come on, let's go sit."

With his hand on the small of my back, he guides me to a couch in the living room. It's filled with people playing a video game. We find a spot on a loveseat under the windows.

"Why'd you lie back at the store? Still think I'm out to get you?"

"No. I..." Can't tell him Vincent would get upset. "I don't know."

"What did you tell your parents?"

"Who says I told them anything?"

He gives a disbelieving look.

"I told them I was at Cherry's tonight."

"Why are they so strict?"

I shrug. "Mom is afraid I'll turn out like her. I don't know. They never let me do anything. It's like an act of God to let me spend the night with Cherry sometimes or concerts. It's like I can't do much of anything without my brother. That's why I'm so focused on school." At least I used to be until recently.

"That sucks. I'm sorry."

I shrug. "I work around it."

"Do you want anything to drink?"

I hesitate. "Sure. A Coke."

He gets up from the loveseat. I watch the buttons and lines speed past on the TV as four people bang away on Rock Band. I didn't think people still played this game. The guy who sings is way too pitchy, but it seems like it's his favorite song. I laugh when he gets down on his knees.

A guy with short brown hair and green eyes takes a seat next to me on the loveseat. He seems familiar, but I can't place him.

"Hey. My name is Adam. What's yours?"

"You should move along."

He shrugs and gets up.

"Who is he?" Casper holds two drinks.

"Adam."

"You know him?"

"Not a clue."

He laughs. "Sorry. That tends to happen at these things." He hands me a cold Coke in an unopened can. It's a small gesture, but most guys from what I've heard, can't wait to get you to drink something so they can spike it with who knows what.

"Now that you're sitting here, they'll leave me alone. Unless you find someone." I take a drink of the coke.

"I'm only here for one reason."

I meet his eyes quickly and look away.

"How was your date last night?" he asks and seems genuinely interested.

"Oh, I hung out with Cherry. Girl's night."

"Cool. So, have you written anymore?"

He asks about my story, and we launch into an easy conversation. It's like we've been friends our whole lives. I enjoy being around him and I'm surprised we never hung out until now. There's a nagging guilt inside the back of my mind, though, that I'm doing something very, very wrong. Like I should be at home waiting for Vincent's call or something. I shouldn't be out having fun while he's not.

"Karaoke." Cherry squeals as she and Luke walk toward us. "Do you wanna sing?" She looks at me.

"Not really."

"Oh, come on. I'll sing with you," she begs.

Casper smiles. "I'll play the drums if you sing."

"See? Even he wants you to play."

I can't figure out what is with her. She hates that I invited Casper but seems okay that I'm hanging out with him. She's starting to get on my nerves. I feel like she brought me along to show off Luke in front of me.

A guy hands me a microphone and gives another to Cherry while Casper takes the drums. I can't believe I'm about to do this. We sing a Tegan and Sara song, one of mine and Cherry's favorites. I'm actually having fun which is nice.

Once we finish the song, Cherry and Luke go back to the dance floor, at least I think they do. I can tell she's had some liquid courage and I wonder if they're going to find a bedroom. Casper and I return to the loveseat.

"You're a good singer," he says.

"That was Cherry. I mumbled through most of it."

"I heard you."

I blush. "Thanks. Cherry and I sing a lot in the car."

"Megan, I know you're with Vincent, but I think—"

A cold liquid splashes all over me as two girls fall near the loveseat. I gasp and stand.

"Sorry." One of the girl's slurs as she and her friend giggle away in the floor.

"You okay? I'll get a towel," Casper says.

"No, it's cool. I'll clean up in the bathroom."

"Sure."

I slip up the stairs and pass several couples making out. Glad they can't see my beer-stained dress. I enter a bathroom that is attached to a room, grateful no one has claimed it. The rooms in this place are endless like at Casper's house. The bathroom is long and has two sinks and infinite counter space and cabinets. At the very end is a shower and garden tub separated.

I grab a towel from the closet and run cold water over the stain. Of course, it looks worse now. I groan, hoping the dress will dry soon. Cherry will kill me if it's ruined. Not like it was my fault. I feel the cold beer inside the dress and in my shoes. *Ugh. Stupid drunk people.*

I jump once I hear the door close.

Looking up, I see Adam, the guy from earlier, smiling as he leans against the door. "I moved along, but I came back," he slurs.

I swallow hard. "I'll leave so you can use the restroom." I make my way toward the door. He doesn't budge. "Are you going to move?"

"Do you know how adorable you are?"

"Can you please move?"

He pushes off from the door and walks me against the counter. I try to go around him, but his hands are on my arms in an instant, planting me in front of him. The countertop digs into my back. I can kick him and go around him. I can scream so loud he has to release my arms to cover his own ears. I have to get away from him. I don't like the way he towers over me or the tight grip he has on me.

"It's hard to believe it's been so long since I've seen you."

"We've never met. You have the wrong girl." Even though he does look familiar, I don't know where I've seen him.

"I'm afraid not, Megan." He smiles, but it isn't friendly. How does he know my name? "Looks like you're spending time with the enemy."

Twenty-Three

My mind is going a thousand miles a second. He knows my name and he accused me of being with the enemy. Like the guy in my dreams. My heart pounds. I can feel the walls caving in. "What are you talking about? Who are you?"

Adam glares at me. A menacing smile stretches across his face. He roughly lifts me onto the counter. My breathing labors. I kick and push. Nothing works.

"Please, sto—" He cuts me off with his mouth bearing down on mine. I jerk back and smash my head against the mirror.

I try to block him with one hand. The other pats against the counter for something to throw at him. I find nothing. He grabs my wrists raising them above my head and slams me against the mirror so hard I hear it crack. It leaves me briefly dazed. I let out a scream. He smashes me against the mirror again. Broken bits of glass stab my back and arms.

"Shut up," he demands.

I kick him hard enough in the right place. He releases my hands with a groan.

I jump down from the counter and run for the door. His hands are around my waist, and he throws me to the ground. My head bounces off the tiled floor blurring and doubling my vision. But I see the unmistakable outline of a gun. He straddles me and I struggle against his eager hands. The strap to my dress rips. I scream again through the cloudiness. He shoves the gun at my throat.

I hear the door burst open and someone tackles Adam, pulling him off me. The gun drops and slides across the floor. I cower near the bathtub and see Casper punching and threatening Adam, his eyes wild with rage. Within seconds, Adam falls unconscious.

A couple of guys rush inside the bathroom and talk to Casper. I don't know what they're saying. They grab Adam and take him out of the bathroom.

Casper turns to me, and his brown eyes soften. He moves next to me and checks me for injuries. I can't stop the tears or the violent shaking. He wraps his arms around me, pulling my head against his chest.

"It's over," he whispers. "It's okay."

I cling to him.

He picks me up and carries me out of the bathroom. I can probably walk, but I don't want to let go of him. My head thumps with the bass of the music so I rest it against his shoulder. He walks down the stairs, sets me on my feet, and fetches my coat. At least, I think that's what he said.

The music is too loud. There are too many people surrounding me. The lights blind me. I have no idea where Cherry is. I have to get out of here. I can't breathe. Holding the strap to my dress, I walk out the front door. A few seconds later, Casper places my coat around me.

My head throbs. My back stings like it's been cut and my face tingles. Somehow, we make it to his car. I don't remember the walk. Every little noise makes me jump and I can't stop shaking.

I don't know what to do. I want to curl up in a ball and cry.

"I'll take you to the hospital."

He opens the door for me, but I reach for him, wrapping my arms around his neck.

"Thank you," I say through thick tears.

"You're welcome. I'm glad you're safe."

My arms are still around him. It's like I can't let him go. He holds me tight around the waist, almost protectively.

"I don't want to go to the hospital."

"You have to. You're bleeding. We have to tell the police."

"I don't want my parents to know."

He exhales. "I'll take you to my house. My mom can help. And don't argue."

He helps me in his car. I lean against the seat, but it hurts too much. It feels like the glass from the mirror is stuck in my skin. I shuck off my coat, hoping there isn't too much blood on it. Casper climbs in and starts the engine.

He curses and removes his shirt, revealing a white t-shirt underneath and lightly presses it to my back.

"You're bleeding badly." He speeds away racing to his house.

I have to call Cherry. I reach into my bag and pull out my phone. I click on her name. She doesn't answer. I call again. No answer. I call again. No answer. I type in a text for her to call me.

Casper and I are quiet on the way to his house. I bite my lip hard, trying to keep myself from crying. I don't want to cry. I can't. I refuse.

I wish Cherry would call me. I need to talk to her. When we pull into Casper's driveway, my phone rings. I relax a little when I see Cherry's name.

"Meg!" she shouts into the phone, and I can tell she's had more alcohol. "Sorry I missed your call. We were...well, you know. Where are you?"

"I left already." I bite my lip to keep it from quivering. "I—"

"What? Why? Are you with Casper?"

"Yes. I was—"

"You went home with him?"

I clench my teeth, but I quickly lose my anger. "Cherry, I was...attacked."

She gasps. "What? Where are you? Are you okay? What happened?"

"I'm at Casper's. His mom's a nurse."

"What? Aren't you going to the police? What happened?"

"I'll tell you about it tomorrow. I wanted to tell you where I was."

"I don't trust him. You shouldn't go there. Let me take you to the hospital."

"I'll be fine. I promise. I'll call you tomorrow."

"Megan."

"I'm okay."

"Fine." She hangs up.

My heart sinks. I can't help the tears as they fall like escaping ants. I cover my face with my hands.

I feel Casper's hand on my shoulder.

Most of the lights are out in Casper's house. We come in through the kitchen again, but this time he leads me upstairs to his room. The last time I was in his room, he yelled at me because he thought I was performing some sort of witch magic on him. Now he saved my life. I can't imagine what would have happened had I not invited Casper.

He shows me his bathroom, which is enormous. The bathroom has double sinks, a garden tub with a window, a separate shower, a closet toilet, and a closet further back. If this is his bathroom, I hate to see what the master looks like.

"I'm gonna get my mom," he says. "Here are some towels." He rushes out of the room and a few seconds later comes back with a woman my height with blonde hair like Casper's. She has brown eyes that are immediately worried when she sees me. She is beautiful even without makeup, has high-arched eyebrows with a straight nose and full lips.

"Are you okay, Megan?" she asks in a caring, yet professional voice. "What happened?"

I bite my lip.

"Casper, get your father's bag." He leaves the room. "Megan, it's nice to meet you finally, even under these unfortunate circumstances. I will take care of you, okay?"

I nod and my chin quivers. "I'm so sorry."

"Don't apologize." She goes into his room and brings back a chair. She instructs me to sit sideways in the chair and Casper returns. He sits on the edge of the tub facing me, while she goes to work on my back.

I feel her pulling the small bits of mirror from my back. I try to ignore it but wince every time. Casper holds my hand.

"Can I ask what happened?" Mrs. Truitt asks.

"This asshole—"

"Language, Casper."

He shakes his head. "Even that word isn't the right one to describe this guy. He had her on the floor, Mom. He was going to—"

"Calm down," she tells him.

"No! Something worse could have happened."

"I think you took care of him," I whisper and flinch as Mrs. Truitt rubs a liquid on my back.

"What did you do, Casper?"

"Nothing that he didn't deserve."

Mrs. Truitt places a hot towel over my back. I lay my head down into my arms on the back of the chair. She sifts through my hair checking my head.

"Casper, go into Cora's room and get her some clothes."

He obliges. Now I'm alone with Mrs. Truitt. She works methodically in silence for a little bit and speaks.

"I know this is a very difficult situation. If you need anyone to talk to, I can recommend a counselor. She's a good friend."

"Thank you."

"Should I call your parents? Anyone?"

"No. Please. I'm not...I don't want anyone knowing."

"Don't feel ashamed for one second," she says facing me. "This was *not* your fault. You did nothing wrong. I'm sorry this happened to you."

I clench my teeth to hold back the tears and she returns to her work.

"I want you to know how happy you've made my son. It's been a while since I've seen him smile for a girl."

I'm not sure what to say to this. Lucky for me, Casper comes back in time with gray sweats and a long-sleeved shirt. When she finishes, she hugs me and tells me to come back if I need anything. Mrs. Truitt leaves the room. I stand holding my arms in front of my chest inspecting the damage in the mirror. I'm a mess. A battered back. A cut on my head. A torn dress. It's overwhelming. His mom taped bandages to my back. I look terrible.

"I'm so sorry, Megan." Casper peers at my reflection.

"It's not your fault. C-could I take a shower?"

"Yeah, of course." He walks behind me to the closet, pulls out a fresh towel and sets it beside the shower. "There's shampoo in the shower. Let me get some other soap."

I nod and I'm alone. As I stare into the mirror, a sudden rise of panic surges through me. I see a flash of Adam slamming me against the mirror.

"Here." Casper's voice startles me in his return. "Sorry. Didn't mean to scare you. I found some soap or lotion or whatever this stuff is from Cora's bathroom." He places several bottles on the counter.

I raise my eyebrows and try to smile at his naïveté, but my lips won't budge.

"Yeah," he says, awkwardly and turns for the door.

The panic returns. My heart lodges in my throat. I'm terrified that someone can easily walk in as I shower and attack me. I know I can lock the door. What if someone breaks in through the window? "Casper."

"Yeah?" His eyes meet mine.

"Um, I have sort of an odd request."

"What is it?"

I bite my lip and move my hair behind my ear. "Could you...could you leave the door open and talk to me?"

His eyebrows furrow. "Yeah."

"I'm sorry. It's that I'm—"

"It's okay. Really. I understand. I'll be right outside the door."

"Okay."

I watch him take a seat on the floor outside the open bathroom door. I turn the shower on, waiting for the hot water to come through. I ease out of the dress and chuck it in the trash. I want to burn it. I shower, washing every bit of my attacker off and change into the sweats Casper lent me. After towel drying my thick hair, I walk out, and he immediately stands. I give him my towel, and he tosses it on the bathroom counter.

"Do you want to stay here tonight?" he asks.

"Um, I don't think that would be okay."

"You can sleep in Cora's room. It's late."

Well, I can ask Casper to take me to my car and I'll go home and somehow explain in the morning why I'm not at Cherry's. Especially after I begged to stay the night. Or I can stay at Casper's.

"I'll leave early in the morning."

"You can stay as long as you like."

"Thanks." I follow him to Cora's room. It's big like his. A lot of the decorations have been removed since she's away at college.

"If you need anything, I'm next door." He shuts the door.

Pulling back the baby pink blankets, I slide underneath. I fall asleep rather quickly only to find myself looking out over a lake. It's dark, but the crescent moon reflects in the black water. The stars glitter in the black sky. Casper and I have managed to live for years together. No one has come after us, and we have no idea the results of the war or anything. It's like our private world. We don't know if we're going to return to his home or not. We fear leaving and being found by the Sprites.

I hear rustling behind me and smile. "Casper, it's so beautiful here." I turn around. My smile disappears and I freeze.

A tall, lanky figure saunters toward me with dark eyes and a menacing smile. In the darkness I can't make out the features of his face.

"Who are you?" I ask.

"You don't belong here. You belong with us."

"I belong with Casper."

"You mean nothing to me, but it's my duty to bring you back. Dead or alive." As he walks closer to me, I move backwards but he catches my arm and draws me against him. "I've always wondered what the clamor is with you."

I punch his chest, trying to release myself from his tight grip. "No, please!"

"He never loved you. You're nothing to him. He's using you, traitor."

Suddenly, I feel myself slipping from him. From the lake. From the moon.

My heart beats crazily as I look around the moonlit room. My body shakes and I can't calm down. I sit up in bed and cry. The attack comes back to me. My dreams consist of someone trying to kill me. I can't take it anymore. Is someone after me? I don't know why they would be. I don't know anything except that I don't want to be alone right now. I'm terrified.

Adam was in the dream. Has he been in them before? Are my dreams predicting the future? I've felt like something bad would happen, but I never imagined this.

I grab my phone and dial Vincent's number. I need to hear his voice. I need some comfort. He doesn't answer and can't help but feel disappointed. I know he's probably in the hospital and can't answer the phone or maybe he's asleep. I wait a few minutes, but he doesn't call back.

Slowly pushing the blankets aside, I climb out of bed, wondering if Casper is asleep. I open the door and wait outside his room, trying to debate if I should knock or not. I stand there for a few seconds feeling awkward and scared. I bring my hand up to his door and knock softly. I don't think he'll hear it, asleep or not. I hold myself and let the tears fall quietly. I cover my face with my hands and suddenly I feel arms around me.

"Megan," he says.

"I was attacked in my dream. You weren't there."

His arms tighten around me, and he pulls me inside his dark room. We sit on his bed until I finish crying.

He invites me under his covers, and he climbs on top of the covers. I lean against the headboard, but it hurts my back, so I lay on my side. He moves down to my level.

"I'm sorry. I don't want to be alone right now."

"Don't apologize. It's okay. You can stay." He takes my hand and caresses it.

We lay like that for a long time. Casper's fingers still rub my hand, so I know he's still awake.

"All I kept thinking was that I have to get out of this." He squeezes my hand. "Someway. Somehow. But I couldn't." My chin quivers and a tear rolls over my nose and onto his pillow. "He was too strong. I'm weak. I wish I knew how to fight for myself. How to be stronger like in my dreams. I mean, even Amber can beat me up. I always thought I would know what to do if I ever found myself in that situation. I shouldn't have gone tonight."

"This wasn't your fault, Megan. I'm sorry this happened to you."

"I wouldn't have gotten out of there if it hadn't been for you." I look up, but I can't see his eyes. His smooth voice calms me.

"You would have gotten out. You are strong. No matter what, he'll get what's coming to him."

"How do you know?"

"I have to believe in that."

"I'm not sure what I believe anymore. He knew my name."

"What?" His voice sounding alarmed.

"I feel like I've dreamed of Adam before. He looked familiar. Unless my mind is playing tricks."

"How is this possible? Are we predicting life now?"

"I don't know but I'm scared. I don't want to have these frightening dreams anymore."

I feel his fingers lightly touch my cheek then his soft, warm lips on my forehead. I exhale in relaxation.

He abruptly pulls away. "Sorry. I-I can't believe I did that."

"It's okay." I smile, but I know he can't see it. I shouldn't have enjoyed that as much as I did. Cherry's comment comes to mind. "I lied to you earlier because Cherry doesn't like that I'm friends with you."

"Why?"

"She thinks you're going to hurt me." I don't know why I'm so honest with him. "She thinks I'm gonna cheat on Vincent."

"You don't deserve that."

"I can't talk to her about my dreams. She always tells me to ignore them, but I can't. No one likes the fact that we're friends. It's like in our dreams. No one wants us to be together."

"I'm sure you'll clear it up with her tomorrow. I'm sure Vincent hates that we're friends."

"Um...he doesn't know."

Casper lets out a sigh. "Megan."

"I know. It's terrible, but he's so unpredictable."

"You have to tell him, or it'll be worse."

"I know. I will. I don't want to wake up feeling scared."

I feel him move closer to me and he's careful not to hurt my back by placing an arm around me. I bury myself in his chest and I'm content. This is wrong. I shouldn't be here, but it feels right.

Twenty-Four

The bright sun casts light through two giant windows and into the room. It takes a moment to remember where I am. And why. My body is sore and achy. The bed is empty, aside from me, who apparently took up the entire middle. I sit up and see Casper playing a video game from a chair at the end of the bed. I watch him for a second. He's intent on the game, pressing buttons and getting frustrated. When something goes right, he throws a fist in the air.

I snicker causing him to turn around and smile.

"Good morning. Did you sleep well?"

I nod. "I don't think I had a dream."

He turns back to his game. "I didn't have one either. We stayed up pretty late."

I remember lying in his bed, talking. It was unusual, but therapeutic actually. I seem to recall him kissing my forehead.

"What are you playing?" I ask, to keep my mind from thinking about the kiss.

He shrugs. "Football. Wanna play?"

I glance at the clock on the side table. The red numbers tell me I have twenty minutes to get ready for work, but the thought of work doesn't settle well with me. "Sure." My parents never come to the grocery store I work in, so I'm safe. I check my phone for messages and see a few from Vincent and Cherry. I text Cherry telling her I'm skipping work and that I'll call her tonight. She asks where I am and I'm hesitant to say, but I tell her the truth. Then I don't hear from her.

Vincent asked about the party and apologized for missing my call. I want to tell him what happened, but not through texting or a phone call. I need to see him. He tells me he'll be at the hospital, but he'll try to visit me when I get off work.

I spend my Sunday with Casper playing video games and texting Vincent. It's a little weird, but it also feels like Casper and I have been friends forever or something. I'm supposed to work until six, so that's when Casper drops me off at my car. I don't want him to leave. When he hugs me, it reminds me of how right it feels. As I watch him leave, I'm overcome with sadness.

"So, it's true." I hear Vincent's voice behind me.

I freeze, cursing internally. Turning around, I'm met with a cold look. "What?" I want to rush up to him and let him hold me, but his demeanor stops me.

"You stayed with Casper last night."

"Who told you?"

"Cherry."

My stomach twists. Why would she tell Vincent that? Is she against me?

"From the looks of it, she wasn't lying. You two seemed pretty close. What's going on?" He folds his arms across his chest.

"Nothing."

"Don't do that."

"Do what?"

"Tell me there's nothing going on when clearly there is."

"It's not what you think."

"Of course, it isn't."

He's got it all wrong. My stomach weaves into knots. "I tried calling you last night because I needed to talk to you, but you didn't answer."

"So that gives you the right to cheat on me? I can't believe you."

My heart falters. Is he serious? "I didn't—"

"You went home with him last night. I'm pretty sure I can guess what happened."

I slap him. "How dare you?"

The muscle in his jaw twitches as he moves closer. I move back.

"Then why'd you go?"

"He's my friend." Tears blur my vision, and my chin quivers. "Nothing more. If you can't handle it, then we're done."

His eyes widen and I see fear set in them. "Megan, no." He takes my hand, but I snatch it away. "I'm sorry that you feel that way. Casper isn't a good person. Why would you stay with him?"

"I was attacked, and Casper saved me. I had nowhere else to go so he let me stay in his sister's room." I try so hard to keep the tears back, but I can't.

"Wait, what? Someone attacked you?" His manner completely changes from cold and calculating to sincere concern.

"Yes. All I thought of was trying to break free and wishing you were there. But you weren't."

He steps closer to me. "Are you okay? Who attacked you? Are you hurt?" He tries to hug me, but I push him.

"It doesn't matter."

"Don't do that. Tell me what happened."

My phone rings. Mom's name flash on the screen. I glance at the time. *Crap.* It's past six-thirty. I answer. "Mom, I'm on my way."

"Where are you? It is six forty-five." She yells so loud I recoil.

"We got busy, and I just got off."

"You know you're supposed to call me."

She frustrates me so much. "I know. I'm sorry. I'm on my way. I'll see you in a few." I open my car door, hoping that Mom won't ground me when I get home. It won't matter though. Cherry hates me and so does Vincent. "I have to go home."

"Wait."

"I can't. I'm already in trouble."

"Call me. Please."

I have no patience right now to hear his pleas and excuses. I get in and slam the door shut. I immediately lock it and feel Vincent's eyes on me. Anger seethes inside me that I peel out of the parking lot. I have never done that before.

I can't believe he would actually think I slept with Casper. Especially after getting attacked. Doesn't he understand the severity of the situation? Why doesn't he trust me? What is so wrong with Casper that I have to lose my best friend and boyfriend?

I want to see Casper again. It's like I feel better the instant I see him. When I get home, I put my stuff down on my bed, not without Ron yelling at me because I barely greeted anyone when I walked inside. I can't win for losing.

I join my parents and Jonathan at the table. When Mom's in the mood, she cooks on Sunday nights, and tonight she prepared homemade lasagna and garlic bread. My favorite. I don't want to be around anyone right now but being with my family is actually comforting. While I have my moments with my mom, there are times that I still feel like a little girl and want her to hug me and tell me that everything will be okay. I can't tell her about the attack. She can't know I lied to her and went to a party. She can't know I wore a dress like that and certainly can't know I stayed at a guy's house.

I can't go to the police because my parents will find out. Adam's face and his words keep circling my mind. He said he knew me. How?

"Megan?" Mom asks. Her reddish-brown hair has grayed at the roots, and wrinkles have formed around her eyes more. She works hard but hates her job. She never takes any time off because I guess her employer doesn't like it. She needs a break.

"Hmm?"

Mom scoops out a portion of lasagna on my plate. "How was work?"

"Oh. It was busy."

"Are you okay?"

"I'm fine. Tired."

Afterward, I take my shower, careful not to get my back wet, and curl up in my bed with Savannah. She licks my face like she knows something's wrong. Adam pops into my head again, but I focus on how safe and *right* it felt being with Casper. It was easy, comfortable.

My phone beeps and it's Cherry messaging me.

Thanks for leaving us swamped today. I hope your night with Casper was awesome.

I sigh at her sarcasm. I don't reply because I know I will say something I don't mean. I lay in bed, cuddling with Savannah and listening to music. It seems to be the only thing that comforts me. Vincent calls a few times, but I don't answer. Why is it when I want to talk to him, he never answers but now that I don't, he calls. I don't know why Vincent would automatically assume I slept with Casper. Why did Cherry tell him I stayed? She knows I was attacked. Doesn't she care? I can't stop crying. I want to leave. Run away. Forget everything and start somewhere new. Maybe Casper and I will run away in real life. I can't keep living like this.

Twenty-Five

'm so out of sorts, I can't remember if I have a test or an assignment due. My mind is in a fog. I want to skip school, but it's the only normal thing I've got right now. Sort of. I need to focus on my studies more. That will help keep things normal.

I take my time because I don't want to face Cherry yet. I slow to a crawl when I reach my locker. Vincent leans against it with a sad look and a mixed bouquet of flowers in his hand. His eyes are bloodshot and there are black circles underneath them. His brown hair is disheveled. My stomach drops. Is his mom okay? "Is something wrong?"

"I'm a stupid fool. Are you okay?" He hands me the flowers.

I'm about to fall apart. "I'm okay."

He takes my hands in his. "Did he hurt you? What happened?"

"I'm not ready to talk about it."

He nods. "Cherry told me you stayed the night and I got crazy. I didn't know anything else happened."

I can understand that. If someone told me that Vincent stayed at a girl's house without knowing the full story, I probably would have freaked out. "I forgive you. I'm sorry you had to find out that way."

He pulls me into an embrace, and I wince a little.. He kisses my forehead, and I'm content by the warm way he holds me. I can feel his heartbeat racing.

I draw back a little to face him. "Look, I know you and Casper hate each other for some reason, but had it not been for him the other night, who knows what would have happened. The guy had a gun."

He tenses and I see the muscle in his jaw twitch. He looks pained and remorseful, like he blames himself.

"You don't have to deal with Casper at all, but he's my friend. I love you, Vincent. Not Casper, so please don't be jealous."

He searches my eyes for a moment. "Why are you his friend? He's been awful to you. I thought you couldn't stand him."

"I've gotten to know him."

"Okay," he says, but I can still see doubt in his eyes. I hate it. What happened to him that made him so untrusting? "Let me walk you to class."

When I meander into chemistry, the teacher gives me a tardy slip, and I take my seat. I feel Cherry staring at me, but we don't talk. It's so stupid. Why is she being difficult?

I don't go to lunch because I'm not hungry and I don't want to sit by myself. Instead, I hang out in the library with my head on the desk. I hate that the only thing I can think about is Adam and the attack.

By English, I'm worn out and ready to go home. I'm so grateful that I'm off tonight. I can't work.

"Hey." I hear a smooth voice beside me and my pulse edges higher.

I turn and meet Casper's brown eyes. "Hey."

"How are you holding up?"

I shrug. "I'm okay. I don't wanna be here."

"I'm sorry. Is there anything I can do?"

I shake my head. "Vincent and Cherry think we slept together."

"What? Didn't you tell them what happened?"

"No details. Vincent apologized, but Cherry still refuses to talk to me. She's the one who told him I stayed at your house."

"Damn. I can see why he'd be pissed."

"Both of them hate you and think it's a bad idea for us to be friends. Why can't they see you the way I do?"

"How do you see me?"

I don't expect that. "You're completely different than I ever imagined. You're thoughtful and you always seem to be there when I need you."

"You didn't always feel that way. We've only started being friends."

"Why is that? If you've liked me for as long as you say you have, why did you wait so long to say something to me?"

"I may not be shy, but that doesn't mean I have the guts to walk up to the prettiest girl in school."

"That doesn't make sense. I mean, if you felt that way, you would've stopped the rumors about me."

"I never said I was a smart guy. I'm not perfect. Why do you even care about the rumors anyway? It's insecure people being bored with themselves."

"So easy for you to say when you're you and I'm me."

"What's that supposed to mean?"

"You can get away with anything and no one cares. They'll still think you're awesome or cool or whatever."

"Why do you even care what they think?" He leans over closer to me lowering his voice. "You're better than them. You're amazing, strong, beautiful, sexy, and thoughtful. If no one else sees that then they're missing out. I bet Vincent sees it."

I feel my cheeks redden, loving the warmth I feel throughout me. "Why would you say that? Don't you hate him?"

"I don't hate him. Don't particularly like him."

"Didn't you once tell me to stay away from him?"

"Yeah, but as much as you may not believe this, I want you to be happy. If he makes you happy, then that's all that matters. I meant what I said that if all we can be is friends, that's good enough for me. Besides, it's your life. You make your own decisions."

"I don't believe you."

Casper sighs. "I'm trying here, okay? Yeah, I like you a lot. Maybe you're right. Maybe it is because of the dreams that I feel this strongly toward you." He shakes his head. "Do you enjoy hearing my misery?"

"No. I'm curious."

I want to hear his words, what he feels for me. I feel like I'm being unfair to Vincent. I love Vincent and I feel a connection. Why is he so jealous? Because he's afraid I'll leave him? Okay, staying at Casper's wasn't the greatest idea on my part.

On the other hand, I'm drawn by Casper. I enjoy being around him. Our shared dreams could be the one thing pulling me to him, but I feel like it's something else.

What am I supposed to do? I've never been in this position. No matter my decision, someone gets hurt. How is it possible to feel this way for two different men?

Twenty-Six

ay to go, Casper!" someone shouts when Casper and I walk out into the hallway. People stop and stare at us. I clutch my books to my chest as my throat tightens.

"What?" Casper asks, confused.

"Way to hit that," someone else yells.

Heat fills my cheeks. What are they talking about? Girls look at me like I'm some rodent.

I can't believe she slept with him.

Why would he go for someone like her?

I hear their whispers and rush out the door.

"Wait, Megan!" Casper calls after me.

How does the entire school know I stayed at Casper's? I know Cherry didn't say a word. Angry or not she would never hurt me like this. Though, she did tell Vincent. Vincent hates Casper, but he wouldn't hurt me like this either. Did Casper seriously tell his friends we slept together?

It's freezing outside, yet somehow, it's not as cold as it is around that crowd. I need to get out of here. I feel a hand on my shoulder, and I jump. I turn around to see Trinity Taylor. She has a frown on her freckle-filled face and her large brown eyes are sad.

"Are you okay?" she asks.

"I'm fine. Why?"

"Is it true?"

"Is what true?"

"Did you and Casper...you know?"

I'm so appalled. "No. Why does everyone think that?"

She takes a deep breath. "Casper told everyone at lunch. He practically gloated."

No. She's lying. Casper wouldn't do that to me, would he?

"Look, I'm sorry. He did the same to me."

"Why are you being nice to me?"

"Because I know what it's like to have rumors spread about me. Amber's out to get you, too."

"Aren't you friends with her?"

"I put up with her because we're on the dance team. I pretend to be who she wants."

"Why does she have it out for me? I haven't done anything."

"She's with Casper. Sorta."

"I gotta go." There's a pang in my chest and a lump forms in my throat. I'm sick of these people. Why are they so cruel? I turn around and almost jog to my car. I wanted a normal day. I needed to return to normal, but it's impossible.

Tears blur my vision, but I can still tell there's something black on my car. As I move closer, I slow down and gasp. I realize the black is spray paint. I let my books fall. In black paint, *slut,* is scrawled across the side, the hood, the roof, everywhere on my car. Tears roll down my cheeks. To make things worse, my tires have been slashed. This is a new low for Amber. I can't believe she attacked me like this. So...*violently.*

I can't handle this anymore. I pull my phone out of my pocket and dial Vincent.

"Hey you."

"Vincent." That's all I can say before I break down.

"What's wrong? Where are you?"

"I'm at my car."

He hangs up and I lean against my car.

"Megan, are you—what the—?" I hear Casper behind me.

I twist around. "Your psycho girlfriend."

"*Amber* did this?"

"Who else would?" I bite my lip. I hate that he sees me crying. I hate that even after all that happened it hurts to tell him this. "Casper, I appreciate everything you did for me Saturday. I do. But I can't. I can't..." I shake my head and swat the tears away.

"I didn't tell a soul about Saturday. I swear I don't know how anyone found out. Brad told me he heard it through the rumor mill."

"Stop lying. Trinity told me you gloated to them about it at lunch."

"What?" His face reddens and veins pulsate in his neck. He shakes his head. "I'm so sick of this."

"She said you and Amber are together."

His face displayed a mixture of disbelief and disgust. "This is ridiculous." He softens. "I never said a word. I would never do this to you." His brown eyes are pleading.

"We can't be friends. Even if you didn't say a word, these things are going to continue to happen because you don't set anyone straight. You say you don't care, but you're still friends with the same people who are doing this. You're no better than they are."

I want to leave and forget him. The strangest feeling overcomes me. It feels like a magnet pulling me to him, wanting to be near him or his arms around me. It terrifies me because I don't know why I should feel this way. He is nothing to me. Nothing but a liar. I have to overpower this extreme sensation.

"You're right. I will make this right. I promise. As for your car, I'll take care of it."

I want to believe him, but I can't. All this drama with Casper is getting old. Cherry and Vincent know the real Casper. So, what if we share dreams. It doesn't mean anything. I have to let one of them go. I can't have both.

"You should go."

"Megan, please. I care about you."

"I don't know what to believe anymore."

"What's going on?" Vincent says from behind Casper.

I run past him and into Vincent's arms. He holds me close, and Casper walks away.

"Who did this to your car?"

"Amber."

He meets my eyes, wiping my tears with his thumbs. "We'll fix this. You deserve so much more than this. Come on."

"I can't leave my car."

"I'll handle it. Come on."

Vincent turns down the street to my house and I'm disappointed. "Why are we here?" I ask.

"You live here." He pulls into the driveway.

"I don't want to be here. I want to be with you."

He frowns. "I have things I have to do tonight."

"Like what?"

"It doesn't matter. Just things I have to take care of." He looks away.

What's up with his elusiveness? Is he doing drugs again? Is that why he's hot one minute and cold the next? A tear falls down my cheek and I wipe it away.

"Please don't cry." He squeezes my hand.

That's when I break down again. I'm tired of people hurting me and it seems to be happening a lot lately. Doesn't Vincent want to be around me? Am I diseased or something?

"Talk to me."

"Everything is falling apart. I got into a fight with my best friend. You. Casper. I trusted him. But you and Cherry were right. He told everyone that we had sex Saturday."

"I told you he isn't a good person."

His comment angers me for a second, but I let it go. "Why can't you hang out when I want to? Why does it always have to be when you want?"

He sighs. "I'm sorry you feel that way. You know things are difficult with me right now." He reaches over and pulls me into a hug. He kisses the top of my head and when he exhales, I feel the air travel over me.

I was attacked and I feel like I'm being punished for something. For liking two guys at the same time. "Please stay with me."

He holds me tighter. "I can't tonight. I will see you tomorrow, I promise."

"What am I going to tell my parents about my car?"

"Tell them the truth."

"I can't."

"Lying won't help anything. I have a history of constantly lying and it's never good. Go inside, tell your parents the truth, and relax tonight. I'll call you later."

"I love you, Vincent."

"I love you, mon trésor."

Inside, my dogs almost trample me. They're always happy to see me and I admire that. At least someone still likes me. I'm on edge and I want to punch something. I know Ron is going to freak out when he sees that my car isn't in the driveway. Vincent suggested I tell them the truth, but he doesn't get it. I don't need Mom making a huge deal out of it and call Amber's parents or whatever.

Instead, I tell my parents the car stopped working and I had it towed. Ron reminds me that whatever it costs, I'll have to pay for it. Not sure how since he gets all of my paychecks. Asshole. I hate him. He and Mom go out to dinner, leaving Jonathan and me alone, with hardly anything to eat.

I stay in my room the rest of the night without dinner. I can't stomach food and I can't concentrate on my homework. I don't feel like working on it. It's strange not calling Cherry and venting to her. I hate feeling alone. Casper texts me a few times during the night but I don't reply. I want to sleep and not dream of him or someone trying to kill me.

Of course, I dream of Casper and it's all sickly sweet. I'm annoyed by them now because I don't understand how I can be in love with someone like Casper.

Twenty-Seven

The cold hurts the cuts on my back. I'm not sure why I endured riding the bus and came to school. I tried normal yesterday and that didn't work. I guess it's better than staying at home and getting yelled at for skipping. I have to work tonight, but I'm still sore. The bumpy bus ride doesn't help.

Vincent is waiting by my locker. I want to cry because I'm overcome with emotion. Rushing up to him, I wrap my arms around him. When he hugs me, I wince, but I ignore it. Being in his arms relaxes me and I don't care if anyone sees our intimate scene.

"I promise I'll take care of you. I won't let anything happen to you again." He holds me at arm's length and gazes into my eyes. He leans down and kisses me, slow at first, but his lips soon move urgently with mine. I see a vision of us again. I'm running into his arms, and he catches me. It's filled with so much emotion as if we haven't seen each other in a long time. When we pull apart, my heart is still beating, and the noisy hall comes back to me.

"That was intense." Vincent presses his forehead to mine.

"It always is."

"How are you feeling?"

I shrug. "I missed you last night. What did you do?"

I see a flash of annoyance in his eyes. "I told you I had something I had to do. Don't worry. Please. Tonight, we'll do something."

"I have to work."

I feel his hands on my hips and he draws me closer. But I hesitate.

"Call in. It's been too long since I've spent time with you." He brushes my hair aside and his dark blue eyes hold mine. His gravelly voice puts me in a trance-like stance.

I don't feel like working. Spending time with Vincent is exactly what I need. "Okay."

"Come on. We should get to class."

I don't want to be here again, but I force myself to stay.

When I get to chemistry, I slide in my chair next to Cherry. I'm tired of the nonsense. "You were right," I tell her. "About Casper. I don't want something stupid like that to come between us."

Cherry frowns and her eyes water. "I'm stupid. I should've been there for you Saturday and yesterday. I heard the rumors and about your car. I'm so sorry, Megan."

"Why did you tell Vincent that I stayed with Casper? Why not the rest? He thought we slept together."

"Because I'm an idiot. I was upset that you chose Casper over me to help you."

"I didn't choose him. He was there. He saved me and I tried calling you."

"I know. I'm stupid and childish. It felt like you wanted to be with him more than anything." A tear slides down her cheek.

"That's how I felt about you with Luke. Why did you even want me at the party?"

She shrugs. "I just did. I didn't know it was going to be that big and I didn't think Luke was going to hang out with me because it was his party. I should've been there for you no matter what. I'm sorry if I messed up anything between you and Vincent, but I'll fix it."

I shake my head. "It's okay."

"Lately, it feels like all you want to do is be with Casper because of the dreams or Vincent. I mean, we hardly hang out."

"I'm sorry. Vincent's going through a lot and needs me."

"I get that, but what about Casper? You can't date two people."

"I know that. I'm not dating him, and we're not hanging out anymore."

"Good."

I'm glad we're not fighting anymore. Especially since it was over Casper. Vincent texts me after lunch telling me that my car is in its parking space fixed. I'm in awe by his kindness.

My stomach is in knots when I walk into English class. Casper doesn't show. I work on our assignment alone, wondering where he is. Not that I should care. I kinda miss him, though.

My phone buzzes with a text message from Cherry and I discreetly read it.

Vincent and Casper got into a fight and they're both suspended.

I freeze. This doesn't settle well in my stomach. I don't like knowing they fought. Was it because of yesterday or that I stayed at Casper's house?

What happened?
I dunno.

This has to stop. They have to stop fighting over me. What is their problem? Why do they hate each other so much?

After class, I call Vincent. He tells me to come over and he'll explain. We've been together four months, and it's the first time he's ever asked me to come to his house. When I reach my car, I stop. It looks amazing, like it was repainted completely.

Vincent's house isn't a drug lord mansion like Casper's, but it's still bigger than mine. It's a two-story red brick modern house. The porch is enclosed by white columns and the shrubs that line each side of the porch are perfectly round.

When Vincent answers, I gasp and cover my mouth. His eye, black and red, is swollen shut and he has a small cut on his cheek.

"Am I that hideous? Don't hold back." He gives a crooked smile.

"What happened?"

"Come in." He pulls me inside the warm house. There are a couple of lamps on, but it's mostly dark. Family pictures grace the walls and I feel sad when I see his mom. She looks like Vincent except her hair is longer. He takes me to the kitchen and offers me a glass of water and I accept. He takes my coat and hangs it on the back of a round backed chair at the table in front of the bay windows.

"Thanks for my car. You didn't have to do that."

"I know. You're welcome.

"What happened?"

"I asked about the guy who attacked you and he said I shouldn't worry since he took care of it. He said I wasn't right for you and that I need to forget about you. That you two were together now that you slept with him."

Blood drains from my face. "What?"

"I told him he needed to leave you alone and not hurt you anymore. He swung at me, and well, we started fighting."

"Why would he say that?"

"Probably because I have you."

That sounds possessive. "Um, what?"

"He's making up all this crap about you because he's jealous that we're together. He's jealous of me. He's a piece of work."

"Why is he lying about me? Why is he so set on hurting me?"

"Because Casper is a jackass and a selfish prick."

I let out a sigh. "Why did you fight him? You're better than that. It's not worth it."

He closes the space between us and takes my hands in his. "Well, I'm not going to let some asshole beat me up. You take a swing at me I'm going to fight back. I can't stand him. After everything he did to you, you shouldn't be friends with him. He's dangerous, Megan. I mean he wailed on me. I love you and I don't always say the right things but I'm falling deeper in love with you."

My heart thrums against my ribcage. I can't decide if it's because of the intense look or the words he said. "You don't need to fight anyone."

"Are you mad because I fought him?"

I silently curse. It's like I can't say the right thing with him. "No, I don't like fighting. I don't like that you got hurt."

"It's nothing. You should see the other guy." He smirks.

"I can't believe he said those things."

"Stop worrying about him. I took care of it."

I give him a pointed look.

"What happened Saturday? Are you okay? Were you hurt physically?"

I shift uncomfortably.

"It's okay." He kisses my forehead. "Tell me when you're ready."

I exhale. "He came in the bathroom," I say in such a soft voice it doesn't sound like my own. "He kept saying he knew me, but I've never seen him before. He slammed me against the mirror and it broke. I have some cuts on my back and head. I tried to run but he caught me, forcing me to the ground and held a gun to me."

Anger flashes in his good eye and his face turns red. A vein in his neck protrudes and I can see it pulsing. "Why did you go to the party?"

"Cherry wanted me to."

He pulls me to him, a little roughly, and I wince as he touches my back. "Baby, you have to be more careful. You weren't wearing anything revealing, were you?"

I was and I know I shouldn't have. "No."

"You said he knew you?"

"He knew my name. He said his name was Adam, but I don't know who he is." I feel his arms tighten around me. "What if he finds me again?"

"He won't. I promise you're safe now. I'll make sure no one hurts you again." He kisses the top of my head.

"I don't want to think about it," I murmur into his chest.

We stay like that for a little while. I love the feel of his arms around me, holding me protectively, and the way he buries his face in my hair. Why can't I ever dream of Vincent? I pull away slightly and press my lips to his wanting to see another vision or feel that rush. He kisses back with the same fervor, and I want it to be like this always. No more dreams of Casper. But I never see a vision.

Vincent pulls away breathless. "Is this normal?" His lips graze my cheek.

"What?"

"Us. The intensity. The fact that I can't stand being away from you and you're always on my mind. Do you feel the same?"

"Yes."

"Good." He smiles and my heart flips. "Are you hungry?"

"A little."

"Do you wanna go out or wanna order in?"

"Let's order in. Where are your parents? Was your mom released?"

He nods. "Yeah. They're at my aunt's. My mom has good days and when she does, she always likes to get out. It makes me nervous though. My dad's with her so I know she's okay."

I squeeze his hand. He orders Chinese and we hang out in his kitchen until it arrives. He makes me laugh and I feel better immediately. We eat and goof around a little. I love how easy it is being with him and how he instantly takes my mind off of everything.

"So, are you ever going to play that song for me?" I ask.

He cocks an eyebrow. "I don't know if you can handle it."

I laugh a little. "Why? Will I faint from the awesomeness?"

"You might."

I roll my eyes. "I think I can handle it."

"Okay." He takes my hand, and we go upstairs. We are the only ones here and it's a little scary. We enter his room, which has music posters plastered to the walls. He has a sleigh bed and a TV on a table facing the bed and a dresser next to that. The bed sits in front of the windows. I peer out and groan when I see rain pouring down in sheets.

He comes up beside me, grabs his acoustic guitar, and sits on his bed. I sit next to him, and he strums a couple of chords, tuning it. He plays a song and it's sad but somewhat uplifting. I close my eyes, focusing on the lyrics, and I see a flash of something. It's so quick I don't know what it is, but the song sounds familiar. It's like I'm having déjà vu.

"I feel like I've heard this before. It's so strange."

"It might sound like another song. I don't know. It's hard to be original these days."

"You wrote that for me?"

"Yes." He places his guitar back in its holder. "Do you like it?"

"Of course. It's beautiful."

"You need to have your ears checked. Nothing is more beautiful than you, Megan."

I roll my eyes. He takes my head in his hands and kisses me with an edge. His lips are almost possessive of mine. I see a vision of us running and laughing. We are happy in the vision, and we kiss as if nothing else in the world matters. He is mine and I am his.

Vincent pulls away and clears his throat. "I'm still trying to get used to that."

"Me, too. It's like we're meant to be together."

"We are." He kisses me again. "Do you want to watch a movie?"

I give a small laugh. "Sure." I know he wants things to progress physically, and I do too, but I'm not ready especially after Saturday night. I shouldn't have come up here.

Vincent pops in a random movie and gets on the bed. He leans against the headboard, pulling me into his lap.

I chuckle once I see *The Fox and the Hound* playing.

"What, it's a good movie."

"I'm gonna cry."

He kisses the side of my head.

We watch maybe the first fifteen minutes and I feel his lips against my neck, sending chills all over. His lips move behind my ear and warmth floods my body. He moves to my shoulder. I turn my head and his lips are on mine. He moves on top of me, and I wince.

"What is it?"

"My back."

"I'm sorry. I should find that—"

I cut him off with a kiss not wanting to ruin the moment with his anger. He slides his hands up my shirt. Heat radiates inside of me. My pulse vibrates inside my ears.

"I want you," he whispers in my ear. His hands and lips are everywhere. I can't keep up.

"Vincent," I hesitate. Adam pops in my mind.

"It's okay. I'll be gentle."

My breathing is shallow. I need to stop. Things are moving too fast for my brain to process. He stops long enough to remove his shirt exposing his smooth chest and a couple of bruises. His nuummite dangles from his neck.

"Did he do that?" I ask.

"It's okay."

"I'm sorry."

"Don't worry." He kisses me, but I stop him. "What? Please don't stop."

I swallow hard not wanting to upset him. I look up to see the raw fire in his eyes. He moves in to take my sweater off and I let him. He tenderly raises it over my head careful not to let it snag on my bandages. He takes my head in his hands and kisses me with such desire it's overwhelming. His tongue finds mine and heat rises inside me. Feeling his bare skin against mine does things to me that I've never felt before. I want more. Especially when his fingers skim the edge of my bra.

He grinds against me and inches his fingers under the bra band.

I don't want to stop him, but I can't go much further. I'm trying so hard not to think Adam straddling me and I hate that it invades my mind.

Vincent tugs my bra strap over my shoulder and his lips graze my bare skin. It feels good. My hands run up his back and I hope he can't tell I'm shaking. I try with everything to push Adam and that night from my mind. Then I think of Casper kissing my forehead and how it made me feel.

Oh god what is wrong with me?

Vincent kisses my collarbone, and his hand tenderly squeezes above my hip. My breath hitches. He moves his mouth back to mine and I kiss him hard trying to focus on him. His hand worms its way upward and sneakily finds the back of my bra. I press my hands against his chest.

"Vincent—wait." I stop his hand.

"What is it?"

"I can't do this."

He groans and sits up. "Megan."

"I want to. Just not yet."

Vincent smiles and runs his finger down my arm. "It has been four months."

"I know. I'm—"

"It'll happen when you're ready." He kisses my forehead and stands from the bed. He checks his phone on his nightstand as I replace my sweater and straighten my hair. He looks angry as he peers at his phone. "You should go. I've got things to do. I'll call you later, okay?"

I don't expect that. "What's wrong?"

"Nothing."

Why is he suddenly cold? "Are you kicking me out because I stopped?"

Vincent looks up from his phone and brushes my hair aside. "No. I have things to do."

"Obviously those things could have waited if we kept going?"

"Megan, please."

"I called into work to hang out with you and now you're blowing me off?"

"Stop overanalyzing this."

"Well can you imagine how I'm feeling right now? I asked you to stop and suddenly you want me to leave?"

He lets out a sigh. "You're always like this."

I don't think he knows me well enough to know what I'm always like. "Like what?"

He shakes his head and I see in his eyes that he's holding something back. "Not you. Girls in general. Look, I need to go. I have something to take care of and everything will be fine."

"Are you going to get drugs?" I shouldn't have asked. Especially when I see his jaw clench. His hands tighten around his phone. He's acting strange and has been the last couple of weeks.

He takes a breath and calms down. "I told you I've been sober since June. Don't be so paranoid. I'll call you later, I promise." He brushes his lips against mine.

I slide off the bed, grab my coat, and leave the room, feeling completely disoriented and unwanted. Apparently, walking me to the door is out of the question. I can't figure him out. One night he asks me to never let him go, yet tonight he can't wait to get rid of me. Why is he being so secretive? I should follow him. I open the door, run out into the rain and into my car. I pull out of the drive, drive down the street, and turn out the lights.

This is so unlike me. But the unusual way he went from hot to cold in a matter of seconds concerns me. The logical part of my brain asks if he is going to get drugs, do I want to be there.

Nevertheless, as he backs out of his driveway and turns at the stop sign, I follow. It's still pouring yet somehow, I'm able to keep up. He isn't speeding or recklessly driving, not sure why I thought he would. He turns into the hospital and parks. I feel sick. Is his mom in the hospital again? Did something happen? I feel low. Vincent isn't a bad guy.

It doesn't make sense though. If something happened to his mom, he would've told me. Instead, he said he had something to take care of, then everything would be fine. My curiosity won't rest until I know the truth. I'm acting crazy and paranoid, but I don't care. I have to know.

I follow him inside, up to the intensive care unit. From afar, I watch him press his forehead and palm to a window. A doctor comes up and squeezes his shoulder and they exchange a few words. I feel awful witnessing his pain. I feel even worse that I doubted him.

Vincent never goes inside the room, but once the doctor leaves, he turns to walk down the hall toward me. I whip myself out of the way and have to think fast of where to hide. Nothing around me but rooms. My heart assails my ribcage and my palms sweat. I open the nearest door to me and quietly walk into a dark room, closing the door. The soft beep of monitors is the only sound. I hide behind the door and see his shadow peeking through the window. *Crap.* He saw me. Any minute I know he's going to open the door. Instead, he walks away.

I exhale and someone moans. I hope I don't wake up the patient. I open the door and peek out in the hallway to make sure Vincent and no one else sees me. It's clear so I swing out and before I close the door, I glance at the patient and freeze. My hand clutches the door handle.

Twenty-Eight

Several pillows prop him up in the bed. Tubes connect him to monitors. I flip a switch and a dim light shines. Bruises and bandages cover his face. He wears a neck brace. His left arm is in a bandage, and I fear what the rest of his body looks like. His blonde hair is even more ragged.

"Casper." My heart breaks at the horrific sight. I can't believe it. What did Vincent do to him? He never mentioned putting him in the hospital. I move in a daze toward him. He seems heavily sedated, or my worst fear is that he's in a coma. My mouth waters, but I can't swallow. Tears brim over and I wipe them from my cheeks. I want to hold him or kiss him or be like the Megan in my dreams.

I have to leave, but I don't want to leave him alone in this place. I reluctantly walk back toward the door and close it behind me. I don't remember getting on the elevator or walking past the front desk. I step outside into the cold night and inhale a shaky breath. The rain has slacked. I can't believe it. Casper's in the hospital beaten to a bloody pulp.

"I never pegged you as a stalker." I stop mid-stride clutching onto the strap of my bag that crosses my chest.

"I never pegged you as a liar, but here we are." I twist around and see Vincent sitting on a bench under an awning, arms stretched along the length of it. His dark blue eye focuses on me though he isn't angry, but sad.

"Liar?" He gets up and moves toward me. I stand my ground but tense. "My dad sent me a text telling me that Mom was admitted again. She isn't awake though." He frowns and his eye waters.

I feel like the lowest of low. I feel my shoulders sag. I'm a terrible person. "I'm so sorry, Vincent. Why didn't you tell me?"

"Because. I already don't like being known as the kid with the cancer mom. I don't want people to pity me. I blame myself. I worried her so much with all my reckless shit that she got sick. I'm sorry I don't tell you every little thing. It's still hard for me open up to people."

"But it's me."

"I know."

Here I am getting upset with him over something so trivial and his mom's in the hospital dying of cancer. Maybe he's so angry and Casper came at the wrong time. "Were you taking out your anger on Casper?" My voice is barely above a whisper.

He tilts his back and gives a hard laugh. "If I took out all my anger on him, he'd be dead." The look in his good eye tells me he means it.

I shudder. "You almost did."

"What? A couple of bruises and a black eye hardly seems like death. Why are you so worried about him now?"

"He's in the ICU." I point back to the hospital. "I know you're under a lot of stress, but that's no reason to beat someone up like that. Why did you do it?"

Vincent narrows his eyes, and his face contorts with confusion. "ICU? For what?"

"He's got bruises and bandages all over his face. His arm is in a cast. He's wearing a neck brace. You didn't have to put him in the hospital."

He holds up his hands in surrender. "I didn't do that. I got a couple of punches on him before the coach pulled us apart. We went to the principal's office, and they suspended us both. I went home after that."

Maybe it's best that I don't have contact with either one of them. My life was fine until these stupid dreams and visions and fights. I've seen more violence in the last month than ever before. I have school to focus on. I have to get a scholarship and get out of this place.

"You're so quick to accuse me and defend him." He shakes his head in disappointment.

Remorse overcomes me. I don't know why I'm so quick to blame Vincent. I love him with everything I have, but I don't treat him well. Worrying over Casper doesn't help him. "What do you think happened to him?" I whisper as a small tear rolls down my cheek. I'm crying at what Vincent said, not Casper. Maybe I'm crying for both.

"I don't know." He lets out a defeated sigh. "We can go find out if you want."

I shake my head and my heart drops. "No. We aren't friends anymore. He hurt me. I'm so sorry for being the worst girlfriend ever. I'm such a terrible person."

He takes my hand and brushes it against his lips. "You are anything but. You gotta learn to trust me though and you gotta stop worrying about him."

I swallow the lump of guilt in my throat and wrap my arms around him. His arms wind around me and instead of feeling the cold mist of the rain soaking us, I feel his warmth. "You deserve better."

"No, I don't," he says with conviction. "I love you. Probably more than I should, but I do. You keep me grounded and out of trouble." He clears his throat. "With the exception of today." He pulls back to peer into my eyes and cradles my face in his hands. "I promise I will never hurt you or fight anyone." Vincent kisses me and it brings another vision. We are standing in the rain, somewhere. I'm crying and he's comforting me. He whispers something, I can't hear but I read his lips. *Don't forget me.*

When we pull apart, I whisper, "I won't forget you."

He tightens his arms around me. "You should get home. I don't want you getting sick."

"Are you staying here tonight?"

He scratches his head and avoids my gaze. "Yeah. I'm gonna sleep here."

"Tell your mom I said hi."

He gives a pained smile. "I will."

I stand on my toes and kiss him. "I love you."

He walks me to my car and on my way home, I feel sad. I can't imagine being in his shoes. I want to be there for him and take away his pain. But I can't.

Then there is Casper. What happened to him? Maybe someone knows something. I'll find out tomorrow. I can't help wanting to be there for him as well.

Once home, I take a hot shower and it warms my body from all the cold rain. I put in my earbuds and start playing music. A soft piano song begins, and I slide under the blankets. I close my eyes and let the song lure me to sleep.

"I could listen to you play forever." Casper smiles and walks toward me. My fingers unconsciously and blithely move from key to key on the upright piano as I perform a beautiful number. I stop playing once he sits next to me on the bench. Candles dimly light the little cottage and his face glows in the beautiful orange light.

I smile.

He leans into me and presses his soft lips against mine. His hands tangle with my long black hair as I fold into him. Warmth rushes within me. He tugs on my lower lip. I moan as I reach inside his shirt, running my hands across his smooth chest.

The door bursts open, breaking our passionate kiss. Three figures advance, but I can't see their faces. Covered by hoods. Somewhere deep down I know it is them. How did they find us?

"Take her," the man in the middle demands. They come at me without hesitation.

Casper shields me with his body. "You will never take her."

"We've been down this road before. She doesn't belong to you. Yet, each time I see you with her."

"I love her."

The man lets out a hard laugh. "What does your kind even know about it? You vile creature. You have no feelings, no soul, no heart."

"What are you talking about?" I ask, peeking from behind Casper. I clutch onto his hand, refusing to let go. "He has more of a heart than you will ever have. Why can't you leave us alone? I love him."

"You've been manipulated, my dear, but we shall fix that."

"She doesn't want you."

"I will not discuss this any further. Take her," the man says and turns for the door.

"No." Casper pushes the guards away, protecting me, and I grasp onto Casper with everything I have.

The man turns around and fires the gun. Casper cries out and collapses. The guards seize me, dragging me away from him.

"Casper! Please, Casper!" I kick and scream and wrestle with them. My eyes lock on Casper's brown eyes as they slowly close.

Twenty-Nine

With a gasp, I bolt upright to see the morning sun has barely risen. Grabbing my phone from my table, I scroll down to Casper's name, but stop. He's in the hospital, I remember. What did the dream mean? Are my dreams connected to real life or vice versa? Is Casper okay? Is he dead? If I call the hospital, will they tell me his status?

Maybe I'll sneak in the ICU later and see him to see if he's okay.

I turn off my alarm before it sounds. I have an annoying dull ache in the back of my throat that is scratchy. *Great, now I'm on the verge of getting a cold.*

I jump when my phone beeps. It's a text message from Vincent.

School can wait. Want to spend the day with me?

A smile stretches across my face. I reply yes. I know it's bad, but I don't want to go to school. Vincent says he changed the number on my file so that the school will call my cell phone, instead of my mom's. I'm glad he thought of that.

I dress in jeans and tuck them into my black boots and put on a maroon sweater. I grab my backpack to let my parents think I'm going to school.

Driving to Vincent's, I promise myself I won't let things get out of hand. Of course, I said the same thing the night before.

"You're just in time," he says.

"For?"

"I'm making breakfast."

"Wow. Thanks."

I follow him into the kitchen and halt in the doorway. A man in a grey suit is sitting at the table in the kitchen, sipping coffee and reading a newspaper. He looks up and flashes a smile. He has the same blue eyes as Vincent. His hair is dark like Vincent's but with grey mixed in. Vincent opens the refrigerator and pulls out some eggs.

"Megan, this is my dad. Dad, this is Megan."

"Stan." He reaches out his hand and I shake it. "So, you're the reason for my son's constant beaming."

I smile and feel my cheeks redden.

"He told me about the fight yesterday. Although, I'm not exactly pleased with his suspension, I'm proud of him. I probably would've done the same thing for a girl I loved."

I shift uncomfortably. What an odd thing to be proud of.

"Dad." Vincent groans.

"Just stating the facts. Do you have time to eat? School starts soon." He looks at me expectantly.

"I'm making her breakfast because she's getting my homework and such. She's got time."

"All right. I have to go." He stands and finishes his coffee. "I'll meet you at the hospital later," he tells Vincent in a low voice. "Megan, it was a pleasure meeting you. Maybe next time we'll actually get to talk longer."

"It was nice meeting you, too."

Stan leaves and as soon as Vincent hears him back out of the driveway, he grabs me and pulls me into a hug. "That was embarrassing." He kisses my cheek and walks to the fridge.

"I didn't know your dad was going to be here."

"He wanted to meet you."

"He seems nice."

"Yeah." Something about the way he answers that makes me doubt how kind his dad is. "Scrambled?" He holds up eggs.

"Yeah. How long is your suspension?" I lean against the counter and watch him stir the gooey mass of eggs.

"A week."

"So, you get to sleep in for an entire week? Nice."

"Doesn't exactly help my permanent record."

Well, you should've thought about that before you fought, I want to say, but I don't. He finishes scrambling the eggs and divides them on two plates that already have sausage and biscuits.

"Thanks for breakfast."

He beams showing a dimple. "Anytime."

We sit down at the table and eat while chatting about random things. School, how he's been dealing with his mom in the hospital, which isn't too well. He fears for his mom but knows she can overcome it. I hold his hand without saying a word. I know nothing I say can help.

"Is it not good?" He points to my half-eaten plate of food.

"I'm not hungry." And it hurts to swallow. The pain in my throat worsens. I prop my head against my hand while I lean on the table.

"Are you okay?"

"I'm tired. Not exactly a morning person."

With a sly smile, he lowers his head to my level. "There's a bed upstairs you can sleep in."

I sit up. "I'm okay." I am *not* going up there. I know what will happen.

"I'm kidding." He gently touches my cheek, then moves his hand to my neck and forehead. "You're burning up."

I moan.

"I was going to take you to the art museum, but I don't think you need to be going out."

"Art museum?"

"Sure. My mom has a photograph there."

"Wow. What is it?"

He scoots back his chair and leaves the room. A few seconds later, he returns with a thick black frame. The picture inside is a black and white photo of Vincent. His body is shadowed as he walks into a tunnel, but his face is turned toward the camera. His eyes look sorrowful, but he looks sexy.

"I don't show people that." He clears the table.

"Why? It's beautiful." I can't stop looking at it. I'm a fan of black and white photography, and the way she captured him makes me ache.

His shadow covers the picture frame blocking the overhead light. "Hmm, you think I'm beautiful?"

"Just the picture." I tease.

"Oh, I see." He takes the picture frame from my hands and places it on the table. He proceeds to tickle me. I fall back in the chair, but he catches me. Chills run over my body. I feel tired and sluggish. I rest my head against his stomach.

"Come on." He pulls me to my feet and takes me to a chocolate suede couch. He lowers me down onto it and grabs a handmade afghan covering me with it. "You should probably go home. But I don't want you to."

"I don't want my parents knowing I skipped."

"They won't. I worked it out. Besides, your parents are too strict anyway. Do you want me to get you anything?"

I shake my head.

Vincent puts on a movie and crosses back to the couch. He sits in the corner of the L-shaped couch and pulls me to him. "Have you been writing more in the story?"

"Not a lot."

"Can I show you something?"

"Sure."

He reaches over and grabs a notebook opening it. There are pages and pages of text.

"Wow."

"I've been writing, too. Your story is so inspiring especially right now and I find it fun to write. Especially since I've nothing better to do in the hospital. I know it's all fantasy, but it's something to dream about. Two people who are stuck in a world they can't escape and do what's necessary to be together. I named the immortal world Arvada."

I start reading and I'm amazed with the intricate details of this world that he's written. Part of me is a bit jealous at the beautiful, detailed descriptions. I wish I could have come up with this. He places a pillow in his lap while I rest my head on it. His hand rakes through my hair softly, repetitively and I close my eyes.

I find myself inside a dark and cold room. The bed is lumpy and very uncomfortable. I hear the door unlock and a glowing candle enters the room with a hooded figure.

"You're safe, now," the voice whispers.

"W-who are you?" My teeth chatter.

The figure removes the hood revealing his face. I gasp and bring my hands to my mouth. Haggard and drawn, he looks much older than I remember. "Vincent?"

He rushes to me, placing the candleholder on the table next to my bed. "You're here. You're here, Megan." He takes my hands and kisses them. "I've missed you terribly." He hugs me tightly and holds my head between his warm hands. His dark blue eyes are red from tears, and he presses his forehead to mine. "I thought I lost you forever."

"Vincent." Tears well in my eyes. After four months, he has returned from his mission. "You're back." I hug him and plant kisses all over his face. My heart swells from the sight of him. I've missed him.

He draws back with a stunned look on his face, and I see the hurt in his eyes.

"What is it? Why am I in the cellar? When did you return? Why did you think you lost me?"

Vincent's eyebrows furrow. "You don't remember?"

"Remember what?" I ask, but something feels wrong. I remember him telling me he had to leave. He was to be gone four months, but here he stands. I can't recall anything of the past four months. It makes me uncomfortable that my mind is nestled in a thick fog. What happened to me?

"Megan, please tell me you haven't forgotten. Please."

I chew on the inside of my mouth, but I can't give an answer to the pleading man. "I'm sorry." I lower my head.

"No, don't be," he says with clenched teeth. He lifts my chin with this finger. "Can I try something that might make you remember?"

"Yes." I know he will show me a memory of us. It's his gift.

His fingers gently caress my cheek down to my chin and his lips are on mine, hungrily attempting to awaken my memory. I can never forget the way his mouth moves with mine and how he pulls me so close against his body with such ardor.

I see a vision of us in the garden. He asks for my hand in marriage, and I accept. He lifts me, holding me close, and gently places me on the ground. He leans down and whispers, "*Don't forget me.*" I tell him that I could never forget him.

Vincent pulls away searching for an answer in my eyes, but it isn't there. I have no recollection of this. He sighs and drops his hands from my face. "I've lost you," he says painfully.

"You haven't lost me." I place my hand on his. "It might take time. What happened for us to be apart?"

"What do you remember? Anything about your life here? Or is all you can remember your life with *them*?"

"With who?"

"You don't even recall them? What did they do to you, Megan?"

"I don't know. Who are 'they'?"

"I saved you from them. *He* took you from me, but I brought you back. I killed him."

"W-who?"

"He's not important. Come with me. I will tell you everything I know. I should banish those who placed you in this retched room."

I let him take my hands and we walk out of the cold room. The higher we go in the dark stoned building, the warmer it gets. As we climb the spiraling staircase, we pass windows that show a beautiful golden wheat field under a faultless blue sky. The field reaches for miles over rolling hills. I stop and watch the blades softly bend in the direction of the wind.

"Do you recall something?"

I shake my head.

Vincent frowns. He takes my hand, leading me up through another hallway and into a vast bedroom with long red velvet curtains and a canopy bed with sheer red drapes. The furniture is a dark wood, and all of my little trinkets are still here. The room is mine; I remember. Nothing looks out of place.

"I can't believe you're here with me. I've searched for you, centuries it seems. Now you're here."

He leans down and kisses me once more providing me with yet another memory, but it is unclear. Then I don't feel his arms around me or the kiss.

Thirty

My eyes flutter open and it takes me a minute to remember I'm at Vincent's. The TV is on and I'm still in his lap. His notebook is still open, and the room is dark as rain pours outside. I sit up slowly, feeling more tired than before. Heat fills inside me and chill bumps scatter all over my skin. My throat is still sore.

"If I knew my writing would put you to sleep, I wouldn't have given it to you," Vincent says.

I groggily look his way. "No, sorry. I'm tired is all."

"Are you feeling better?"

I shake my head and feel my throat. It's definitely swollen. My head is throbbing. "I had the strangest dream."

"What was it about?"

I hesitate unsure if I want to tell him I've been having a constant storyline in my dreams. "Um, you and me. The details are foggy."

"Okay," he says. "Did I at least kiss you?"

I smile.

"I'll take that as a yes. I must be good if I'm in your dreams."

I roll my eyes. "What time is it?"

"It's a quarter to three."

My eyes open wider. "What?" Did I sleep the whole time I've been here? "I slept for seven hours?"

"Yeah. Which tells me you're getting sick." He frowns and moves closer to me.

"You were seriously passed out."

"I'm a pretty heavy sleeper. I'm so sorry."

"Don't be. You need the rest. You're not going to work, tonight, are you?"

"I have to."

"Meg, you don't look so good."

"I don't feel great."

"Then I'll take you home."

"No, I can drive."

He lifts an eyebrow. "You shouldn't. Let me take care of you. Tell your parents I drove you home from school because you were too sick."

I want to check on Casper because for some reason I miss him. I shouldn't drive since I can barely keep my eyes open. "Vincent, it's okay."

"Are you sure?"

"I'll be fine."

"Too bad you can't stay here. I'm great at taking care of people." He grins.

"I wish I could."

We walk out to my car, and he kisses me. I slide into my seat and check my phone for messages. I got one from Cherry.

Where are you today? Did you hear Casper got into an accident? They say it was pretty bad.

Accident? Now I feel bad for blaming Vincent. Poor Casper. What happened? I need to see him. The dream I had last night left me with a stabbing pang in the pit of my stomach. With the world spinning around me, I force myself to focus on the road.

Seeing Casper in the hospital last night and getting shot in my dream, I have to see him. This need won't go away until I know he's okay.

Calling Cherry, I make my way toward the hospital.

"Hey, are you okay?" she asks. "Why weren't you in school today? You don't sound good."

"I played hooky with Vincent but ended up sleeping most of the time because I'm coming down with something." My voice sounds terrible. Like suddenly I've developed testosterone and it's deepened.

"Hooky with Vincent? Yum. What did you do besides sleep?"

"We hung out.

"Did you ever find out why they fought?"

"He has some deep hatred for Casper."

"And you don't? Especially after yesterday?"

I release a sigh. "I can't explain it."

"I feel like anything Casper does you choose to ignore it. Are you still dreaming about him?"

"Yes, but that's not the reason."

"You told me yesterday that I was right about Casper. That all he's doing is messing with you."

"I don't understand why they hate each other so much. They don't even know one another. It can't be because of me."

"You're kidding me, right? Of course, it's because of you. Casper is pouting because he can't have what he wants."

The comment almost makes me lash out, but I don't. "I know you don't understand it. Sometimes I don't either. Casper isn't who we thought he was." If he was the one who spread the rumors, then he's exactly who I think he is. Then again, he completely attacked Vincent. I don't know why I have to see him again.

"Has he brainwashed you?"

"No. You should see the way he acts around me or hear the things he says. It's hard to explain."

"Yeah. That's called manipulation. I worry about you. You're with a great guy. Why ruin it by being friends with Casper?"

"Why can't we be friends?"

"He *attacked* Vincent. He told everyone that he slept with you. Why do you ignore the signs?"

"I don't know what it is, Cherry. He saved me the other night. I don't know how everyone found out that I stayed at his house."

"Casper told them. Why do you defend him?"

"There's something off and I don't know what it is. I need you to be my friend."

"I am."

When I pull into the hospital, I end the call with Cherry. Huddling inside my coat, I make my way toward the entrance. The elevator dings, I get off and make my way toward his room.

I quietly enter, relieved that no one else is in here. He looks the same as the night before. I move toward him and reach for his hand, which is warm, and rough from several cuts. My fingers lightly caress his hand. Almost like an automatic response, I lean over and kiss his forehead. I have this sudden urge to curl up

and lie next to him, but I shake the thought away. I can't help thinking of my dream last night. He was shot and the image keeps circling my mind, and now he's unconscious.

Chills envelop me and my ears ring. I need to go home and lie down. My body is weakening every second. I'll sleep it off and come back tomorrow. I squeeze his hand, trying to keep the tears away.

"Please Casper. Wake up." My vision blurs. I don't care that I'm crying. My heart is broken at the sight. I want to do something, anything to wake him up. Like that day I ran to his house and woke him. I want to see his brown eyes or hear him tell a stupid joke. I don't care that he spread rumors if he did. I need him to wake up. I kiss his hand and press it to my cheek, pretending it's him touching me. I know it's wrong to want that, but I do.

Mom wakes me at some point and makes me eat a bowl of chicken noodle soup. I'm glad that the sickness covers up my sadness because I don't want to tell her the boy I've been dreaming about is in a coma. I miss him. The ache in my throat and body is nothing compared to the ache in my chest. I go back to sleep, letting the dreams continue.

I wash and dress in a low-necked dark green gown. The elbow-length sleeves have a ruffle trim. I study my reflection in the tall mirror. Long black hair. Milky skin. Oval face. Blue eyes. My name is Megan, and I am a Sprite. An immortal being. I live at the Chateau de Fées, a beautiful palace in France. It's 1758 and I'm seventeen. I love Vincent and always have. Florence is my best friend. When I try remembering the last four months it's all black. I struggle with my mind, digging through memories, but it's like a hollow void.

Vincent enters the room and stands behind me. His dark blue eyes watch me through the reflection. His heavy gaze feels as though he is drinking me in. There's so much passion, yet pain in his eyes.

"I can't tell you how good it feels to have you in my arms again."

I smile. "I'm trying to remember everything. When did that vision take place?" I turn to face him. "The one you showed me yesterday."

He's reluctant to answer, but I take his hand in mine. "Please, tell me."

Tears well in his eyes. "Seven years ago."

I stiffen. I can't breathe. Maybe it's the corset suffocating me or the sudden knowledge that I have lost seven years of my life. My knees buckle.

Vincent grips my arms and holds me upright. "You're here now. You're safe. I won't let you go."

"Where was I?"

He leads me to sit at the small table in front of the window. He opens the curtains to let the brilliant sunlight into the room. He always told me he loves the way I look in the sunlight. I peer out into vast rolling hills and mountains in the background.

"When I came back from my mission seven years ago, you were gone," he says. "Rumors surfaced of you spending time with another man while I was away."

My eyes widen. "Are you sure?" I shake my head. It doesn't sound like me at all.

"When I realized who it was, I knew why. He was an Elf. He brainwashed you into leaving and he kept you for seven years."

"What? Was he the reason I can't remember anything?"

He wavers. "I must confess something to you."

I reach for his cheek, but he catches my wrist and kisses my palm.

"What is it?" I ask.

"When I found you, you looked gaunt, like you hadn't eaten in days or weeks. You were dirty and didn't want anything to do with me." A tear falls down his cheek and my heart aches for him. He looks into my eyes. "I erased your memory of them torturing you. I erased the last seven years because you begged me to. I couldn't stand for you to be in pain, but I messed up because you can't remember things that occurred before I left."

I can't believe this. Spending my days with an Elf while Vincent was away? Our only enemy? The same ones who have declared war on us several times and killed so many of us? I feel the tears coming. I never thought Vincent would erase my memories, but I'm glad he did. The Elves manipulated and fooled me with their charm.

"Why were they here?" I ask, hearing the building anger in my voice.

"Looking for the Nuummite Jewel."

"Why did they take me? Did they take anyone else?"

"From what I gather, one of them manipulated you into trying to find the Jewel for them. He made you fall in love with him. They must have run out of time and one of them fled, while the other took you with him to use you as a pawn thinking we'd give up the Jewel since they stole you. But we found you."

"Where did you find me?"

"He held you captive in some building in the woods. We shot him."

Something in my mind tries to push its way through at the mention of a shooting. I keep hearing a gunshot in my head. I jump once I see an image of a dark figure walking toward me with a gun.

"Megan? What is it?" Vincent takes my hand.

"I don't know. I saw a glimpse of someone with a gun. I think he was trying to kill me."

"What?"

"I see bits and pieces of an image."

"The Elves. Perhaps the man who took you. Torturing you." Vincent shakes his head. "Do you forgive me?"

"Of course, I do. I wish I could remember those last few memories of us though. You did the right thing. Do you forgive me?"

"You did nothing wrong, mon trésor." I smile at his pet name for me but I feel guilty. How could I have let another man fool me into loving him?

Vincent gets to his feet. "Let's visit your family. I'm sure everyone will be glad to see you."

I nod. I know he doesn't want me thinking these things because they are traumatic. It's best that they stay hidden. Somewhere deep inside me wants to remember everything and who did this to me. Why did they do this? I feel lost. I have to find out the truth. I want to find the man who did this to me. Vincent said they shot him, so perhaps he's a prisoner. I must confront him.

Thirty-One

I feel like I'm in a *Lord of the Rings* novel. Next, I'll be seeing dwarves. I feel like the dreams are trying to tell me something. Casper is bad and manipulating me into loving him. It's a warning. The crazy dreams make my head spin and make me nauseous.

Mom gently pushes open my door and places her cold hands on my forehead. She sticks a thermometer under my tongue and a minute later she gasps. "I gotta take you to the doctor. Do you think you can get dressed?"

I mumble something incoherently.

Mom takes me to the doctor, and they tell me I have mono.

Great.

We get home and I retreat to my room, curling up under the covers with Savannah. A few minutes later, Mom plows through the door. When my eyes finally focus, she stares at me with an intimidating look, arms crossed, lips tightly pressed in a straight line.

I prop myself up on my elbows trying not to panic. I've done so many things lately, I don't know why she's upset. "What's wrong?"

"Megan, I know you don't feel well. I called your work to tell them you would be out for a while. They informed me that you'd been out for quite a few days. How many days have you missed?"

Sorting through all the lies and truth, I can't remember what I've said and not said. I swallow and wince from the horrible grainy feeling in my throat. "I called out a couple of times because..." *Think fast.* "Cherry needed me."

She frowns and rolls her eyes. "I'm sure Cherry was fine and that you didn't need to call out of work. Where did you get the money to cover what you lost?"

I feel like crap, and she wants to yell at me. "Nowhere."

"Don't lie to me. Where did you get it?"

I bite my lip. "Vincent."

"You're going to pay him back. I can't believe you asked him for money to cover your irresponsibility! Give me your phone. You're grounded."

"What? No, Mom, please."

"It shouldn't be that bad of a punishment since you're sick anyway and can't go anywhere. How many times do I have to tell you to stop lying to me? Why do you feel the need to lie?"

"I don't know. Because you never understand or care what I go through."

She scoffs. I know she's offended. I want to tell her about my attack, but I feel like she'd tell me I shouldn't have gone to the party and that she told me so or she'll want me to go to the police. I don't want to because I'm afraid Adam will find me again.

"What is going on with you? Ever since you started dating Vincent, you've been missing work and you're hardly ever here. When you are here, you're always in a mood. Give me your phone."

"Mom—"

"Megan, I'm tired and you're sick. We're not arguing about this."

I let out a sigh as my chin quivers. I reach over to my nightstand, grab my phone, and hand it to her. She takes it and leaves the room.

I let the tears fall. Either I tell Mom what happened or suffer through another grounding. What am I supposed to do?

Thirty-Two

ours later, I make my way to the living room to talk to Mom. She and Ron are watching TV as usual. Mom cackles at something funny. She laughs like she's in the best mood ever. I bite my lip and grip the doorway. "Mom?"

She turns still smiling from the TV. "Why are you up? You need to go to bed."

"I need to talk to you."

"Okay."

I look at Ron who laughs at the show. I hate his laugh. It's like a high-pitched giggle. Then he starts coughing like he's hacking up a lung because of the smoking he refuses to admit he does.

"Can I talk to you alone?"

She releases an irritated sigh. "You're not getting your phone back."

"Mom, will you please talk to me? I have to tell you something."

She groans and follows me into my room. She acts like I'm the biggest nuisance ever. That's another reason why I never tell her anything. Anything that deals with me is always such a problem for her.

"What is it?" she asks as I sit on my bed.

I clasp my hands together trying to find the strength to tell her. The best way to get this out is to say it. No sugarcoating. "Saturday, I left work early with Cherry. We went to a party and things were fine until someone spilled beer on me. I went upstairs to get the stain out and I was...attacked."

She crosses the room and sits next to me. "Megan, are you okay?"

"Nothing happened. My friend Casper stopped him in time. I didn't go to work Sunday or any day this week because I needed time to deal with it."

"Why didn't you tell me?" I see tears in her eyes.

"I was scared you'd be upset that I lied."

"Yeah, I'm upset about that, but Megan, you were attacked. Did he hurt you? Did you call the police? Who was it?"

Seeing the tears in my mom's eyes makes me break down and she holds me. We stay up pretty late talking and crying about what happened. I come clean. I tell her everything that happened that night. Including staying with Casper. Her reaction surprises me because I expected less. She's not pleased that I lied, but it's the first time Mom and I have bonded like this in a long time. I feel like I can come to her with anything now. I wonder how long it'll last. She wants me to go to the police. I'm too scared he'll find me.

Mom gives me my phone back and says she will have a tighter leash on me. I don't care. I got everything off my chest and I can still talk to Cherry and Vincent while I'm sick.

When Mom leaves to go to bed, I check my phone, which has several missed text messages.

Cherry: **Megan! Are you ok?**

Cherry: **omg! Why aren't you answering your phone? Something's wrong, I can feel it.**

Vincent: **Are you okay? I miss you so much.**

Casper: **Megan, we need to talk.**

My heart skips a beat when I see Casper's name. My heart swells. He's awake and I'm so relieved. I immediately send him a message asking if he's okay.

While I wait, I reply to Cherry and Vincent letting them know what's wrong. Cherry tells me she'll drop by after school to give me my homework. Vincent tells me to get better soon so he can see me. I don't hear from him more than that. His texts sound rather formal. I can't figure him out. Anytime I can't see him, he gets weird and upset.

My phone rings and it's Casper. I answer in a mumbled voice. My throat feels like sandpaper when I talk. It's late and I should get some rest, but I long to talk to him. It's been a while.

"Casper, are you okay? What happened?"

"Someone's after us." He speaks with a gravelly voice. He sounds weary and angry, but I detect a hint of sadness.

"What?"

"I only remember bits and pieces. I was driving home from school after the fight with Vincent and next thing I know, I wake up in a hospital. I remember feeling mud though. The police said there were several bullet holes in the car. They think someone might have thought I was someone else or something. One of the bullets hit my shoulder. I'm okay."

My breathing accelerates. Bullets? Someone tried to shoot him. Casper could have died. The thought overwhelms me. I don't know what I would do without him. Where did that thought come from? "Someone shot you? Did you see anything?" I'm shaking all over.

"I don't remember. They said my car was crumpled in the ditch and that I must have crawled out. They've been questioning me. I'm no help and there weren't any witnesses."

A breath leaves my lungs. Someone attacked both of us like in our dreams. "Adam," I say.

"What?"

"It had to be Adam. You attacked him so he came after you."

"Why would he be after us?"

"I don't know."

"How can we find out?"

"I'd make sure someone guards your room. He could still come after you."

"I'll be fine."

"What if he comes after me again?"

"He doesn't know where you live. You'll be safe."

A few minutes pass in silence. I'm trying to figure out a way to find Adam. I can ask Vincent to help, but I can't mention Casper's accident. Why is he after us? I completely delusional and have no idea what's going on? That's possible. With the dreams, the medications, all of it makes my brain foggy. I take a breath and focus on what's important. "I'm so glad you woke up. I was so scared."

"I'm much better now."

"Good medication?"

"Uh, yeah. Sure, that's it. Did you ever." He pauses. "Visit me in the hospital?"

"Um, yes."

"I knew it. I felt you."

"What?"

"It's hard to explain. I had this overwhelming sensation. I felt you and I think it gave me the strength to pull through. You saved me."

I'm speechless. I remain quiet, biting my lip.

"I have to ask you something. Did you send Vincent to fight me?"

"What? No! Why would you think that?"

"He threatened me to stay away from you. Said you were his and wanted to make sure I understood it. Told me to stop hurting you and spreading rumors about you. I never said a word to anyone about you staying."

My chest aches. "Then how did everyone find out? What am I supposed to think? Vincent and Cherry didn't say anything." My heart is pounding and I'm crying which wears me out. "Vincent said you told him we slept together. Why would you say that then wail on him?"

"Of course, he said that. He threw the first punch. You believe what you want. And I never said we slept together."

Did Vincent lie about the fight or is Casper lying to me now? "Tell me what happened."

"You won't like it."

"Tell me the truth."

"He asked me about Adam. I told him what I knew, but that he didn't need to worry about it because I took care of it. We said a few choice words. He punched me and we fought."

"That's the truth? You aren't lying?"

"Megan, I have never lied to you."

My stomach twists. I keep thinking about the two versions of the story. I watched Casper attack Adam, so I know it's possible for him to beat up Vincent. It seems like he would need a good reason. I've never seen Vincent violent, but I've witnessed his jealousy which seems somewhat possessive at times.

"Aren't you supposed to be in school?" Casper asks.

"I have mono."

"Oh, wow. Sorry."

"It's okay. I feel terrible."

"Do you want me to let you go so you can rest?"

I should say yes. "No, it's okay. What happened? When did you wake up?"

"Last night or the night before. I don't know. My days are mixed up."

"Are you okay?"

"Yeah. About to go crazy from boredom in the hospital room. Luckily, my mom brought my phone. It's hard to stay awake for very long because it feels like every bone in my body is broken."

"I'm so sorry, Casper."

We talk more and joke around. I hear him laugh and I miss that. I miss this. Him. In my dreams and out. This can't be healthy. He's my friend, and I care about him.

He says he doesn't dream of me. He was shot but didn't die. His friend found him, and they returned home. He describes his home as if it's his.

"It's beautiful in my homeland," he says. "It's hard to describe. It's like it comes straight out of a book. The colors are so vivid and extraordinary. The greenery is so lush. There's a garden that's filled with fireflies and it's so dark at night, you can see thousands of stars. It's unreal. Like nothing I've ever seen. I wish I could show you. Maybe you could add that to your story."

I love hearing the passion in his voice. It's strange that our dreams are still connected even though we aren't dreaming of each other.

"I think about you constantly," he says. "In my dreams. It's bad. The hurt and grief and sorrow. It makes me so depressed when I wake up."

I know how he feels because I feel the same way when I wake up.

"Where did they take you?" he asks. "I mean, what is your homeland like?"

"It's an enormous palace. All I've seen so far are bits and pieces of the palace, but it's all very familiar to me. It's very Rococo. It seems as though it's the late 18th century France. What do you think this all means?"

"I have no idea. You mentioned Vincent in your dreams. Do you share them with him, too?"

"No. But," I trail off. I chew the inside of my mouth.

"What?"

Am I about to confess this? Who better to tell it to than the person I share *dreams*? Heat pricks beneath my cheeks. "When we kiss, we both see visions. They look like events from our past and it seems to match what's in my dreams. He also wears a nuummite stone his mom gave him." What is going on with my life? It makes absolutely no sense whatsoever. I'm on the verge of crying. More or less, I think I'm freaking out. I can't sleep without having something to worry about since there seems to be a life inside my dreams. "Are all of us connected in some way?"

"I don't know, Megan."

"I'm scared to talk to Vincent about it. I mean, we talk about the visions, and he's as freaked out. Because he's jealous of you, I can't tell him about us."

"I know. I don't think you should tell him. I wish I had answers. I wish I could see you."

I wish I could see him, too, but I'm not going to tell him that.

This is dangerous territory I'm encroaching. I can't help the way my heart feels when I hear Casper's voice. I need to stop, but I can't. We talk more about Adam and how we can proceed to find out more. With Casper in the hospital and me confined to a bed, our options are limited. I'll talk to Vincent. He can help. I don't want Adam coming after Vincent, too.

Vincent parades me around the large palace and most of the people seem so glad to see me, however, there are some who seem to dislike the fact that I'm back. I hear their whispers. Saying I'm a traitor and how I don't deserve to be back. The ones that are glad to see me tell me how much they missed me. I have known these people my entire life, yet I feel out of place.

"Megan," a loud voice calls behind us. "Is that you?"

I turn meeting the green eyes of a woman with large blond curls and a voluptuous body. Florence, my childhood friend. It's so good to see her.

Her jaw drops and she smiles widely. She rushes up to me and hugs me. "Megan, I cannot believe it's you."

"Florence." She pulls away. Her smile is infectious.

"You remember me." She gushes, glancing at Vincent.

"Yes. I don't remember the last seven years."

"What did they do to you? We have so much to catch up on."

"Maybe some other time, Florence." Vincent tugs me along. I silently apologize to Florence and walk with Vincent out of the room.

"What's wrong?" We stride down a long hallway with a red rug.

He smiles impishly. "I'm selfish right now." He pushes open ornate double doors, and we make our way out into the hedge maze.

We meander along the gravel path, my hand intertwining with his. I remember playing in this labyrinth with Vincent. We have so many memories together. Perhaps we can make new memories. He's all I need.

"I don't want you to be sad," he says.

"Why would I be sad? It's Florence."

"The man who took you had a friend who was seen with her. People say they saw her with him, in love. Before we returned from the mission, the man left, but he wiped her memory of him completely."

"Why would they do that? We know they exist."

"So, she wouldn't remember what they looked like or where they hide out."

"Why did some of the people in the palace give me such dismayed looks?"

He sighs. "Some of them think you're a traitor."

"Is that why I was in the cellar? Because they think I betrayed them?"

Vincent nods and I look away.

It's unsettling to think that people I have always known now see me as a traitor. Something else is disturbing. Not only have I lost the last seven years of my life, but something heavily weighs on me.

We reach the end of the maze and walk through the tall wheat field. Something tugs at me when I see the golden wheat sway in the wind. As my hand caresses the tops of the blades, I stroll through them, knowing Vincent is behind me at a distance. The wind is brisk, and the scent of lavender fills me. The blond color of the wheat has an unusual effect on me. It makes my heart beat fast. I can't make sense of it. How can a simple color make me feel this way?

I feel Vincent's hands on my shoulders. He turns me slowly to face him. "Having you here is so surreal."

I touch his weary face. "I have missed you. Though, my mind feels like it's only been four months."

"You can't imagine the pain I went through when I came back only to find you gone." Tears well in his eyes. "I tried so many times to come for you, but they told me I couldn't risk it, so they sent others to find you."

"Risk it? Didn't they know I'd been kidnapped?"

"Yes. We all thought you had been taken back to Belle Palais."

Belle Palais is where our enemies live. I had known that my whole life. I have never been there, but I wonder why the Elf didn't take me back there himself. "Why didn't he take me back?"

Vincent shrugs. "I'm not sure."

"Will they come back for me?" I tense.

"I killed the man who took you. We are at war with them, so we have extra security here."

"War?" Tears pool in my eyes. I know that can only mean one thing: Vincent is sure to leave again.

"It won't come close to here. You are safe. We are fighting with them at sea. Please do not worry, mon trésor." He draws me closer to his chest.

I'm not worried about being safe. I worry about him leaving. I meet his eyes. He tucks a few strands of hair behind my ear. I reach behind his neck pulling him to me until our lips meet. He gives me no vision this time. I want him like never before. I feel his arms around me, pulling me closer. I love the feel of his soft lips on mine, almost possessive yet tender. Something feels wrong and I don't know what it is.

That night after I blow out the candle next to my bed, I think of the blond color again. It drifts through my mind in an endless stream like water smoothing over stones. The color leaves me with something— the feeling that I loved something more than life itself.

I can't understand the intensity of it, but it weighs in my stomach like a brick.

Something wedges its way into my mind but vanishes. It's frustrating trying to remember, only to have it stripped from me. The flashes of a man with a gun enter my mind again. I close my eyes and the gunman saunters closer. I hurriedly crawl backward, away from him, but he only takes his time.

"Megan!"

My eyes bolt open and my heart pounds. Someone else is there with the man calling my name.

Thirty-Three

om brought me soup after she got home from work. Savannah jumps on the bed and curls up against me. It's nice having company.

"Cherry stopped by after school." Mom helps me into a sitting position. "She gave me a list of your homework. So, when you're feeling up to it let me know." She sets the soup down onto a pillow and shoos Savannah away from it. "I've called the school, so they know you're going to be out for a while. Hopefully not too long though."

I nod. I want to take a shower and get the sickness off me, but I can't move.

Mom stays with me while I eat and talks about her day at work. I feel bad for her because her boss is a jerk but somehow, she manages to suck it up so she can have a paycheck. I've told her several times she can easily find a better job elsewhere. We don't talk like this. It's kind of new territory for me. I like it.

Mom gives me more antibiotics and leaves for the night. I reach for my phone and my heart picks up its pace when I see a text from Casper. This isn't a good sign. It bothers me that Vincent hasn't sent another message. Is something wrong? Did something happen with his mom?

I open Casper's message.

How are u? I know ur probably sleeping, but I hope u get well. I miss u. In my dreams and out. There's something I need to tell you.

My stomach ties in knots. What's he going to tell me? I hope he isn't going to confess anything. Not like he hasn't already. Only one way to find out.

Hi Casper. I'm ok, very tired. How are you?

I only have to wait a few seconds before he responds.

I'm ok. Im so glad to hear from u. Can u talk?
Sure.

A few seconds later, my phone flashes with his name and I answer.

"Hey."

"Is it weird that we talk so often?"

"No, I don't think so," he says. "How are you?"

"I've been better."

"Has your back healed?"

"Yeah. I've taken the bandages off. Have the police found anything new about your accident?"

"No. How are your dreams?"

I clear my throat which feels like gravel raking across it. "More and more bizarre. I feel so out of place since a lot of people think I betrayed them."

We talk about the events of our dreams, but after a while I want something else to talk about. They're getting too involved, and I don't want to pretend they're real anymore. "What did you want to tell me?"

"Oh, that. I don't know how you're going to react to this."

I tense, but secretly want to hear what he feels for me.

"My mom was reading the newspaper to me to give me company on her break."

This isn't what I expected.

"She scanned through it and made a comment about some kid who died from a gunshot."

My heart picks up its pace. Why I think of Vincent immediately, I don't know. It could be that I know he used to be into drugs. If it was Vincent, someone would have told me, wouldn't they? Wouldn't his dad know to tell me? But with a wife dying of cancer and now a dead son, his dad is probably overwhelmed.

Tears brim on the surface of my eyes from my overactive brain.

"It was Adam."

That brings me up short. "What?" I blink away the tears.

"Police found him dead in his home. Investigators are looking for any information as to the killer. What's even more strange is that they don't have any information on the guy. The article said there wasn't anyone else living there, no pictures, no belongings. Nothing. They're speculating a drug deal gone bad."

"I don't know what to say. Does this mean we'll never know who tried to kill you?"

"I don't know. Um, the nurse is telling me to get off the phone. Can I call you tomorrow?"

"Sure. Get some rest." I hang up and hold the phone in my hand, while curling up in the bed. Who killed Adam? Was he into more bad stuff than attacking girls? I hate him, but I never wished for his death. My mind races. Who tried to kill Casper? Was it Adam?

Who was Adam? Why does he seem like a complete nobody who attacked me, yet he knew me?

Once my heart rate returns to normal, I lay there, motionless, allowing the medicine to take over.

Thirty-Four

I stand at the back of the room as Vincent holds a celebration for my return in the palace. The delicately ornate ceiling arches over the dance room while gentle classical music plays. Musicians play violins, pianofortes, harpsichords, and a hammered dulcimer. I have always loved their music and being here in this room. Now I feel awkward.

We're all dressed in our elegant evening attire. I'm wearing a cream, French silk dress with a low neck and elbow-length ruffled sleeves. The gown is padded with bands of blue satin at the bottom of the skirt. Some women wear white wigs and have painted their faces white. My black hair is in springy curls.

I try to be cheerful, but something nags at me. It's been so long since I was here, and the people seem to remember more than me. I constantly think of the voice calling my name in my memory. I have no idea whose it belongs to, but when I hear it, I get the same reaction when I think of the blond color.

"There's the life of the party." Florence flashes a wide smile and takes my hands. "I am so happy to see you."

I peer into her large green eyes that are as vibrant as her smile. A beautiful gold gown adorns her body, and her shiny long blond curls are held back by small barrettes.

"I'm happy to see you as well."

"I'm surprised Vincent let you out tonight." She winks. "He's been miserable, so I understand." She loops her arm with mine and fans herself with her paper fan.

We wander outside the stone palace into the hedge maze, strolling under the midnight sky with bright stars. The only sounds are our footsteps along the gravel path and the low chatter among others.

"I have missed you," she says. "Do you remember anything about the Elves?"

I shake my head. "Vincent says he found me with one Elf in a remote cottage. He doesn't think I even made it to the Belle Palais. He says I was tortured. Why would they kidnap me though?"

"It's a game. They planned to dangle you in front of him, so he'd give up the Jewel. But Vincent found you."

"I wish I knew more."

"Vincent would never let anything happen to you."

He had, hadn't he? By letting them take me away. How had they done it? I can't believe I would even talk to an Elf, let alone spend time with them. "Well now that I'm back, they can't take me again. I won't let them manipulate me again."

"Let's not worry about such things now."

"Megan," Vincent calls from behind us. I turn and he smiles. "May I take her away?" he asks Florence.

"Of course."

He escorts me back inside to the large dancing room. Vincent asks them to play a song. The music stops and a new song begins. He pulls me close. We are among several dancers on the floor. Even though I have been with Vincent my entire life and I love him, something still doesn't feel right being this close to him.

The song sounds familiar as we move with it. We touch hands and follow the steps as they are second nature. Vincent twirls me around and something comes back to me. I envision me in a maroon dress, smiling, and dancing with a faceless stranger. It isn't Vincent, I don't think. But it's someone that I seem to love.

Once the song ends, we applaud the musicians and retreat to a quiet corner in the room. He wraps his arms around me and kisses my forehead. "Let us take a walk." He slides his hand into mine. We walk until we find the gazebo and sit on a swing under the latticed ceiling.

"I will never forgive myself," he says.

"What do you mean?"

"I wasn't here, and it gave them easy access to you. I was off on an important journey. Unfortunately, that's what happens when I'm part of the army. It was agonizing every minute you were gone. Not knowing what they were doing to you."

"Oh, Vincent." A tear streaks down my cheek.

"I had hoped that they would not make you forget me. But I did that."

"I have not forgotten you, mon amour. We can make new memories."

Vincent softly kisses my lips. His kiss turns urgent, overwhelming me. I still feel wrong. I don't know what it is. I love Vincent and I want to be with him and show him. Had they attacked me? Am I repressing some memory that prevents me from being intimate with him?

I press against his chest, and he pulls away, searching my eyes. "You're different."

I frown and drop my eyes from his heavy gaze.

"What have they done to you?" He touches his forehead to mine.

"Please don't be disappointed with me."

His dark blue eyes hold a rueful look. "I could never be disappointed with you. It will only take time. I will kill every one of them who hurt you." Vengeance flashes in his eyes and it scares me.

The days merge, and I can't keep up with what day it is. Each day I await a message from Casper, and I know the more we talk, the more I like him. I can't be doing this to Vincent, but I can't stop. I feel like a terrible person because I'm not a cheater. The guilt eats at me, and I know I should stop talking to Casper.

Every time I dream, it's of Vincent and our life at our palace. We spend our days walking, talking, and kissing. Our nights seem to be consumed by parties at the palace. The voice from my memory still haunts me. Outside of my dreams, Vincent doesn't send me a single message, which annoys me. I know he isn't at school because of his suspension, so where is he? What is he doing? I think something might have happened to his mom.

I text him, asking if he's okay.

No. I miss my girl.
I miss you, too. How is your mom?
Worse.

I'm sorry. Anything I can do?

I hate how simple his messages are. If he misses me, wouldn't he want to talk more?

Get well. I'm at the hospital. I will talk to you later.

I let out an annoyed sigh. I feel bad because I'm acting too selfish. I know he needs to spend as much time with his mom as possible. I hate this. I miss him so much and while he's grieving for his mother, I'm talking to his arch enemy.

My first two weeks of sickness pass and I still feel the same. I wonder if I'll ever feel normal again. With all the sleep, it's like my dreams are the only thing going on in my life. It feels like ages since I've seen Cherry. I miss her and hope she hasn't forgotten about me.

My throat finally stops aching and I'm able to talk again. I'm still contagious so no school. I'm not terribly heartbroken about that. I do a lot of make-up homework and I've written more in my story, including the bits that Vincent wrote.

The days seem endless and I'm excruciatingly bored. To walk outside and feel the cool crisp air would be nice. To see something other than the four lavender walls of my room. I'm tired of staring at my band posters. No one can visit either.

I finally get a message from Vincent asking if I'm still sick, so I call.

"Hey, you," he says, and I can tell he's smiling. "Are you feeling better?"

"I'm fine." I can hear the irritation in my voice.

"It's been forever since I've seen you. Can I come over?"

"No. I'm still contagious. My parents won't let anyone come over."

"I can sneak into your bedroom."

"No, they'd find out."

He lets out a sigh. "Can you help a guy out? I'll be outside your house at around midnight. I need to see you."

"What? You can't come over."

"I'll park down the street. See you tonight."

He hangs up before I can object. I don't care that it's been forever since we've talked. I want to see him. I need to.

Midnight comes and I stayed up so I can see if Vincent did come. I'm not sure how I'm going to open the front door without making a sound and waking up the dogs. Somehow, I creep across the hardwood floor soundlessly and slowly turn the knob on the glass paned door. I step outside and shiver, even though I'm wearing a heavy coat over my flannel pajamas, a beanie, a scarf, thick socks, and shoes. I close the door behind me and walk out into the yard. The full moon is high above and very bright tonight.

I stand outside, shivering and waiting for Vincent. I don't know what I want to say to him. It makes no sense that I haven't heard from him. I hear footsteps and I see him nearing my driveway. I meet him in front of the bush to hide from the house, though everyone is asleep.

Vincent rushes up and circles his arms around me cradling my head against his chest. I keep my hands in my jacket pocket. "It's been so long." He kisses my forehead. "I missed you."

"I've missed you, too." I speak into his warm jacket and shiver.

"My car is warm, come on." His warm hands take mine and once we're inside the car, we snuggle in the front seat with the heat on.

"You shouldn't get this close to me," I tell him, but I enjoy feeling his arms around me.

I feel him shrug. "I don't care. I wanted to see you."

I smile.

"When are you coming back to school?"

"I don't know. My doctor said I'll probably be out for a month."

Vincent groans. "My poor baby's sick. This is brutal. Having you this close and not being able to kiss you."

"You can still get sick being this close to me." I raise my head. "If you get sick, you-you won't be able to visit your mom." I try to move away but he only holds me tighter.

He chuckles. "I'll be fine." He presses my head against his chest and kisses my forehead. "I bet being sick is boring. What have you been doing to pass the time?"

"Mostly sleeping. Writing. Talking to Cherry and Casp—" I stop. *Crap.* I feel his body stiffen.

"Casper?" He pushes me off his chest. His eyes are cold. "The same Casper who lied about you, hurt you all those times, and attacked me?" The anger in his voice reverberates in the car and it scares me because I know nothing, I say now will fix this.

"I was bored. You never called or sent a message. He did."

He narrows his eyes. "I was with my mom, Megan."

"I know. But you couldn't send one message? Not even to ask how I was doing?"

"Why are you attacking *me*? I came to see you."

"I don't understand you. You're always talking about me not forgetting you, yet for two weeks I've barely heard from you."

He rakes his hand through his hair. "I've been visiting my dying mother," he snaps. "I'm sorry I haven't had time to talk to you constantly. I figured you were sick and needed sleep, so I didn't want to bother you."

I bite back tears and look away. I don't want to fight, but I'm frustrated. I don't understand him. Has he ever dated a girl before?

He releases a sigh. "You shouldn't even be talking to him. He's dangerous."

"He was in a coma. I wanted to see if he was okay."

"So, being close to death automatically makes him the good guy?"

"Why are you both at each other's throats over me? You barely know each other. I'm nothing special."

"You have no idea." The intense look in his eyes forces me to look away.

"I wish you two could get along."

"That'll never happen. Why do you still talk to him? After everything he did to you."

"He didn't say those things."

"He's manipulating you. He fought me. Have you already forgotten that part?"

I bite my tongue. "Vincent."

He tilts his head. "You like him, don't you?"

"What? No," I feel the blood creeping into my cheeks. I hope he can't tell.

Vincent shakes his head, frustrated, and drags his hands down his face. "I can never win with you, can I?"

"What are you talking about?" I don't like the gut-wrenching feeling I'm suddenly experiencing.

"I'm always doing something wrong in your eyes. You always think I'm the bad guy. No matter what."

"No, I don't." I reach for his cheek, but his hand snatches my wrist.

"Forget it. You should go back inside." He stares out the window.

"Vincent, no."

He opens the door, refusing to look at me. I want to hold onto him. I don't want him to let me go. He never says a word. I slide off his lap and out of the car. He keeps the door open for a moment.

"Please don't go." My eyes water. My heart is tearing apart. His eyes meet mine and all I see is anger and pain.

"Go inside, Megan." His voice is low, but not gentle. He closes the door and drives away.

Each time my heart beats against my chest, I feel it shatter into pieces. I'm not sure what happened. Did he break up with me? Have I been foolish? Why did I have to mention Casper?

Dejected, I creep back inside the house and into my room. I sit on the edge of my bed, still dressed, holding back tears. My phone beeps. For a brief moment I get excited. Maybe it's Vincent and we can talk about the whole stupid ordeal and move on from it. If he asks me to never talk to Casper again, I'll do it. When I pick up my phone, I frown at Casper's name.

Hey. How are you? I hope you're coming back to school soon. I kinda miss you.

Part of me wants to chuck the phone across the room. Instead, I clear the message and place it on my nightstand. I want to be talking to Vincent. I don't know when we'll speak again. I have to end my friendship with Casper. It's the only way all of this hatred and stress will end.

Thirty-Five

eering through the window watching the heavy rain fall in sheets, I can barely see the mountains in the distance and the beautiful vast field. My mind tugs at a memory. Running in the rain. Feeling lips on mine sending a shock throughout me. The door opens, startling me. Vincent appears with sad eyes.

He waits in the threshold for a moment. "Every morning, you're so forlorn. Are you unhappy?"

I shake my head and let the curtain fall, blocking the window. "No. I fear the unknown."

He hesitantly crosses the room and intertwines his fingers with mine. "It's such an unpleasant day but

I hope to cheer you up." Vincent smiles and reaches in his pocket, pulling out a black cloth. He peels it back to reveal a beautiful yellow gold link necklace with a central scrolling foliate motif. It's set with an oval garnet with three golden scrolling drops. It's the most gorgeous thing I've ever seen.

"Vincent."

He lifts it from the cloth, and I turn around, raising my hair. He gently places it around my neck. My fingers brush against the satin-like texture. I feel his lips brush behind my ear. My skin tingles. "You make it look gorgeous." He moves to my neck. Vincent tightens his arms around me and my breath hitches. I twist around and he presses his lips to mine, kissing me so tenderly and lovingly.

He rests his forehead on mine, holding my hands against his chest. I see the muscle in his jaw twitch.

"Vincent, what is it?"

Melancholy flickers in his eyes. "I must sail out in the morning." He lowers his gaze to my hands and kisses them.

My stomach drops and I shake my head. "No. You can't."

"The war has started. I promise I will return to you."

"How long must you be gone?"

"I do not know."

I start crying and he pulls me hard against him.

"I cannot believe that the second I find you; I must leave."

"Why must you go? What am I to do?" Panic fills me.

"I'm part of the army. I must obey orders."

"Please don't leave me. My days without you are empty. I cannot rest easily when you are gone. I always have nightmares."

"You said the same thing the last time I left." He gives a pained smile. "This will be the last time, I promise. You must be strong once more. I know you can do this."

"They all think I'm a traitor. What if something happens?" I hear the terror seep into my voice.

He takes my face into his hands. "Please don't worry. Nothing will happen, I assure you. There are several people who will protect you if something should happen."

"But the Elves. They could come back—"

"Trust me, Megan. You will be safe."

I shake my head and cling onto him. I kiss him as though this is our last one and he responds as fervently. I feel my dress coming loose and I let it fall to the floor. He plants tiny kisses along my jaw as he removes my undergarments until I am left wearing nothing but the necklace.

Vincent holds me close to his body and carries me to the bed. "I love you with every beat of my heart."

"I love you, Vincent."

I refuse to let anything ruin this moment, this night with Vincent. He is mine and I am his.

Everything is perfect. I do not think of anything else but him. We are meant to be forever.

As I gather in a parlor with a few other women, I peer out the window, watching men rush about. I look to my right and a woman named Sophie stands holding a baby with tears in her eyes.

A few moments later, I feel a soft hand grab mine. I turn and face Vincent.

Clad in a red coat with long tails, and black pants, he looks handsome. "It is time."

My chin quivers, and I can't hold back my tears. No matter how many times we've been through this, it never gets easy. Being immortal, we've shared many lives together. Having him go to war with those vile Elves all of the time from a hatred that runs deep, I still fear his outcome. I fear the day he doesn't return to me.

He frowns and pulls me close. "I will miss you, mon trésor."

"I don't want you to go."

He crushes his lips against mine. In his seductive kiss, visions of us run rampant through my mind. Dancing, laughing, kissing, frolicking, almost every intimate moment we have ever shared, including last night. I am filled with an unparalleled love. This man makes me whole and I need him. When our lips part, he removes his black ring and slides it on my middle finger. "Please remember me." He brushes my chin with his finger and walks out of the parlor.

I watch though the window as he and several other soldiers mount horses and salute goodbyes. I run outside to see them gallop away. My heart plunges into the depths of darkness.

Thirty-Six

wake in a sweat, my shirt clinging to me, my heart pounding. I think I finally broke my fever, but I still lack energy. Vincent is gone in my dreams. Is that true for my real life? I let the tears fall, soaking my pillow. I don't think my body has much energy to cry, but I can't stop. The overwhelming sadness I feel in my dream and how I felt after mine and Vincent's fight makes it worse. I'm miserable, tired of being sick and tired of the weird dreams that make no sense.

I grab my phone. It's mid-morning but with how dark it is in my room from the stormy skies, it feels much later. I'd gotten two messages. One from Cherry and one from Casper.

Cherry asks how I'm doing.

Not well. Vincent and I had a fight last night.

What? Why?

I don't even know. I let it slip that I'd been talking to Casper and he got mad.

I told you it wasn't a good idea to talk to Casper. On the other hand, Vincent seems like a jealous guy. You guys will make up though.

I don't know. He won't talk to me. He said everything he did was wrong in my eyes. But that's not true. I don't even know what he's talking about.

Didn't explain it?

No.

I'm sorry. I wish I could give u a hug. Want me to kick him in the balls tomorrow?

I smile. **No.**

I will. You say the word. When are u coming back to school? I'm miserable without u!

Soon. Stop sending me so much homework.

I can't help it! U know it's getting closer to exam time and they're trying to squeeze in all this stuff before the end of the year. We miss u at work, too. Luke asks about you, too.

I miss u so much.

Me too! You've got to hurry up and get better for the prom! Anyway, I gotta get back to class, love. I can feel Mrs. Tanger's third eye on me. Feel better and I'll send you a message when I get out.

I don't even want to think about the prom now. I don't read Casper's message. I get out of bed and move to the living room to watch TV. Something to keep my mind off Vincent. I stay up for the rest of the day and briefly talk with my mom when she gets home from work. I eat something other than chicken noodle soup and I stay with my parents a few hours longer watching TV until they go to bed. Mom advises me I should do the same.

I'm grateful for my illness because it masks my depression over Vincent so no one will ask what's wrong. I shower and cry. Afterwards, I amble to my room. It's the last place I want to be. I don't check my phone because I fear the messages from Casper, and I don't want to be let down when I don't see Vincent's name pop up. I decide to woman up and send him a message, apologizing and asking to talk.

Eventually, I fall asleep, waiting for his text that never comes. In the dream, I weep for Vincent. I miss him and I have no idea what to do. I stay in the parlor and peer out the window, watching for their return. I attempt to read a book, but I can't concentrate.

Florence enters and joins me at the table near the window. She flashes a beautiful smile. "You aren't going to sit around all day pining for Vincent, are you?"

I open my mouth to answer, but she waves her hand.

"I won't have it. Let's go for a ride." Her green eyes light up like a little girl on Christmas. "Sadie has missed you. No one's ridden her in seven years since you...well since *they* took you. I've been keeping her company."

It sounds better than sitting around. Florence leads me outside and across a large field to the stables. Horses quietly stand in their respective stalls, looking bored, eager to roam, or to be free like me. Florence opens their stalls and lets them out to roam freely in their enormous meadow. She begins harnessing a grey and white speckled horse. "This is Ginger," she says. "In case you forgot."

"I remember. I lost the last few years. I can't even recall Vincent proposing to me."

She hands me a saddle and I walk up to the tall solid white horse. Her large brown eyes watch me. I tenderly place my hand on her cheek and soothe her. Moving my hand down her neck to her withers, I heave the saddle onto her back. I grab the harness and place it over her head. I don't know how long it's been since I've ridden Sadie, but I missed her, and by the way she burrows her muzzle into me, I can tell she missed me too.

Florence steadies the beautiful Sadie, while I pull myself up onto her back.

Florence smiles. "I see you haven't forgotten our secret way of riding." She winks. My legs straddle the horse, like a man would ride. She hoists herself onto Ginger and leads the way. We move slowly at first, but soon we gallop through the woods laughing and giggling the whole way. It's a freeing experience. Invigorating. I feel my heart breaking free of the heartache and confusion. The cool air whips through my hair leaving me high.

We ride for hours and soon find a quiet place that overlooks a beautiful sea from high above. It seems like a familiar place.

"I wish you could remember something," Florence says. "I want to know what it's like with them."

"Why should you care what it's like? They tortured me."

She wrinkles her face. "I don't believe that."

"Why?"

"I have never believed they were our enemies."

"Why are you saying this?" I begin to feel wary of her. Unsure of what she will do to me.

"This is the only place we can truly tell each other what we're thinking. They're constantly watching us." I know this, but I never worried because I never did anything wrong. Her eyes gaze off into the direction of the distant palace and she bites her lip. "He didn't kidnap you, Megan. He didn't manipulate you. You willingly left with him."

I gasp. "What? How dare you make up such stories? Why would you say such a thing? I thought we were friends." I stand to leave.

"Vincent left like now." She raises her voice and there's a hard look in her eyes. "The Elves came posing as Sprites and you fell in love with one of them."

"No. That man charmed me into loving him." I grab the reigns on Sadie.

"His name was Casper. You told me all of this before you left."

I open my mouth to speak, but my mind clings to the name. *Casper.* My heart leaps at his name and my body freezes. How do I recognize that name? I have the same reaction that I did when I saw the blond color. *Casper.* I turn back to face her. "What did I tell you? What happened? Vincent told me you were with an Elf too, but he erased your memory."

"I lied. I had to so Vincent and his men wouldn't erase my memory of Edmond."

Another name that I recognize. "What? Why would Vincent erase your memory?"

Florence presses her lips together. "Same reason I presume he erased yours. So, you won't remember the truth. That you fell in love with Casper."

Again, his name almost brings me to my knees, but I'm outraged by her allegations. "No." I shake my head. "Vincent erased my memories of them because they tortured me. He would never hurt me. He loves me."

"I'm not sure I'd call it love. More like he's possessive of you."

"You're wrong."

"Why do you think he calls you his trésor?"

"Stop! Why do you say such things? Did the Elves get to your head?"

Florence stands and grabs me at arm's length. "Listen to me. I can see part of you is arguing with yourself. When Vincent left last time, you met Casper and I met Edmond. You spent every day with Casper. They came to take back the Jewel. When Casper met you, he stopped looking for it. You eventually tried to help him find it. When you caught word that Vincent was returning, you both decided to run away. You left in the middle of the night and when Vincent found out, he sent men after you. None of them ever came back. You were gone for seven years until Vincent found you."

My gaze shifts to the palace. I can't believe what she's telling me. *Casper*. Every time I hear his name, my heart swells, and my body fills with a prickling sensation. "Vincent said Casper was trying to kill me. Why would we have been in love if he was trying to kill me?"

"Of course, Vincent says that. He doesn't want you near Casper. It's a simple tale of star-crossed love. Now he erased your memory completely of Casper so you can't remember anything."

"Why would I leave Vincent like that?"

"Because you love Casper. He is more to you. From what you told me and from what I witnessed, you looked at Casper differently. You were truly in love."

I shake my head. "No. I love Vincent."

"You love both of them, but nothing compares to your love for Casper. Casper never manipulated you. Elves only fall in love once and it's for good. You are Casper's true love. I'm only repeating what you told me. I saw it too. Casper made you feel alive, and you were more yourself instead of this caged bird that Vincent forces you to be."

"He doesn't make me feel like that." Though as I say the words somewhere deep inside me knows she is right. "Vincent said he was dead."

Florence widens her eyes and drops her jaw. "What?"

"I remember a gunshot and a struggle." I let out a frustrated sigh. "Everything is hazy. I can't remember anything."

"He killed Casper?"

I don't know the cause of her anger, and I see a single tear squeeze from her eye.

"Now I know the cause of this war. The Elves are after us and the Jewel."

"We're safe from them, right? I mean, Casper and Edmond wouldn't have us killed."

"That is if the Elves know of us. I wonder if you and Casper made it to his homeland. And Edmond." She bows her head. "I don't know his fate."

"This doesn't sound like me at all. I love Vincent with all my heart." But as I say the words, that immoral feeling washes over me. *Casper.* Is this true? Did I fall in love with another man? An Elf no less? I must try to remember the truth.

I want to scream. Throw something. I'm so sick of all the dreams and the confusion I feel for both Vincent and Casper.

I pick up my phone from the nightstand and search for new messages. I want to talk to someone, but I know Cherry is asleep. Vincent hasn't texted me back. I finally read Casper's message from earlier.

I miss u. I do. I can't find you in my dreams. The days at school are long, even though I only see you during one class. Hope ur well.

I wonder if he's awake. I shouldn't be sending him messages if I want to work things out with Vincent, but he made it clear he doesn't want to talk. Besides, shouldn't I be able to talk to whomever I want? Even if I'm in a relationship? Okay, so Casper isn't perfect, but I believe him about not telling anyone that I stayed at his house. Maybe someone from school overheard my argument with Vincent in the store parking lot. Casper saved my life. That counts for something right? I argue with myself for a while before I finally send a message to Casper. I know he won't respond until the morning.

Hi Casper. Sorry it's been a while. I hope you're well.

My heart is beating ridiculously fast as I close my eyes, holding my phone. When it beeps, my heart accelerates.

I'm so glad u sent me a msg! I can't sleep.
Me either.
How are you feeling?
Not great.
Still? Do you need to go back to the doctor?
My illness is getting better. Vincent and I had a fight.
Why?!
Because I told him I'd been talking to you.
I'm really sorry. We can stop talking of you want.
The thing is I don't want to stop. As much as I hate to admit, you've become a friend. I wish he hadn't gotten so upset.

I hit send and I'm not sure where these thoughts and words come from. It's as if I am listening to my dreams more than I should be. They are dreams. They mean nothing. But I keep telling myself they have to mean something if I share them with Casper. What if he's some mythological creature manipulating me into love? I shake my head. That's ridiculous.

Casper calls and I answer in a low voice so no one can hear me.

"I'm sorry, Megan." I hear the genuine sympathy in his smooth voice. I love his voice. It calms me and I know he cares for me deeply.

"It's okay. Hopefully, we can patch things up. He's been busy with family things."

"I wish I could do something."

"Is there something between you two that you haven't mentioned?"

"No. I never liked him."

"Why?"

"He gives off a weird vibe. I don't know."

"I wish I knew why you both hate each other. It can't be because of me. There has to be something more."

"Why does there have to be more? You're worth the fight."

My lips twitch with a smile. "I'm pretty sure you won't have to worry about him starting a fight with you. I wish he would talk to me."

"I'm sorry."

"It's not your fault."

He chuckles. "It kinda is."

"Let's talk about something else. No dreams. No Vincent."

"Have you finished your homework?"

"Seriously?" I laugh and he chuckles too. "I wish I could get out of here. I hate it. Do you know how boring my room is after two and a half weeks?"

"Probably about as boring as mine. Except I started school this week."

"How's that been?"

"Okay, I guess. People are glad to see me. Amber constantly wants to help me or whatever."

"Does she flirt with you or still act like you're going out?"

"You jealous?"

"No." Warmth rushes to my cheeks. "Why would I be?"

"No reason." I can tell he's smiling. "I told Amber to leave me alone and to stop messing with you."

"What?"

"Had to be done."

"Thanks, I guess. Have you heard more about your accident?"

"No. My parents are pushing the police with the investigation. It's hard to figure anything out when there's no evidence and I can't remember anything."

"How are you feeling?"

"I'm fine. I guess memory loss helps with that. I wish I knew what happened. It's killing me not knowing. I sit here trying to remember and sort through the chaos, but all I see is nothing."

We stay on the phone so long that my cell phone is warming my face. At one point, I peer at the clock on my nightstand, and I can't believe it's already five in the morning. Have we seriously been talking for two hours? "Don't you need to get *some* sleep tonight? You'll be exhausted for school."

"I'm not worried. That's what coffee is for."

"At least you get to leave your house."

"I'll be thinking of you."

My pulse quickens. "I should get some rest."

"Feel better."

"Thanks. And thanks for talking with me."

"Anytime. Sleep well."

I hang up unable to calm my heart.

My phone beeps and I click on Casper's message. **It was nice to hear your voice. Sweet dreams.**

Ha-ha. I put my phone on my nightstand and roll over. It was nice to hear his voice and I realize I miss him. What about Vincent? What am I going to do?

Thirty-Seven

"Why are we at war again, Florence?" We sit close to each other, leaning against a tree while our horses graze the grass behind us.

Her thick lips press in a straight line. "Vengeance, especially since Vincent killed Casper. Vincent and his men have killed too many Elves for them to stand by. They want the Jewel. You know it belongs to the Elves, right?"

"That's impossible. We've always had it."

"You ever wonder why we have it? We're immortal. Why do we need it?"

"It protects us from death," I say. I'm not sure where she's going with this. We've always known that of the Nuummite Jewel. "It keeps us immortal."

Florence shakes her head. "We are immortal without the Jewel. I guess it does protect us from death, at least from dying at the hand of an Elf."

"What are you saying?"

"The Sprites wants the Elves dead, obviously. We hold the Jewel because it keeps *them* mortal. Thousands of Elves are dying as we speak because they are aging. They are only immortal with the Jewel. When it's in their home, it connects each of them. Without it, it weakens them. There are other uses from this Jewel."

"What does it look like?"

"It's a black stone with different bandings that has an iridescent glow. Sometimes you can see several colors in it. It's the most beautiful thing." She pauses. "Whoever has the Nuummite Jewel has the ability to access other times and existences. The Elves fear that in the wrong hands, someone could destroy the future by messing with the past."

I take a deep breath and stand. I can't believe what she's telling me. I feel like everything I have ever known is a lie. I wander by the ledge watching the water crash against the rocks below. There is something familiar about it. My mind keeps flashing with a dark scene.

"What is it?" Florence comes up behind me.

"This spot. I recognize it."

"It's where you and I used to come all the time."

I shake my head. "No, it's something else."

"What?"

My mind flashes again. I'm looking over the edge like now except it is night. I'm staring into blue eyes before I am pushed. Quickly, I grab the ledge. A man with blond hair and angular features saves me.

I open my eyes and step back from the ledge. "Someone tried to kill me here and someone else saved me."

Florence gasps. Her green eyes water. "Someone tried to kill you?"

"I see flashes."

"Who saved you?"

"I don't know. He had blond hair and brown eyes."

"Casper."

"Who would want me dead? And why?"

Florence brings a shaky hand over her mouth. "I don't know."

"I must know everything. Will you help me?"

"Of course. We will learn the truth together."

I sleep until noon and let my dogs roam in the backyard. It's a rainy, cold day. I want to run around or do something and briefly it seems like I have the energy to do a lot. After pouring myself water and letting the dogs back in, I'm tired. I sit down at the kitchen table and let Savannah hop in my lap. Her paws are wet, and they soak through my pajama pants.

"Thanks for getting me wet," I tell her, and she licks my nose.

There's a knock at the door and the dogs go crazy, barking so loud it rings in my ears. I push my way through them and close the foyer door so they can't attack whoever's at the door. I answer it. It's a deliveryman holding up a glass vase with beautiful white calla lilies and yellow roses. *Vincent.* My heart swells. I'm so happy. He knows exactly how to cheer me up.

"These are for Megan Devereux." He smiles when he sees my eyes widen.

"Thank you!" I take the vase and close the door.

I inhale the floral scents and grab the card, eager to read what Vincent wrote. When I read it I almost drop the vase.

Thought these would cheer you up since you can't go outside. – Casper.

I can't believe he did this. I'm absolutely floored. It's such a generous gesture. I'm disappointed that it wasn't Vincent, yet a strange excitement rushes through me knowing Casper sent them. How did he know these were my favorite flowers? Why did he send them? He knows Vincent and I are still together. We had a fight. That's all.

My dreams are so against Vincent like he's the one who killed Casper. Is my subconscious trying to tell me something?

I shake my head. How could I *ever* think something like that? Vincent would never shoot anyone.

Maybe I should visit Vincent. I can go to his house and wait for him to come home from school.

Hopefully, I can make it back in time, so my parents won't know I left. I slowly dress in a lot of layers and slide into the freezing cold car. My teeth chatter and my body aches, begging me to return to bed. I back out of the drive and go to Vincent's. I leave the heat on in my car and wait for him to arrive. I curl my legs against my chest and close my eyes.

I jump when I hear a knock at my window. Vincent opens my door and I step out. I'm so happy to see him. I missed him so much.

"Why are you here? Shouldn't you be in bed?" Concern fills his dark blue eyes. I feel relieved that at least he still cares about me.

"I had to come see you. I hated that fight. Please tell me it's not over between us. Please."

"No, Megan. It's not over." His eyes soften and I relax. "I had to leave that night because I don't want to be around you when I'm angry."

I take his hands in mine. "I never meant to hurt you. I know you and Casper have some weird hatred toward each other." I can't believe I'm about to say this. "I'll stop talking to him."

He raises his eyebrows and looks at me as though I've given him the greatest gift ever. "What? You would do that?"

"Yes. I love you. Only you. I would do anything for you."

Vincent's eyes darken with desire. He lowers his lips to mine, but I stop him.

"I'm still sick."

He rolls his eyes and presses his lips to mine with fervor, his hands cradling my face and my heart beats so fast. He slows his lips and pulls away. "I love you so much Megan. I never want to be away from you. I've missed you."

I swallow my guilt. "I'm sorry. How is your mom?"

His eyes turn sad. "Cancer's spread. She has breast cancer. She had a mastectomy. That's why I haven't called. They found more cancerous cells in her lungs."

My heart falls. Tears burn at the back of my eyes. "I'm so sorry." I don't know what to say. He draws me into an embrace, and I fold into him. I feel him kiss the top of my head.

"Don't be. It's not your fault. But thank you." He unburies my face and holds it between his hands, his blue eyes locking onto mine. "You are mine and I am yours."

He kisses me and his tongue grazes mine making my heart workout. I feel as though I'm running out of breath, but I don't want to stop. I love the feel of his velvet lips against mine. His kisses always leave me wanting more and I feel his love. He never holds back.

When we part, he grins. "Should we wait until you're better?"

"It wears me out," I admit. "I don't want to get you sick. I have missed you."

"Me, too."

"Will you come see me tonight?"

A sweet grin stretches on his lips. "I'll come see you every night if you desire."

"I don't wanna fight anymore."

His eyes hold mine and there seems to be something in them that hesitates.

"What is it?"

He holds me at arm's length. After a moment, he breathes a sigh. "I'm so scared of losing you again. I wish I knew what to do to not lose you."

"Vincent, you didn't lose me, and you never will."

He nods slowly. There is still pain and doubt in his eyes. He pulls me into his chest. "You should probably get home. I don't want you to get worse." When I draw back, he lifts my chin and kisses me.

I'm glad we patched things up, but I wonder what makes him hesitant. Does he not believe that I can stop talking to Casper? I can do it. Can't I?

I stare at the beautiful flowers on my dresser. I should thank Casper for the gesture. I need to put him out of my mind for good.

"Are you sure they weren't trying to kill Casper?" Florence questions. We're still sitting at our spot by the cliff that overlooks the treacherous waters. "What did he look like?"

"I don't know. It was dark. My mind is blurry. Could it be one of the Elves?"

"Megan, why would any of them want to kill you?"

"Because I'm their enemy. I don't know. Maybe they weren't keen on us being together."

Florence shakes her head. "*You* were not an enemy. You brought them hope."

"How is that?"

"If you and Casper married, it could help end the wars. Bring the two sides together."

"If Casper is an Elf, there would be no way I could fall in love with him." As I say it, I somehow know it isn't true.

"That's not true. You have to remember."

"There's nothing I can do if Casper is dead." When I say that, I feel my heart shrink like it never wants to see the light of day because of Casper's death.

"We can stop the war. We can look for the Jewel and give it back to the Elves." Her eyes are serious.

"I don't even know where to begin looking, let alone know where the Elves are."

"I think I can get someone to help us."

"Who?"

She seems to struggle with her words. "One of Edmond's friends. I know where they are."

"Where?"

"I promised I wouldn't say."

"Don't they know what happened to Edmond? Why didn't you go with him?"

"I'm not as brave as you. I can't run away from everything I have ever known. Now, I want to."

"I can tell you've changed."

"I have had time to learn a lot of truths. When Vincent sent out people looking for you, I got scared that they'd find me. I was about to leave because they never found you, Vincent announced you returned. I knew I couldn't leave. Now that Casper is dead, I can't handle it if I learn that Edmond died." Her eyes water.

"Oh, Florence. I had no idea."

"You did at one time." She smiles wistfully. "I'm going to meet my friend and he will help us after we get the Jewel, bring it to the Elves. In the meantime, I need you to hunt for this Jewel."

I search her eyes. Is she telling the truth? I have no reason to distrust Florence. The more we talk, the more I become wary of Vincent. How can he do this to me? How have I never known the truth about the Jewel? Vincent has always been my love. Why would he ever harm me? Perhaps because I had fallen in love with an Elf. I almost can't forgive myself. I also don't want their entire race to die because of us. "Okay," I agree.

Florence places an arm around me and pulls me close. "I'm leaving tonight."

"I should come with you."

"No. You have to stay here. You have to try to find the Jewel. Do not mention the Elves or Casper."

"How long will you be gone?"

"Three days maybe."

"How am I going to find this Jewel? I think Vincent left people to watch me."

"You have to be careful."

"Be careful." I echo. That sounds easier.

"Everything will be fine. Soon we will be living with them."

I'm not sure if I want to live with them if Casper is dead.

Lightning flashes in the distance and thunder rumbles above.

Florence grabs my hand, and we get to our feet. She tows me toward the palace. We carry on as usual so as not to give anything away. Later that night, we hug and say goodbye. I tell her that I will try to find the Jewel and for her to be careful. Then she leaves.

A beep from my phone wakes me. It's Vincent telling me he's outside. I quietly make my way outside and meet him behind the bushes. He takes my hand, and briefly, I'm cautious because of my dream, I guess, but I shake it away. He smiles and my heart melts.

"I hope you don't get worse by doing this," he says.

"I feel fine." But I shiver uncontrollably. Even though it's now late March, it's still cold outside.

"My car has heat, come on."

"I can't wait until I'm done being sick."

"I can imagine."

Like the other night, we cuddle in the front seat with the heat on. I feel safe again. There's something deep inside of me like a caution light. I don't know what it is. Ignoring it, I nuzzle against his chest, and he strokes my hair.

"What did you mean earlier about losing me?" I ask. "You say it a lot."

"Nothing."

"Please tell me."

"I don't want to think about it now. I want to enjoy being with you right now."

I reach up and touch his cheek pulling him to look at me. "Please. Let me in. You act like you're going to lose me any minute. I don't understand why. Did you have bad luck in prior relationships?"

"Something like that." He sighs. "She left me for someone else. No warning. No time for explanation. I hated every minute she wasn't there. Now that we're together, I'm scared the same thing will happen."

I raise my head. "You have to trust me. I'm not gonna leave you." I search his eyes, and there is the same doubt as before.

"I wish I knew what I did."

"Maybe you didn't do anything. Maybe she was fickle. I don't know. Don't think I'm like her. She's not here. I am."

He studies me. A mix of pain and desire flash in his eyes. "You *are* different."

I lean in, intertwining my fingers around his neck and kiss him. He kisses back with an urgent fervor. His warm fingers brush against my stomach sending a hot ache throughout my body. I want him closer, and I hitch a leg over his. I tire and have to catch my breath.

He kisses my forehead and presses my head against his chest. "We should hold off on that. I want you to get better." He lets out a long sigh.

"What?"

"I can't believe you're here. I've been looking for you for so long."

Why does he say such things? We are so young. I don't understand his intensity. "Why are you so intense?"

I feel him shrug. "Does it bother you?"

"No. I don't understand it."

"I know that I love you and I can't stop thinking about you. I don't know what I'd do without you."

"You are so incredibly sweet. How did I get so lucky to find you?"

"I'm the lucky one." He brushes his lips across my forehead. "I wish I could be the one taking care of you."

"Come over during the day. Hide your car."

"Don't tempt me."

"You might have to hide if one my parents come home."

He shakes his head. "So ridiculous."

I don't know what he finds ridiculous. I get why my parents don't want me alone at home with a boy.

That doesn't mean I have to abide by it. "You'll come over tomorrow?"

He smirks. "I do have school, you know."

I kiss his cheek. "Skip."

I move to his ear and nibble. He exhales a breath and squeezes my hips.

"Okay," he says through a pant.

I smile. "I should go inside now."

"Sleep well, mon trésor," he whispers in a sexy voice. Whenever he says that, it makes my insides turn to mush.

"Good night, Vincent." I get out of the car and make my way back inside my warm house.

"How are you?" Vincent comes inside the next day. He places his hands on my waist, drawing me closer.

"I'm okay. How are you not going to get sick?"

"I've had mono before." He inhales a slow breath and runs his fingers along my arms which sends shivers all over. "Are you cold?"

I shake my head. "You should probably go to my room. I gotta let my dogs in."

"Ah yes, I forgot you own a zoo."

I playfully hit his shoulder and he laughs. He heads down the hall, and I can't believe Vincent is in my house. Alone with me. I open the door and all five dogs almost knock me over to get inside. I go to my room.

"Who got you these?" Vincent points to the flowers.

My heart jumps to my throat. "Cherry," I lie. Thankfully, I hid Casper's note.

He frowns. "I wish I had thought of that."

"You've had a lot going on."

He crosses the room to me and puts his hands on my hips. He brushes his nose with mine and kisses me chastely. I feel his fingers slip between my pajama pants and my skin. I stop his hands.

"Behave."

"I can't help it." He grins.

"It'll happen. Not right now. I'm all icky and sick."

"It could make you feel better. You're definitely not icky. You're beautiful."

Heat pricks beneath my cheeks.

His knuckles brush my cheeks. "Mon beau trésor. Come on. Let's get you back to bed."

Vincent pulls the blankets back and removes his shoes. I slip under the covers, and he comes in after me, pulling me close to his body. His warmth radiates and I begin to relax.

"If you hear anyone coming home, dart like hell to hide."

He laughs. "Of course." He kisses my neck, and he holds me tighter. "Thank you."

"For what?"

"For this. I've been so stressed for so long then I met you. You have given me nothing short of absolute happiness and you are the hope that stood at the end of my long, dark tunnel."

His words make me feel guilty. He hasn't had the best life and still, as his mom lies in the hospital, he's here with me.

I kiss his hand and twist around to face him.

His eyes well and my heart breaks.

I pull his mouth down to mine and kiss him. I want him to know that I love him, that I care for him, that I wouldn't want it any other way. He brushes my hair back and caresses my face as he deepens the kiss. His lips are hot against mine making my heart pound faster. Heat pours over me as his hand slips under my top and touches my bare back. I catch my breath as his lips wander to my neck down to my shoulder and to my stomach. I clench my eyes and grip his hair at the soft caress of his lips on my naval. I feel my heart throbbing everywhere. I have to stop him, though I don't want to. I want to feel his love like I do in the dreams.

Something keeps nagging at me.

Vincent drags his tongue along my skin upward toward my chest sending that hot ache throughout me. He pulls my shirt back down and kisses my cheek as I pant.

When I open my eyes, he's gazing at me with a sweet smile, and I blush.

"Are you okay?" he asks, probably because I'm shaking.

I nod.

He pulls me close. "It's okay. Take a deep breath." His silky-smooth voice calms me.

I chuckle once my breathing levels. "I liked it. A lot."

"Me too. I can't wait," he whispers. "Je t'aime, Megan."

I smile as my heart swells. "I love you." I want Vincent to be my first. Cherry said when you know the one, you know. Prom will be the perfect night.

Thirty-Eight

"Megan." Someone is shaking me, and I open my eyes to see Vincent leaning over me with a concerned look. "Megan, are you okay? You're crying."

I sit up and wipe my cheeks. I was searching for the Jewel in my dreams, but a man caught me. He tossed me in a cell, called me a traitor, and threatened to use me as his own secret rendezvous. I realize the man was Adam. I can't catch my breath.

Vincent pulls me to him, stroking my hair, and I clutch onto him inhaling his spicy scent.

"Good grief, you're shaking. What happened?"

"I had a dream." That's an understatement.

"What about, baby?" He brushes his lips over my forehead.

"It-it was." It takes me a moment to get my words together. "Adam."

Vincent stills. "You don't have to worry about him anymore."

I breathe a sigh of relief, but the ominous tone in his voice scares me a little. Adam was shot. He is dead. Did Vincent read about that, too? "You heard?"

"Heard what?"

I meet his dark blue eyes. "He was shot and killed." I see the shock register in his eyes, but it goes away.

"Oh. No. I hadn't heard that."

I don't know why, but I feel paranoid or something. Is it from my dreams and how different I feel about Vincent that's leaking into my real life? "What do you mean I don't have to worry?"

"Because I'm here to protect you. Why?" He looks at me and a crease forms between his eyebrows. "You think I had something to do with it?"

I shake my head enthusiastically. "No. I'm on edge. The dream freaked me out."

I feel him relax beside me. "What happened?"

"Nothing. I don't want to talk about it." At least not with him. I can't get rid of this stupid pesky feeling. What is it? It's seriously messing with me.

"You know I'm here for you."

"Thank you."

"Tell me what to do."

"There isn't anything you can do. There's nothing anyone can do."

"Have you talked to someone about that night?"

"I told my mom." I haven't thought about that night or Adam in a while and I'm not sure why I dreamed about him. I can't help this sinking feeling that somehow Vincent knew Adam.

He holds me a little while longer, then he leaves. I'm on edge. I'm locked in a cell in my dreams, and I've been stuck inside this house for several weeks. I can't stand any of it anymore. I start pacing my room like a mad woman. I don't want to sleep. I don't want to lay down. I want out of this house.

I walk outside in the backyard to watch my dogs run and frolic with each other in the mist.

"Megan, what are you doing outside?" Mom asks from the door.

"I needed some air."

"Get back in here."

Rolling my eyes, I follow my dogs inside and she shuts the door. They jump on her and bark, excited that she's home.

Once they calm down, Mom checks my temperature and says I'm running a fever. Of course. I can't stand this.

"Take this and go lay down, sweetie." She hands me some medicine.

I swallow the pills and head back to my room. I need to talk to Casper about the dream, but I promised Vincent I wouldn't talk to him. He's been texting me since the lilies came and I've not replied. I pick up my phone and thumb down to his name. My heart vibrates inside my chest. I can't. I shouldn't. Instead, I rest my phone on my nightstand.

The cell is dark and cold, and I never hear any voices. Not even squeaking mice. It's enough to drive anyone crazy. As I've been here for however long, my mind has constantly been flashing with memories of Casper. The man I'd fallen in love and ran away with. The one whom I felt safe with no matter the circumstances. Slowly, I begin to remember everything and I'm not sure how that is possible. To think Vincent killed him makes my heart ache like I've never felt before. The only thing that keeps me sane is thinking of Casper.

The first time I laid eyes on him, I couldn't help but stare. Vincent had left and I missed him terribly but there was something different about the man with beautiful, brown eyes. His bleach blond hair was tied back in a ponytail at the nape. He was tall with lean muscles and his skin was the color of the sun. I had never seen him before, but we had Fairy Sprites come and go often.

When he touched me, I didn't want him to let go. I felt safe. Comfortable. Like I was where I was supposed to be. It was an extraordinary feeling—one that I had never felt before. We danced to several songs, laughing, and our eyes never strayed from one another. I never wanted the night to end. What a silly notion. It was crazy to be feeling such intensity toward a man I didn't know. I had been with Vincent my whole existence—there was no one else.

Until now.

The night Vincent stole me away from Casper, I asked him to take away my memories. Vincent had set the lantern on the small table and glared at me with cold, wounded eyes. He looked so worn-down and weak. As did I. I hated being on the run, but it was worth it.

"Vincent, please," I begged him.

"All this time I thought you had been tortured." He ran his hands through his dark hair. His voice was rough as if he hadn't slept in days. By the looks of him, I didn't think he had slept much in the past few years. His blue eyes pinned to mine.

"I'm sorry. I never meant to hurt you." It was the truth. I loved Vincent, but not like Casper.

He shook his head. "Seven years, Megan. Seven years I thought they stole you and tortured you or worse killed you." Tears pooled his eyes. "You were having some affair with *him*." His jaw twitched as he gripped the handle of his sword that hung on his belt. "You left me without a single word. No warning. Nothing. You vanished."

My chin quivered. It never occurred to me to leave some sort of letter. "Why would you send your men to kill me if you thought they kidnapped me?"

A crease formed between his eyebrows. "What are you talking about? I would *never* have you killed." He took a step closer. "Is that why you left?"

I shook my head. "No. I don't know why I left. You were always gone, and I-I fell in love with Cas-"

"Don't say his name," he spat.

I got to my feet. "I don't know why. It was all so sudden. I love you, Vincent. I can't explain what happened."

He stared at me for a long moment, then he let out a relaxed breath and closed his eyes. "I can't believe this."

"What?"

"The man manipulated you. Elves use their charm to get what they want. Did he have some ulterior motive as to why he was here?"

I felt my knees weaken. Had Casper manipulated me so he could find the Jewel? Was that why I fell in love with him so deeply? It couldn't be true. He spent seven years with me running and not searching for the Jewel. Now he was dead and the pain in my heart was too much for me. I had to tell Vincent something. I had to stay alive so I could find the Jewel for the Elves. For Casper. I didn't want to hurt Vincent any more than I already had. "He was looking for the Jewel."

"Of course. He charmed his way to your heart so he could get the Jewel. I should've known they would've tried something like that."

"Why would they do that to me?"

Vincent stepped closer and pulled me into a tight embrace. "Megan. Of course, your love for him wasn't real. He fooled you. I thought I lost you forever. I thought I had done something undeserving of your love."

I shook my head. "No, you did nothing. Tell me what I can do to make it better." I drew back, searching his eyes.

"Having you here in my arms and knowing that you love me is enough. I never want to lose you. You are everything to me."

His words only made me cry harder. I had never felt such a heavy guilt, but my grief for Casper weighed on me more. Our love was real, it had to be. I wanted to hold on to that forever, but I would never truly be with Vincent with that knowledge. I had to let go of Casper. I had to be free of him I couldn't live knowing he was dead.

"Please don't cry."

I wiped the tears from my cheeks and peered up into his eyes. "Take my memory away."

Vincent stilled. "What?"

I drew a ragged breath. "Take it all away. Why should that Elf even possess an inch of my mind? I don't want to remember how I was made a fool." I hated the words I spoke, but I needed to be with Vincent. We were supposed to be together. I loved him, even if that love didn't compare to what I felt for Casper. That was what I was supposed to do.

He cradled my head in his hands, staring into my eyes with a heated gaze. "I'll take it all away. Every last memory of him."

And Vincent erased it all.

Now my memories returned. As I sit in this cold cell alone, they are all I have. I know for a fact that my love for Casper was real and that his love was real. I do not wish to cause Vincent more pain, but his men have tried to kill me repeatedly. I have to pretend none of the memories have returned if I am ever saved from this cell.

I will have my vengeance one day.

For now, I hug my knees and weep for Casper. My heart has never felt so broken. The pain overwhelms me. It fills my lungs like water from the ocean. I cry so hard and scream so loud, knowing no one can hear me. No one can hear my heart breaking into pieces or me drowning in the tears. I hold onto my memory of Casper. I have to be strong.

If Vincent releases me, I will continue to pretend to love him with all my heart and all the while, I will look for the Jewel. Once I find it, I will return it to the Elves. For Casper. For the man who will always be the true owner of my heart.

Thirty-Nine

 ibbling my lip, I get out of my car in the high school parking lot. It feels so good to be outside and smell the fresh air, not in my front yard or in Vincent's car. Weeks of being cooped up in my house drove me crazy. I feel good. Except for the stupid dreams. I can't decide which made me crazier, the dreams or my sickness. Why are my dreams so against Vincent? Is something trying to tell me something about him?

I'm eager to be at school. To see Cherry. Vincent. And yes. To see Casper. I will never admit that to him. He sent texts a few times, and I ignored them. I feel bad that I've not replied, but I told Vincent I wouldn't.

Every time I think about it, there's a strange ache in my stomach. It's so stupid.

The last few weeks I spent my nights with Vincent in secret. After my most recent dream, I feel like the worst person ever. How could I leave Vincent like that? I know they're dreams, but it makes me feel like a shady person. How could I fall in love with someone else?

I shake my head hoping to free my mind from these absurd dreams. I grab my backpack and shut my car door.

"There's my girl." Vincent makes his way toward me.

"Hey."

He kisses me softly using an inch of his tongue which is enough to make me turn to mush. "How are you feeling?"

"I'm good." I look to the school building. "I feel a little awkward, though."

"Why's that?"

I shrug. "I don't know. Feels like it's my first day of school or something. I've missed so many days. I did all my work, but it still feels weird to be here."

"Trust me. You'll feel like you used to in no time. Dreading to be at school. Shall we?" He offers his hand and I take it.

We walk inside and posters of prom are all over the walls. I wonder if Vincent will ask me. When I reach my locker, Cherry squeals and pulls me into a tight hug.

"Omigod! It's been forever! I know we talked all the time but whatever." Her face lights up and it makes me smile. I missed her.

"I know. It feels weird being here."

"I bet."

"I'll leave you two girls to it." Vincent curls his lips into a sexy smile and walks away.

"He's so hot," Cherry mumbles as she watches him walk down the hall.

I clear my throat and cross my arms in a joking manner.

She turns back to me. "What? It's true."

"Can't deny that."

"I wanted to wait and tell you this in person." Her blue eyes are wild and excited. "Luke asked me to the prom." She giggles.

"That's great." I giggle with her.

She hooks her arm with mine. "We have to go dress shopping."

I roll my eyes and turn my head down the hall. I stiffen when I meet those familiar brown eyes. My heart jumps and my breath catches in my throat. I bite my lip, trying to calm down because I don't wanna give myself away in front of Cherry. Casper and I gaze at each other with such intensity. It reminds me of my dream.

I force myself to break his gaze and tug Cherry toward our class. I'm thankful she doesn't seem to notice.

The whole day I think about Casper and that deep look in his eyes. I don't want to go to English, but I have to.

As soon as Casper walks into the room, I have the urge to run and hug him with everything I have. To run my hands through his soft, blond hair or to feel his lips on mine. I close my eyes tight and take a deep breath. When I open them, I focus on the blank piece of paper in front of me. Why do I feel like this? Why are my dreams messing with my head? I take a deep breath and get through the class. I feel his eyes on me the whole time. Like old times.

The bell rings and I'm out the door to my locker. The faster I can leave, the faster I won't have to talk to him.

"Megan." The way he says my name makes me want to wrap myself in his arms. "Why did you stop talking to me?"

I brave a look into his deep, brown eyes. "Casper, we-I can't talk to you anymore."

His eyes narrow. "This again?"

"Vincent and I are together."

"And that matters why? We've been talking this whole time."

"You know why."

"Because he won't allow you to talk to me?"

I look away and close my locker.

"I can't believe you're letting him win."

My eyes cut to his. "This isn't about winning. You know I'm with Vincent."

"You're okay with the fact that he lied to you about jumping me? He's manipulating you."

"Funny. He said the same about you."

He rolls his eyes. "Soon, he won't be jealous of only me. He'll be jealous of Cherry and your family. You're so blinded by him."

"Why should you even care? Ugh. I'm so sick of this."

Casper moves close. Dangerously close. He doesn't touch me, but I feel the tension between us. I want to kiss him. "I know you feel it, too." I can't stop the humming inside my body. "Truth is, I've tried to forget about you, but I can't. You challenge me and make me see things differently."

Heat rushes to my cheeks and I roughly push him away. "I feel nothing when I'm around you. It's an unfortunate circumstance that I dream about you." I'm glad my voice sounds stronger than I thought it would.

Casper flinches. He slightly opens his mouth as if to say something but turns around and walks down the empty hallway.

I had to do it. I have to forget about him.

I'm not sure how long I've been in the cell, but I know my days are numbered. They've barely fed me or given me water and I can feel myself getting worse. Which, a small part of me doesn't mind because maybe I can see Casper in death.

I hear voices. Loud and angry. Coming closer. The door flies open, and light filters inside.

"Megan," I hear Vincent scream. I see a dark figure rush over to me and lift me in his lap. "You fools. What have you done?" he shouts toward the door. He kisses my forehead and lifts me in his arms and carries me out of the dark cell. "I'm so sorry. Please forgive me."

My mouth is dry, my body shriveled into nothing, my heart lost. I have no will to speak.

In the days that follow, I'm nursed back to health, and Vincent never leaves my side. I never doubted his love for me, but I doubt his character.

"Why did they force me in that cell?" I lay in bed, and he sits in a chair beside me.

His dark blue eyes look remorseful. He takes my hands in his and kisses my fingers. "They will never harm you again. They have been exiled. They thought you were a traitor."

"I don't understand."

"They think you willingly ran away with the Elves."

"I was kidnapped," I lie, keeping my innocent

composure.

"I know." He frowns.

"They mentioned Florence and that I was involved in her wrongdoing. What happened? I swear I don't know anything—"

"I know." He presses his lips in a thin line and hesitates. "Florence was killed."

My heart pounds and I feel faint. The dizziness settles over me and I can't stop my tears. "Why?"

"She was trying to escape to the Elves."

"What?"

"I'm afraid it's true."

"How could she do such a thing? Why was she killed?" I have to keep my composure, but I can't believe they killed her. It's hard to keep the truth hidden when I want to lash out so much. Does he lie to me for his benefit or because he erased my memory?

"She resisted our men."

"Why wasn't she punished? Why did they have to kill her?" My voice rises.

"I'm so sorry. She betrayed us."

"How do you know that? The Elves could've used her. She would never willingly betray us, Vincent."

"Did she talk to you while I was away?"

"Of course, we talked. We're friends."

He shakes his head. "I meant about the Elves."

"No. Why would she?"

"Try to convince you to leave with her."

"This doesn't make sense. You said the Elves erased her mind of them. Why would she run back to them if they did that?"

He swallows hard. "You need to rest. Don't work yourself into a frenzy."

I can't help but wonder if he's holding something back. I know he killed Casper, but only because he thought I was being tortured. Right? Now I hear our own kind killed Florence. Why didn't they punish her? Was it the same men who tried to kill me all those years on the run? Who threw me in a cell to rot until Vincent returned?

Is Vincent behind all of this? The man I have loved my whole life. *No.* Vincent would never hurt me. He only did what he thought was right. Something feels wrong.

I know I should move on from the Elves, but I feel like I have to help them now that Casper and Florence are dead. My heart aches. I will help the Elves, even if it means die trying. I can't tell Vincent any of it. I did a terrible thing to him by leaving. I look into his dark blue eyes. He loves me so deeply, but I'm wary of him.

"Vincent, please don't leave me again," I tell him with tears in my eyes.

"I will do everything in my power. Sometimes there's nothing I can do. There will always be wars among us and the Elves."

I nod, understanding.

"Believe me. I hate leaving you."

"I'm so lonely when you're gone. What if they put me in a cell again?" I know I'm making him feel guilty, but I can't help it. I need a distraction, so I won't think of Casper and this Elf thing. Can I even still find the Jewel and bring it back to them? Being in that cell made me lose my willpower it seems.

"They will never hurt you again. I will kill every single one of them if they ever lay a hand on you. You have my word."

I hear the strong conviction in his voice, and I know he means it. A tear escapes my eye.

"Do not cry. I am here. I love you, mon trésor." He kisses me and I wrap my arms around him, wishing with everything inside me that it was Casper. "Now that you are recovering, we shall have a party. A masquerade. Those are your favorites." He smiles.

"Only if you wear my favorite mask."

"Always."

He leaves, and I lose my smile. They killed Casper. Florence. Everyone that I love. Once I find the Jewel, I'm gone. I will never return to this place or to Vincent.

Forty

Vincent leans against my car holding a red rose and a sweet smile on his face. I can't help but smile.

"What's this?" I ask.

"Something nice." He hands it to me, and I inhale the sweet scent. He puts his hands on my hips and pulls me closer. My heart races when he does that. "I was curious if you would like to go to the prom with me." With the way his lips curl into a smoldering smile and the hopeful look in his eyes, I can't refuse him.

"Of course."

His smile widens and he crushes his lips to mine, kissing me so hard it almost hurts. He slightly pulls back. "You're mine," he whispers across my cheek.

"I am yours and you are mine."

Vincent's mouth is on mine. A flash explodes in my mind, and I see Vincent standing near a cliff, watching the waves down below, weeping.

He tries pulling away from me, but I stay with the vision. I recognize the cliff. His grief overwhelms me. His suffocation and the excruciating pain feel like being pulled underwater. His heart is breaking as he peers down at the chaotic water.

We pull apart.

"What was that?" I ask, breathless. The cliff is the same one from my dreams.

I see tears gleam in his eyes, but he doesn't answer. Why was he weeping?

"What was that cliff? I've seen it before."

His eyes flick to mine with an intense gaze. "What?"

"The cliff. I recognize it. You're crying over someone."

Vincent stares at me as if he knows something. He's holding something back. Then I remember something. In my dreams, Vincent's gift was showing me memories. Did my dreams predict that too?

"What are these visions? Are you doing that? Are you making me see things?"

He lowers his head but holds my hands tightly. "Yes."

I stiffen. "What? How is that possible?" I try to pry my hands from his grasp, but he won't let go. "What's going on? What are these visions?" My breathing picks up and I feel everything around me closing in.

"Please, calm down."

"How are you doing that? Why did you show me you weeping? You once told me about a girl who broke your heart. Were you weeping for *her*?"

"I have no control over visions." He pauses. "And yes, for her."

My heart drops and my eyes water. "Why are you still thinking about her? Do you love her?"

The look in his eyes hardens. "Yes."

I draw a sharp breath and suddenly feel queasy.

"Megan it isn't what you think."

I can be rational. I'm not going to get upset. I will let him explain. "Is it your mom?"

He shakes his head.

"Who is she?" I demand trying to keep what little restrain I have left. "Why would you get involved with me if you're still crying over someone else?" I push him hard, but he moves back and puts his hands on either side of me on the car.

"Don't get dramatic. Let me explain."

I push him again and he sighs removing his hands. I open my car door, but he shuts it back.

"Vincent," I shout. I lose the battle with the tears. I'm so angry and hurt and confused. My boyfriend is actually the one causing visions, as if that's even possible, and he's still in love with someone else.

"Megan, it's you," he finally says.

My body stills. "What?"

"I'm crying over you."

"What does that even mean?"

He hesitates and sighs, running a hand through his thick hair. "Don't be upset." He moves closer. "I have no control over what you see. I don't want to fight."

I rub my face and lean against my car. "I don't even know what's going on. What are these visions? You seem to know more than you're letting on."

"I'll explain it. Not now, please. Don't be upset. There's nothing to be afraid of."

Why can't he explain it now? Maybe if I go home, I can keep my distance or something. I want to leave. "I need to go."

"Megan—"

"I-I'll call you."

He sighs. "It's my fear inside me. I don't know why, but I've always had these visions. Ever since I met you."

"Why are you crying?"

He takes a deep breath and gives me a knowing look.

"You still think I'm going to leave you. Why can't you trust me? What have I done to make you not trust me?"

He wavers. "Nothing."

"I don't believe you."

"The visions cloud my mind. I-I can't explain it right now."

"Why?" Why is he hesitant and fumbling over his words? "What's wrong?"

"I'm not ready to talk about it."

Okay, I can respect that, especially if it's as crazy as me sharing dreams with another man. "Fine. Then tell me what do I have to do to prove to you that I'm not leaving you? I can't be with you if all I'm having to do is prove my commitment to you. I'm here to stay."

"It's my subconscious. My mind is crazy because of my mom and with all the stupid Casper stuff. I trust you," he says but I can tell he's still holding back. I know he's scared, but after we talked about it, I hoped he would be done with this. "I'm not an easy person to love. I know that. I'm sorry I'm so fucked up, but I love you, Megan. You are everything to me." He steps closer and cups my chin. "It feels like we've known each other forever. I need you. I would crumble apart if I didn't have you. I'm so sorry for scaring you and I promise I'll tell you soon."

I can't help but soften at his words and the pleading look in his eyes. It's intense. I love Vincent and I have no intention of letting him go. I brush my knuckles on his cheek and he closes his eyes. I pull him closer and kiss him, softly. "You have to trust me." I kiss his forehead.

He nods. "It's hard for me. I promise in due time, I will."

"Okay." I know I should beat it out of him, but I can't. I have my own secrets that I'm not ready to delve right into either. Still, this whole thing is bizarre.

On my way home, I can't help but feel a little weirded out that Vincent admitted to producing visions. Like in my dreams. I can't get over how my life is so similar to my dreams. There's no way the dreams could be true. There's no way any of this is connected.

Then it hits me. Like I've been punched right in the chest. In my dreams, I left Vincent for Casper. Can Vincent see my dreams when we kiss? It's the only answer that makes any sense. Sort of. Maybe he can read my mind or take images from my mind. Maybe that's why he's so scared and so jealous of Casper.

I shake my head and sigh. This is the most ridiculous thing. Ever.

I have to talk to someone. Not Casper. Not Vincent. I have to tell Cherry. I'm losing my mind and I need some kind of sanity in my life. And normalcy.

I call Cherry on my way home and ask for a girl's

night tomorrow. She agrees. I'm on the verge of ugly crying, but I hang up and pull into my driveway. I sit for a moment thinking I will feel better once I tell Cherry everything. All of it. Maybe it will loosen some of the weight off my shoulders. I'm scared of her reaction. What if I lose my best friend because thinks I need to be locked up in a looney bin?

Forty-One

The sun is shining, and the skies are blue with little wispy clouds here and there. It's a beautiful Friday and I'm excited to spend some time with Cherry. Even though we're shopping for my prom dress, I'm not sure I'll even wear it to prom with the way mine and Vincent's relationship has gone.

I've managed to ignore Casper all week since the first day I saw him, but his eyes are still focused on me in class. I don't want to admit it, but I miss him. It was so easy to be around him. So natural.

I'm in English, the last class of the day, counting down the minutes until I can leave this hellhole. Vincent was right. Eventually, my ornery feelings toward school would return.

"For our last project," Mr. Burress says. "I'm going to let you partner up, but I'm going to assign your partner. Clare, you'll team up with Demi." He continues to go down the list and he gets to my name. "Megan, you and Casper will team up since you two did an excellent job on the last project."

I can't move and my heart is pounding. Why is this happening? I can't work with him again. How am I going to explain this to Vincent? He'll never believe that Mr. Burress put us together twice, which he didn't, but that's what Vincent thinks. I hold my head in my hands and I hear Casper plop down in the desk next to me.

He sighs. "Your boyfriend gonna be okay with this or are you gonna have to get a permission slip from Mr. Burress?"

I clench my teeth. He's such a jerk. "Maybe if you stopped lying to me, he wouldn't have such a problem with you."

He glares at me. "That's right. Make excuses for him."

"You're being a jerk."

"Whatever. Why don't you do us both a favor and stop playing Vincent and me. It's quite pathetic that you only talk to me when you're fighting with him."

He thinks that? I soften. Maybe I do only talk to him when we're fighting. I feel terrible. I ignore him the rest of the class and meet Cherry at her house after school, still irritated over Casper, but I hide it.

"I'm so excited that you're here," Cherry says with a wide smile. "It's been forever."

"I know. It feels good to not be at home."

"I can imagine." She bites her lip and I know she wants to ask what I want to talk about, but she won't. She always waits until I'm ready.

"About last night, I'll tell you. I want to get my mind off things first."

"Sure. Wanna see my prom dress?" she squeals. It's hard not to smile from her excitement.

"Yes!"

She tows me to her bedroom and pulls up the plastic cover, revealing a beautiful red ball gown. It's strapless with a diamond zigzag pattern across the top.

"You're going to look like a queen, Cherry."

"I cannot wait. Can you believe we both have dates for prom? The cosmic gods are on our side this year."

I give a small smile, thinking that the cosmic gods have seriously warped my mind. I start thinking about Casper again and his stupid allegations. What makes him think I'm playing him and Vincent?

"Come on," Cherry says. "Let's go."

I nod. I'm letting the anger take over. We get in her car, and I accidentally slam the door.

"Hey! Roberto does not appreciate that."

I sigh. "Sorry."

"What has you so riled up all of a sudden?"

"Who is he to say Vincent is manipulating me? Why should he care?"

"Who?"

"Casper."

Cherry lets out a long-annoyed groan. "Seriously, when are you going to forget about Casper?"

"It's kinda hard to when Mr. Burress put us together again."

"Ugh. I swear that man is a sadistic prick. Why does Casper think Vincent's manipulative? Because he's jealous and wants inside your pants?"

I roll my eyes. "I told him Vincent doesn't want me talking to him."

Cherry's eyebrows furrow. "Vincent told you that?"

"It's no big deal. He hates Casper."

"Well, who doesn't? Still, he said that?"

"It's okay."

"Why don't you talk to psycho Mr. Burress and ask him to switch partners?"

Not that Mr. Burress would ever do it, but somewhere deep in my sick twisted mind, I don't want a different partner. "No, it's okay. We have a couple of weeks."

"Well, cheer up. We're going to get you a prom dress." Cherry flashes a huge smile. "You and Vincent will be the happy couple."

Cherry and I go to the mall and shop at random prom stores, but I can't find anything. I'm beginning to lose all hope, until she drives to a specialty shop. I know when I see the dress, I'm going to buy it. I grab it and take it with me in the fitting room. I strip down to my underwear, unzip the dress, and slide into it. The white chiffon is soft against my skin. It fits perfectly. It's a slim, strapless, floor length dress. Its tube top is embellished with pleats and rhinestones trail the top and at the waist all around. The back is low, and my long hair covers the tiny scars left on my back. I open the door so Cherry can see, and she gasps.

"It's like it was made for you."

"I love it."

"Match made in heaven."

I pay for the dress, and we grab some dinner and some snacks for the movie later. When we return to her house, she pulls up a movie from the screen and I know it's time for me to start talking.

"Cherry."

She turns to me. "Yeah?"

I play with her fuzzy pillow, twirling the long strands of fuzz around my finger. "When I tell you something, will you promise not to laugh or judge me or be mean?"

She moves to the couch next to me and squeezes my hand. "Of course."

"I don't know how to say it or even begin. Hear me out through the end before saying a word. I need to get all of this off my chest before I explode."

"Okay."

"You know about my dreams. Well. Some of them. The dreams started in October and I'm still having them. It's like this elaborate story has unfolded inside my head. They started to get more intense in January." I tell her every detail of the dreams from the beginning.

"So, you and dream Vincent were together, and you left to go be with dream Casper, but dream Vincent thought Casper was torturing you?"

"Yes. In his mind he was rescuing me and killed Casper."

"Wow. Those are intense."

"It gets worse. Casper and I share these dreams. We have the same exact dreams, except when they took me away, I started dreaming my own dreams and vice versa."

Her jaw hangs wide open, but she doesn't say anything.

I stand from the couch, wringing my hands, trying to loosen them up from gripping the pillow too hard. "That's why I've been acting so weird about Casper. That's why he claims he likes me. There's more. Every time Vincent and I kiss, we see visions of ourselves from another time apparently. Last night, I saw a vision of him mourning for someone while he was staring over a cliff. The same cliff from my dreams."

Cherry gasps.

"Vincent tells me he's the one making me see these visions and now I'm thinking he can read my mind and see the dreams I've been having. Everything is so messed up and I love Vincent, but I can't stop thinking about Casper. These dreams are making me crazy."

Cherry gets up and wraps her arms around me while I cry. She rubs my back. "This is-I don't know what to say. I mean, it's like something is forcing you to be with Casper or something or the cosmic gods or." She shakes her head. "I don't know, Megan."

"I don't know what to do because I find myself having feelings for both of them and each one makes me feel different. The dreams are wreaking havoc, making me feel and think things that probably would never cross my mind."

We sit in silence for a while. I know she's at a loss for words.

"I know it all sounds so preposterous. This is my life now. Vincent's afraid that I'm going to leave him. I have feelings for Casper."

"Okay, first of all, take a deep breath. Breathe in. Breathe out."

I do as she says.

"Set aside the dreams and visions. Forget about them for a moment. Tell me how you feel about Vincent and Casper here in your real life."

I take a couple more breaths and close my eyes, focusing on each man. When I open my eyes, Cherry and I return to the couch. "With Vincent, I feel like there's a struggle between us because he never seems to trust me. He makes me feel loved and protected. There's this darkness about him that I'm drawn to, but it scares me a little. He's always serious and brooding. He's kind and caring. But his jealousy is intense.

"With Casper, it's easy. I feel like I can be myself. He's always been genuine and tells the truth no matter what. He makes my insides twist with an ache and whenever we've hugged, it felt so natural. He makes me feel safe."

Cherry lets out a surrendering sigh. "As much as I hate to say this, you like Casper more."

"What?"

"When you talked about Vincent, you gripped the pillow. You seemed like you were on edge, but with Casper you seemed relaxed. Casper challenges you. He makes you feel things you've never felt before. I was rooting for Vincent this whole time, but I was wrong. Vincent is a little controlling. He makes you skip school and work all the time."

"We're teenagers. That's what we're supposed to do."

"Okay, but I noticed something change in you in January. You say the dreams intensified then, but so did your life. Maybe the dreams represent your life. Vincent doesn't seem good for you."

"No, I'm not breaking up with Vincent. We're in a weird patch right now."

"Okay. But Megan, don't deny yourself what you deserve or want. Life's too short to be with someone you're not completely happy with. It may be good, but it's not great. You're fighting hard against something that it's driving you insane. It's stressing you out and the only way you're going to find out is if you give it your all. People unfortunately get hurt, but you have to be selfish once in a while and do what makes you happy. If Vincent is already telling you to stop talking to Casper, that's a red flag. I would never tell Luke to stop talking to his friends, male or female. Sure, I may get jealous, but he's with me. You have feelings for Casper, and you've ignored them this long. You're not a cheater, and if Vincent can't trust you, he never will."

I nod. It feels good to get all of it off my chest. Now I can't stop thinking about what Cherry said. Is she right? Do I like Casper more? Does Vincent put me on edge that much?

Forty-Two

haven't told Vincent that Casper and I have to work on another stupid project. I hate the tension around us. I don't want to deal with a jealous controlling boyfriend right now. I don't want him to get sad again or think I'm going to leave him. We haven't talked about that night with the visions. I'm sure I'm avoiding it because I don't want to know how that cliff was in my dreams and his visions.

My dreams are still rather uneventful, which is nice. I don't need the added stress.

I'm thankful it's Friday. Casper and I only have until Tuesday to finish our project. I'm pretty sure no one's going to work on it over the weekend since it's prom.

We work in the library to dig up more crap about Nathanial Hawthorne. Normally, I would be excited to work on such an assignment but being around a moody Casper doesn't help. We sit across from each other at a table reading and researching.

"Have you found anything yet?" I ask him.

Casper sighs. "Not since you asked me ten minutes ago. Maybe you should stop worrying about what I'm doing and focus on your own research."

I grit my teeth. "Why are you being such a jerk?"

He looks up and meets my eyes. "Probably the same reason you're being one."

I feel my jaw drop. I want to tell him I hate him that he hurt my feelings, but I don't. I don't hate him either. I look back down at the book, feeling the tears burning at the back of my eyes. If I can get through this class, I can cry in my car.

A few minutes pass as we research in silence, except I'm so distracted by him sitting across from me and I find myself looking up and watching him every so often. The way he twirls his hair with his fingers or chews on his thumbnail. I want to take my hands and run them through his messy hair.

He looks up, catching me staring at him. I immediately avert his eyes and feel the heat rush to my cheeks.

"What?" he asks.

"Nothing."

Several awkward seconds pass.

"Are you going to the prom?" I ask, trying to make small talk for some reason.

He flashes a wicked grin. I love it but hate it at the same time. "Why? Are you interested?"

I kick him in the shin under the table. Complete knee-jerk reaction.

"Ow!" he cries in a whisper as he rubs his leg. "What is your problem?"

"I'm trying to be nice."

"Kicking me is your way of being nice?"

"I was trying to have a civilized conversation."

Casper locks his eyes with mine. "No. I'm not going."

I'm surprised by his answer. "Why?"

"Because I don't want to. Why do you care?"

I shrug. "I find it odd that you're not going."

"Why should I? So, I can see the girl I love kiss and hang on some other guy? No thanks."

My heart is pounding against my ribcage. "What did you say?"

He shakes his head. "Nothing. I've gotta go make copies of this stuff." He grabs a few books with him to the copy room. The door closes. He can't be in love with me because we talked about this. What he feels for me isn't real. It's some side effect of the dreams. I don't feel the same no matter what I told Cherry. She was wrong.

I make my way to the copy room. I open the door and let it close. "Casper." I put my hand on his arm.

He turns and there's a desperate yet painful look in his eyes that makes my knees weak. I forget anything I thought about saying to him. His lips are on mine, his hands cradling my face. I should push him away. My hands run through his blond hair and I'm drawing him closer. He kisses me with such a fervor that my back hits the wall with a thud. It's the same passionate kiss as in my dreams. I've never felt anything like it. His lips move against mine, slower now, and I realize how much I love Casper Truitt.

His hands slide down and he presses his body against mine. I'm flying high as little pricks of excitement rush throughout me. My heart is throbbing, and I feel it all the way to my feet.

Casper pulls away and leans his forehead against mine. "Wow," he breathes.

We are both breathing hard, still clinging onto each other.

Then it all comes crashing down on me. I kissed Casper and I loved it. I cheated on Vincent. Tears prick in my eyes, and I put my hands on Casper's chest. He moves back.

"I'm so sorry," he says. "This wasn't your fault. Oh god I'm so sorry."

"I-I." I shake my head. I can't seem to catch my breath as I dart for the door and run out, grabbing my things in the process. There's an ache in my chest and I bury my face in my hands. What have I done? I promised Vincent that I am his. He's so afraid of something like this happening. What am I going to do?

"Megan, please," I hear Casper's voice behind me as I reach my car. "Wait. I love you."

I freeze with my hand on the door handle. Did Casper Truitt say he loves me? I turn and meet his eyes. "How can you possibly love me when you know nothing about me?"

"That's not true. I know a lot about you."

"Like what?"

"You have incredibly controlling parents. You don't like coffee but like the smell of it. You're not a morning person. You like the smell of rain because it reminds you of being happy and you hate fire because it gives you a bad feeling. You cry when you hear a song that moves you. You like running barefoot in the grass."

My heartbeat is so loud it's throbbing in my ears. I can't believe he knows all of this. How can he though?

He moves closer, his eyes pin to mine, which only makes me grip the handle behind me. "I know what makes you shiver," he whispers in my ear, making me tremble. "I know your favorite place to be kissed is the tiny spot behind your ear." My breath hitches, and he pulls back slightly. "I know these things because I know you. Whether the dreams mean anything or not, you're still the same, Megan."

I want to kiss him again and run my fingers through his hair. His eyes lure me closer, and I give in, pressing my lips to his. Heat reverberates throughout me. I am in love with him. His kiss is as chaotic and passionate as mine. Months of tension between us release throughout our kiss.

I have to get out of here. No matter how much I want to stay. "Casper." I draw away, averting his heavy gaze.

"Megan, I'm worried about you. There's something about Vincent that's not right and you have to leave him. Not for me or anyone, but for yourself."

"What?"

"He's thrown up too many red flags. You have to be careful."

"I-I have to go." I open the car door, sink into the seat behind the wheel, and close it. I take a deep breath when I'm out of his sight, but my I touch my tingling lips.

What am I doing? I'm a terrible person. I can't tell Vincent about this. I want to cry. Vincent doesn't deserve me.

No matter what I do, I can't stop thinking about that kiss. It moved me like nothing ever has. It felt real. Right. The cruel wanting that has plagued me for months was filled. For a fleeting moment, I wish I was going to the prom with Casper. I can't hurt Vincent. I can't do this to him. It would crush him.

The night of the masquerade ball, I'm beginning to give up hope. I've been looking for the Jewel for six months and still, nothing. Even if I had the Jewel, how can I run back to the Elves? I have no idea where they are located. I will proudly die in their honor, but I have no Jewel to give them.

The music plays and I push my way through the masked people. Gold, glittery masks, silver ones, green, purple, blue. Every color imaginable. The dresses are intricate designs and big and long. Mine is white with heavy black and silver beads covering it. My hair is pulled up save for three curls that lie against my collarbone and I'm wearing a light blue and silver half mask with an elaborate design made from crystals.

Vincent has business to attend so I am left to wander around. He always has some kind of business lately.

I feel a hand softly take mine and I turn. A man with a gold mask that covers his entire face except for his lips looks down at me. I meet his brown eyes and his blond hair comes just over the top of the mask. He has an angular jaw.

"May I have this dance?" He kisses my hand. Something about his smooth voice is familiar to me. And his eyes...

"Yes."

With a smile, he draws me close against his body and holds one hand at the small of my back and the other holding my hand up. Flashes of color whirl all around us, but I am glued to the brown eyes in front of me. They look at me with such desire and passion that it makes my heart flutter and my breath hold in my lungs.

We move rhythmically among the crowd, all while we gaze in each other's eyes.

"You seem familiar," I tell him.

He leans down and I feel his breath near my ear. I swallow hard. "I found you," he whispers. "You're safe, now."

I draw in a deep breath and my heart pounds beneath my chest. The music seems to fade. The mindless chatter is lost in the air. The dancing people appear to pause. *Casper.* I want to scream his name. Wrap my arms around him. Pull him closer to me and kiss him. Give him my all. How is this possible? All this time, I thought he was dead. Here he stands, holding me, touching me.

Forty-Three

should probably choose a different color if I'm wearing a red dress, huh?" Cherry asks, holding up a florescent pink nail polish bottle.

"Sure."

We're at the nail salon for the start of our girl's primping day since prom is tonight. My mind is elsewhere. Thinking of Casper's lips on mine. The dream. My heart hasn't calmed down since yesterday.

"Are you even listening to me?"

"Sorry. You should get a French manicure." I wince. My dreams take place in France. Why did I have to say French?

"Are you okay?"

"Yeah, I'm good. Why?"

She cocks an eyebrow. "You're the worst liar."

We pick our colors and they set us up in the massage chairs. My phone buzzes in my pocket, but I can't answer it. I don't want to either. I don't want it to be Casper, yet I do. I'm such a terrible person.

"Are you gonna spill the beans? You're about to chew a hole in your lip."

I stop biting my lip. "Sorry. I can't believe we're going to prom tonight."

"I know. I thought for sure I'd go to my senior prom, but junior? I always thought it was a pipe dream. But here we are." She squeals. "I can't believe our junior year is almost over."

"It's strange."

"Next year, we're going to make it awesome. You, Vincent or Casper, Luke, and me will have so much fun. Oh! We should totally go to the beach house this summer."

"Yeah."

Beach house with Casper sounds amazing. *Ugh.* I need to stop.

"How did you convince your parents to let you out tonight?"

"I have to be home by ten."

She gasps. "What! Do they think things like that can only happen late at night? This is prom! Ugh."

"Mom's overprotective. She also doesn't want me to have sex. She thinks if we go to dinner, then prom, then go home, we won't have time."

"Oh, you can make time." She gives a wicked grin.

I roll my eyes. I was supposed to take the next level with Vincent tonight. Butterflies swarm inside my stomach. I feel their wings fluttering throughout my entire body. I try focusing on the lady filing my nails, but all I can think of is Casper soft lips on mine.

"Whoa. Are you okay? You look a little sick."

"I'm fine."

She lets out a frustrated sigh. "Tell me what's up."

"Casper kissed me," I blurt.

She gasps again. "Oh. My. God." We sit in silence for a moment. "When? How was it? What are you going to do?"

"I don't know!" My vision blurs. "It was yesterday. I can't stop thinking about it. Or him. Cherry, I'm in love with him."

"Oh wow."

"I have to break up with Vincent."

"Tonight?" she asks in disbelief.

"I can't. Tomorrow. I don't know. I love Vincent. I don't want to hurt him."

"Megan, don't force yourself to be with someone if you don't want to. Life is short. You love Casper and I know this would tear you up inside if you ignored those feelings. It's been tearing you up for months."

She's right. I know I can't fight this anymore. It's not fair to Vincent or me. I'm only seventeen. How can I feel this way about someone? How can I hurt Vincent's feelings like this? I'm doing exactly what the Megan in my dreams did. She broke Vincent's heart because of loving Casper. I can't get over how similar my dreams are compared to real life. Am I psychic or something? Are the dreams making us feel this way?

My hands shake as I try to pin the stupid boutonniere to Vincent's lapel. I can barely meet his eyes. He looks hot in his tuxedo, and I can feel his dark blue eyes on me. The right side of my neck is hot from all of my curled hair being swept to one side. I curse aloud as the pin pokes my finger.

Vincent holds my hands steady and brings my finger to his mouth, sucking on it. I feel the blush coming a mile away, and this is too intimate considering Mom is in the other room getting her phone camera ready. I remove my finger and finally pin the flower.

I take a deep breath.

"Are you okay?" he asks.

I swallow hard. "Yeah. I'm good." I'm such a terrible liar, hoping he can't tell the real reason for my nervousness. He told me last night he had a surprise for me and wants to make tonight special. I can't help but wonder if he means he wants to take our relationship to the next level. I can't give him what he wants. He grabs my hand and intertwines his fingers with mine giving me a squeeze.

"Okay, get in front of the fireplace," Mom orders and proceeds to take a million pictures of us.

"I can't believe you were able to find a date," Ron jokes as he stands behind Mom.

I feel Vincent tense and I squeeze his hand. I've learned to ignore Ron's dumb comments, but it still hurts.

"Vincent, stand behind Megan and put your hands on her hips. Megan, get in front of him and turn toward me." We do what she says, and I smile, but it's fake. I'm trying so hard to be in the moment, but I can't stop thinking about that damn kiss. From that one kiss, I know that what I feel for Vincent is small compared to what I felt yesterday.

"Be home no later than ten." Mom hugs me. "Be careful."

"I'll be fine."

"You kids have fun."

Vincent opens the door and I gasp. There's a limo sitting in my driveway. "Vincent," I hesitate. He spent way too much.

"Come on. It's fine." The driver nods, opening the back door for us and once we're in, Vincent leans over and kisses me. His lips trail to my jawline to the back of my ear. "You are gorgeous, Megan." My heart goes into overdrive. He kisses me, his tongue mingling with mine and he presses harder like he can't get enough.

I feel sick, knowing I don't deserve any of this. He holds me so close to him, as if he's afraid I might run away. I decide if I want to rid my mind completely of Casper, I should give myself to Vincent. All of me. I can't bring myself to do it.

"Are you sure you're okay?" Vincent squeezes my hand. I loosen my hold, unknowing that I had been gripping that hard. He lifts my chin with his other hand, and I gaze into his eyes.

"Yeah, I'm fine."

"Talk to me." His voice is so soothing, and it almost brings me to tears. I have to come up with something.

"My mom and dad are fighting again," I lie. They tend to fight often over child support or whatever, but it's been a while. I hope he buys it.

He pulls me tighter and kisses my forehead. "You won't have to worry about that much longer. I promise."

I look up into his blue eyes. "What do you mean?"

"You'll be going to college soon, right?"

Oh. "Yeah. I hope. After this semester of being sick and skipping, I hope I can do well on my exams to keep my GPA up."

"You'll be fine. I promise everything will work out."

He sounds so sure. He takes me to an upscale French restaurant. I can't get over the coincidence, but I remember his family originated from France. Is that why my dreams take place there? Something isn't right. It's unsettling and I can't stand this feeling. During dinner, Vincent is incredibly charming as usual and acts so happy. So, in love. It's crushing me.

We arrive at the ancient theatre where the prom takes place. I've always loved this theatre for its architecture. It was built in the late twenties and the renovation kept its beautiful charm and warm atmosphere. The chandeliers hang low and light glitters throughout them. We enter the ballroom and it's decorated in blue and silver.

Cherry and Luke meet up with us and I was right. Cherry owns the prom with her beautiful gown, fit for a queen. Her brown curls are pulled up high with one long curl hanging loosely. Her eye makeup brings out the blue in her eyes. She gives me a knowing look and the four of us head to the dance floor. While the music isn't exactly my favorite, Vincent and I dance to almost every song. I enjoy every minute, and it keeps my mind off of things.

He makes me smile and I'm so lucky to have him. I can't escape this stupid nagging feeling. Why does it bother me?

After an upbeat song, Vincent sighs. "I hate to do this, but I need to call and check up on my mom. Don't go anywhere. I'll be right back." He kisses my forehead and walks away. I'm left alone on the dance floor.

Someone taps me on the shoulder and when I turn, my heart lodges in my throat. "Casper."

The DJ plays a slow song with a haunting piano tune and a beautiful female voice begins singing.

Seeing Casper in a tux makes me want to lose my inhibitions and kiss him. His brown eyes are dark with intent, and I can't seem to move or speak.

"May I have this dance?" he asks.

My heart thunders inside my chest. I nod and he takes my hand and places his other hand on my waist. I shudder from the pleasurable touch and hope he doesn't notice. We move blithely as if we've been dance partners for years.

"I thought you weren't coming."

He lifts a shoulder. "I wanted to see you. You look stunning as always."

I brave a look into his fervent eyes. It's enough to take my breath away. "You can't be here." I avert his gaze.

Casper pulls me closer to him and his lips are close to my ear. "It's my prom, too. I have every right to be here." His fingers interweave through mine with the most tender touch.

"You know what I mean."

"I know. I've been thinking, Megan."

"About?"

"I'm not sorry about the kiss. If Vincent's the one you want, I will wait for you."

"Thought you said to stay away from him."

"I'm not the only one who feels that way. Maybe I'm wrong."

"He's fine. Why wait for me?"

"Because I know deep down inside, I won't ever love another woman the way I love you." He lowers his lips to my ear again. "I know you feel it, too." He draws back and kisses my hand.

The feelings are too intense, and I can't fight them anymore. Cherry's right. I'm pushing away something that feels so right and it's making me crazy. I know what I have to do.

A breath escapes my lips. "It's you."

"What?"

"It's you, Casper. You have to get away from me. I can't be seen with you."

Casper stares into my eyes with an edge. "Megan—"

We stop dancing and I reluctantly pull away from him. I can't let Vincent see us dancing. I have to end it with Vincent without him getting angry.

"I get it," he says, and I don't miss the bitter tone, but he has it all wrong. He walks away before I can explain myself. My heart won't stop its erratic beating. I want to cry. I shake my head and take deep breaths. I hate being so emotional.

"You know, I didn't mean that literally," Vincent says behind me which startles me.

Confused, I turn around to see his smile. "What?"

"When I said not to go anywhere."

"Oh."

"Are you okay?"

I nod.

"Are you ready to leave?"

"Yes."

We ride in silence in the car. I don't want to push the issue, but he never explained the visions to me. I have to talk to him. I expect him to take me home, but he's going the wrong way.

"Where are we going?"

"My house. I have a surprise." He smiles.

"I can't stay out late."

He sighs. "None of that will matter soon."

I'm nervous. I'm not ready for anything and as much as I hate to think it, I'm so ready for this night to be over. I want to tell Vincent about the kiss. Tonight isn't the night and I'm too scared. As I look at Vincent in the soft orange glow of the limo's interior lights, I realize that what I feel for Casper is so much stronger than what I feel for Vincent. I knew this already. I don't want to break his heart, but I have to tell him.

When we get to his house, he blindfolds me and takes me inside. I can hear him flicking a lighter and I start smelling candles. My palms begin to sweat. I wring my hands and feel him behind me.

He unties the blindfold and there are hundreds of red and white rose petals leading upstairs with the tea light candles.

"Vincent," I whisper.

"I wanted to do something romantic for you." He brushes his lips against mine. "Do you want something to drink?"

"Sure," I say, my throat suddenly dry. I put my purse down on the table and he hands me a glass of water. I chug the whole glass.

His lips tickle my neck, my shoulder. Vincent takes my hand and leads me toward the stairs, but I don't budge.

"What is it?"

"I-I'm not ready."

He smiles sweetly. "But it's prom." He shakes his head. "We have all the time in the world for that." I feel a stabbing pain in my chest. "Your surprise is upstairs."

I follow him, losing my grip on things. How can I tell him I don't want to be together anymore? My heart is lodged inside my throat making it hard to breathe or swallow. We get to his room, and I sit on his bed.

He hands me a small box and gets down on one knee. I'm trying not to jump to conclusions, but my whole body is shaking.

"Vincent."

His eyes hold mine. "I love you. I always have and always will. I see no reason why we can't be together forever. You are my soulmate. You are the sun in my life. You're everything to me. Will you marry me?" He opens the box revealing a white gold ring with a sky-blue aquamarine stone surrounded by swirls and flowers.

I can't breathe. I can't speak. Marriage? We are so young! We don't know each other that well. He's completely serious.

"Obviously, we'll wait until we're out of school," he adds. "I've got it all worked out."

"This is crazy." I stand, moving to the window. Dizziness overcomes me, and I grip the ledge. He turns me around to face him.

"I don't mean to scare you. I couldn't wait to ask you. I want to be with you forever."

I start crying. This is getting too deep, too fast.

He pulls me to him. "Please don't cry."

"We need to talk."

As one would assume, his muscles go rigid. He draws back, holding me at arm's length. "What is it?"

"This is too fast. I mean we barely know each other."

"I know a lot more than you think. We are meant for each other. I have plans for us. For us to run away from all of this. Neither one of us is happy here. My mom's on her deathbed. Your parents are insanely controlling and strict. We can have our own life and leave this place."

I try to get the words out, but they won't form. "I love you; I do. I think-I think we should—"

"Don't you dare say it. I'm sorry for scaring you but that's no reason to end this."

I shake my head. "It's not that. I need some time."

"Time for what? You've been distant all night. What's going on?"

I swallow several times as the ache in my heart spreads to my stomach.

Vincent narrows his eyes, and his face grows dark. His whole demeanor changes like a switch went off. "It's *him,* isn't it?" His tone is harsh, and he grips my arms.

"Who?"

"Don't play innocent with me."

This is going downhill in a hurry.

"What are you talking about? I'm talking about you and me." There's no way I can admit to him about mine and Casper's kiss right now.

"What is it about Casper that has you so wound around him? Has he been manipulating you again?"

"What? No. This has nothing to do with him," I lie, feeling ashamed.

"This has everything to do with him. No matter what, you always choose him. Every time."

"What are you talking about? I've never chosen him."

"You always do. Even after everything I do to keep you two apart."

"What are you talking about?"

"*I* vandalized your car and framed him, yet you believed Casper. *I* spread the rumors about you sleeping with him. *I* was the one who killed Adam because he came after you, and you still hail Casper as your hero."

Air traps in my lungs. He *killed* someone? His confessions boggle in my mind like dice in a cup. I feel sick and my knees are weak and I'm starting to feel sleepy. It's too much. I can't even look at him. "Why?" My voice is barely audible.

"Because I would do anything for you. I even tried killing that vile Elf by running him off the road and shooting him. I was at the hospital that night to finish him off, but you ruined that. Imagine my surprise when he woke up because of you. I have given you my heart. I have given you everything you can ever imagine. What more do you want?"

"D-did you call him an Elf?"

"Because that's what he is. The story you and I have been writing is real. You and I are Sprites, Megan."

I shake my head. "It's a story. A story that I created from all these crazy dreams I've been having. Every single night about you and Casper and—"

Vincent bursts into laughter releasing his grip on me. "I can't believe I didn't see this before. That's how you've been finding each other."

I don't know what he's talking about, and I don't know why I'm still standing here. I need to get out of here away from this dangerous and obsessive man. What does he mean the story is real? Does he know why I have these dreams? "What's going on? Have *you* been playing me for a fool?"

He stops laughing and looks at me severely. "Absolutely not."

"Then what's going on? What is all this? I don't understand. Why would you try to kill Casper?"

"I'm sure you'll figure it out soon enough with your precious dreams." He moves closer to me, and I turn my head. His lips are on my ear, and he whispers to me. "I bet you wouldn't even have thought about him twice without these dreams." He pulls back and forces me to look at him, his hand squeezing my jaw. "We had a lifetime once. In this godforsaken world. You never found Casper. We were happy. But there was a part of you that remained distant. I took you home, but you aged and died. I was so lost. I thought I had lost you forever. I didn't find you again until now."

"I don't know what you're talking about."

"Not now. But you will. When I first saw you, I nearly fainted." His eyes welled. "You can't know what this has done to me. No matter what, you always choose him."

I have to get out of here and talk to Casper but I'm so sleepy I'm having a hard time keeping my eyes open or even standing still. This is insane.

"I have to go." I try prying his grip from my jaw, but he doesn't budge. "Let me go."

"Don't you get it? You promised yourself to me. You promised we would run away and be together."

A tear slides down my face, and he loosens his grip. "I need to go home." I fall against him.

I feel his arms around me, and he sighs. "We'll be there soon."

Forty-Four

asper and I are outside in the maze, hidden from view of the others. In the dark sky above, the full moon is our only light. We discreetly make our way through the maze but yearn to move quicker. We make it to the side of the palace where there is a lone white palomino waiting.

Casper swings onto the horse's back and pulls me on behind him. I wrap my arms around him. The horse trots toward the wrought iron gate. Once the horse turns a corner, he breaks into a fierce gallop. Feeling the warm breeze, I hold Casper tight.

We are free.

I don't know how long we race in the night, but when the auburn light barely breaks the horizon, we come to a stop. He gets off the horse and helps me off. Tossing his mask to the ground, my heart skips a beat at the sight of him.

I remove my mask as his lips press against mine. He lifts me by my hips and our mouths release the built-up passion between us. We are together again.

He eases me to the ground, still kissing me. He holds me so tight, and I clutch onto his shirt, never wanting to let him go.

"I tried so hard to find the Jewel," I tell him, breathless, the tears coming now. "I wanted to bring it back to your people. All this time, I thought you were dead. They said they killed Florence and put me in a cell because they thought I was a traitor. This whole time I've been pretending to love Vincent. I can't do it anymore. I can't be away from you."

Casper draws me closer, holding me tightly against him. "I found a way to be together."

"We're together, now."

His thumb grazes my cheek, wiping the tears that escape. "So, we won't have to run."

"How?" I meet his beautiful, deep brown eyes. How I've missed them.

He hesitates. "The Witch."

I gasp.

It takes me a minute to open my eyes. I swear they feel like they've been glued shut. My head is killing me with an ache that could kill a rhino. I sit up but I can't see anything. Not even my hand in front of my face. Wherever I am, there's a damp chill. Briefly, I think I'm dreaming and back in the cell, but no, this is real. All of it is real. Vincent tried killing Casper.

I roll over on what feels like a bed with a lot of blankets. I swear if I didn't know better, I would think I'm blind. I feel for anything that I might recognize. The wrought iron bed frame doesn't feel like mine. The cold, concrete wall feels empty.

The last thing I remember, I was trying to leave Vincent's, but everything beyond that is blank. I remember our conversation. His proposal. His confessions. My blood turns cold. I start to panic. Did Vincent put me in a cell?

"Vincent," I yell. When I get no answer, I stand from the bed, cautiously. I'm barefoot and my feet land on soft carpet. I can tell I'm still wearing my prom dress. I hold my arms out blindly trying to find my way to a door or window. Anything. "Vincent," I shriek.

I back up against the smooth cold wall. I can't keep my breathing leveled and I start crying. I can't stop shaking, I'm so scared and I have no idea how to get out of here, wherever here is.

A door squeaks open, and I jump. Looking toward the direction of the sound, I still see nothing. Footsteps slowly meander down wooden steps. My breath catches in my throat, and I try not to make a sound.

I hear a flick of a switch and I squint from a soft orange glow.

"Vincent?"

"Are you okay?" he asks, pure concern in his eyes. "Are you hungry?"

"Where am I?"

His lips press in a hard line. "In my basement. Sorry it's not the Ritz, but I tried to make it homely as I could."

Scanning the room, I see a bed, vanity, and a bathroom.

"It's just for a few days."

"Days? Why?" I'm trying so hard to keep my voice strong, but it's hard when my psycho boyfriend has me locked up in his basement mere hours after confessing to killing a man and almost killing Casper.

He exhales. "Because I need you to stay here. I have things to do before we can go home. I can't have you going to Casper."

"I don't want to go to Casper. I want to go home. To my house. My parents are probably freaking out by now."

"Stop all of this. This isn't your home. You don't belong here. You belong with me in Chateau de Fées. As soon as we return, I will make sure you don't ever remember Casper for as long as you live."

"Please stop. It was all a story. A fantasy. None of it is real. I have to get home."

He raises his hand to my cheek and caresses it. "It is real. All of it. We're immortals who love each other. I'm sorry you don't remember, but once we get home, it will all come back to you." He takes my hands in his. "You are my life. You are mine and I am yours. You have to trust me." His eyes are full of passion and it's so easy to be swept up in his words. I can play along and maybe he'll release me.

"I trust you. Please don't keep me here. You're right about Casper. He manipulated me."

He studies me and I can tell he's mulling it over in his mind. He closes his eyes. "It won't be much longer."

"What do you have to do? Why can't we go now?"

"I have some things to take care of in the meantime. Everything will be okay." He presses his lips against mine and softly kisses me. He starts walking back up the stairs.

"Wait. Don't leave me here, Vincent. Please." I'm practically begging on my hands and knees.

"A few more days. That's all." He trudges up the stairs, opens the door, and locks it once he closes it.

I have to find a way to break the door down. I have to get out of here. I wait until I hear him leave, but I can't hear any footsteps above me. It's like I'm in a sound barrier or something. I look around the room but there isn't anything I can use to wail at the door. Unless I take apart the bed.

I charge up the stairs and slam my body against the thick door. Of course, nothing happens. I scream and beat against the door until my voice has gone hoarse and my fists are tender. Defeated, I sink to the top stair. I'm such a mess. Crying and shaking and scared for my life. I can't believe everything that's happened. I've been dating a complete sociopath and I defended him. Repeatedly. What does that say about me?

How in the hell does he know about mine and Casper's dreams? None of this makes sense. He knows something that he's not saying. These thoughts race through my mind like the lights on a Simon Says game.

Leaning my head against the door, I think of ways to escape. How I wish I were at home or with Casper. I wish my mom were holding me or Casper could rescue me, not to sound like a damsel in distress. I can get out of this. I will escape.

Forty-Five

"I've found the witch," Casper says. "She can turn us into mortals. No one will ever find us."

"Mortals? How?"

"I don't know the details. She said to come to her when I've found you. I want to be with you forever, Megan. Every time they rip us apart, it nearly kills me."

"I will do whatever it takes to be with you."

He kisses me with hard edge and holds me tightly against his body. I melt from the softness of his lips and from the heat of his touch. I revel in the hope we will be together.

"Come on." He takes my hand, and we walk through the woods to an old shack.

The door opens and an old woman with long white hair emerges.

"I see you have found me." She invites us in with her long bony fingers.

We exchange wary looks, step inside, and sit at a round table with her. It's dim inside with cobwebs and clocks. Clocks everywhere. Each ticking at different times. There are thousands of vials and bottles filled with different colored liquids. Candles light the entire shack, which looks much bigger inside than outside.

"So, you want to become mortals," she says, her voice light and smooth.

"Yes," Casper answers.

The old woman raises an eyebrow. Her blue eyes are glossed over, and her skin is lucid and wrinkled. "Why do you immortals want to become mortal?"

"The Elves and Sprites are constantly at war because of us and other reasons," Casper says. "We wish to be together forever without being ripped apart."

The woman nods with a cunning smile. "How miraculous? An Elf and a Sprite fell in love and doomed us all."

I tense gripping Casper's hand. "Is there no hope for us? We never meant to hurt anyone with our love. We—"

The witch raises her hand to stop me. "I feel your love. It is overflowing. It's radiant like the sun. If only others could see your beautiful aura." She purses her lips and watches us in silence for a few moments. "Perhaps making you into mortals is the right thing to do. You will be gone, therefore, maybe the wars will end, and we can have peace again." She scoffs. "Don't hold your breath. However, I'm willing to try." She turns to her shelves of vials and takes two. She faces us again. "Now, you must listen to me very carefully. Once you are mortal, know that you will die in each lifetime. You won't be a true mortal because you will reincarnate after each life. Dreams will bring you together."

"Bring us together?" I ask. "Won't we already know each other?"

"Being mortal is different. You start a new life and live however long that life is, you die, then you start over in a new life. You may not know each other. You may hate each other or find each other at the very end of your lives or worse never find each other. Years in a mortal life are longer than our immortal ones."

"So, there's no guarantee we'll be together?" My voice shakes and Casper tightens his grip.

"I would say that about anyone else but you two. Your love is stronger than I have ever seen. Even if you ended up hating each other in a life, you would eventually remember who you are. Remember, dreams will bring you together. It might take a while for you to remember what the dreams mean."

"What kind of dreams will they be?" Casper asks.

"Of your immortal life together."

"Once we turn mortal, we cannot return to the immortal world?"

"If you can find me, or find someone like me, you can give up your mortal life and return here. If you possess the Nuummite Jewel, you can return as well. Know this, they will never stop looking for you," she warns.

"They'll never know we're in the mortal world," Casper says.

"No. They won't."

"Except Vincent has the Jewel, Casper. He could find us."

"Only if he knows we are in the mortal world."

"Will you be safe?" I ask the witch. "If Vincent and his men come lurking around asking questions?"

She curls her wrinkled lips into an appreciative smile. "I will be fine. I am more powerful than anyone knows. You deserve happiness and peace. However, be forewarned. If you find each other, and one dies before the other, you must live out the rest of your life. These mortal lives are not to be wasted. I only ask one thing in return."

"Of course. Anything," Casper says.

"Use these lives to find a way to stop the wars."

Casper nods and looks to me as if asking my opinion. I agree and he turns back to the woman. "What do we have to do?"

"Drink this potion." She hands us a clear liquid in a vial. "And say goodbye for now."

My stomach drops. "We just found each other."

"I will give you a minute." She leaves the room.

"Casper." My heart races as I clutch onto him.

He pulls me to him, cradling my head. He peers into my eyes with a heated gaze. "This is the only way, Megan. We will see each other in the next life." He wipes a tear from my cheek. "Don't cry. Know that I will always love you."

"What if we don't find each other? Then what?"

"I'd rather be without you for one lifetime than never have you at all. This is all we have, and I can't be apart from you. I will find you."

I search his eyes. He's right. This is all we have.

We look at each other, potions in hand, and wanting more than anything for a way to be together without interference. It is crazy to think that in each life we'll have to find each other and fall in love over and over. I fear us hating each other or never finding each other.

The possibly of being with him without the Sprites hunting us down and trying to kill us encourages us to drink. After we down the drink, we embrace, clutching onto each other. We kiss like it is our last then blackness.

Forty-Six

I'm still stuck in Vincent's basement and my body hurts from throwing myself against the door. I don't know how many days it's been since he locked me up. He seldom visits, and part of me wonders if he forgot about me.

I remember my dream.

Flashes of memories fill my head. I steady myself against the stair rail as the memories race forth. Everything makes sense now. The dreams. The visions. My whole immortal life with Casper. We found each other. In every single lifetime. Except one.

The one with Vincent. The one where he took me back home, but I aged. Will that happen again if he takes me back?

How did Vincent find us? I have to find Casper before Vincent finds a way to take me back and erase my memory again. He will kill Casper and Casper will start a new life without me. The dreams would torture him. He would search endlessly for many lifetimes. I can't let Vincent do this to us. I have to end this. Is he trying to kill Casper now? He said he had things to take care of. I have to get out of here.

Frantically searching through drawers of the vanity for anything, I dig inside and find matches. I pick up the box. I can set this whole house on fire. I wonder if this is considered suicide, but I have to end this. The war. The fighting. I can't imagine how many more have died because of us.

I light the match and take a breath. I will find Casper in the next life. I drop the match and light another one and drop it on the bed. I empty the matchbox and stand back and watch the flames feed themselves across the room. Soon the room starts filling with smoke.

"Vincent," I scream.

Seconds later I hear the door open, and he clamors down the stairs. "Megan!"

"Help me."

The flames grow latching onto anything they can.

He jumps through the flames and grabs my hands. I tug him and knee him hard in the groin. I snatch a flaming pillow, burning my arms, and press it to his face. He lets out a cry and I dart up the stairs. It's dark and my heart feels as if it's going to burst through my chest. I shakily open the front door and charge for the woods. I can't promise it'll lead me someplace safe, but I don't care. My bare feet step over dead pine straw and sticks. I feel cuts forming but I ignore them. I run as fast as I can. I don't know how far Casper's house is, but I know the way and I won't stop running until I get there.

It seems like days that I run, and I finally reach a familiar street.

I finally arrive at his house. It's dark inside and out. It looks like no one is there. I ring the doorbell and try to turn the knob. This time it's locked.

"Casper," I scream. I'm sure the neighbors welcome the sounds I'm making but I have to find him. I have to tell him everything. I hold myself as my body is shaking but I know it's not only from the unusually cold night.

Headlights blind me as they sweep across the driveway and the car halts. The door opens and I see a man running toward me.

"Megan." I immediately relax when I hear his voice.

I collide with him; my arms wrap around him as

he catches me. He holds me so tight, and I breathe him in.

"I've been looking everywhere for you." He exhales. I feel the air travel over my head. "I'm so sorry. I knew Vincent took you, but I didn't know where." He holds me at arm's length and looks at me.

"Casper, he locked me up in his basement. He's the one who tried to kill you. He killed Adam."

"What?"

"I left him in his burning house. I left him to die."

Casper holds me tight. "It's okay. You're safe. Are you okay?"

I nod. "You were right all along. I love you—" His lips cut me off. Soft, warm, and eager. We finally found each other. I lose myself in his kiss, forgetting, if only for a moment, being held captive and knowing Vincent's confessions. Casper is all I need, and I want him forever.

He rests his forehead against mine. His hands rake through my hair, which feels matted. He takes a deep breath and kisses my forehead. He tilts my chin up. "I love you." He fans my hair out from my shoulders and his fingers brush against my neck, sending a hot shiver up my spine. I can't tear myself away from his brown eyes and I inhale as he leans down, pressing his warm lips to mine. The same rush fills me like in my dreams. There is nothing else but us. I press my body to his, wanting him closer as our mouths slip over each other's. My heart can't be tamed. It's like a wild horse who has escaped, freely running.

A loud crack sounds, though it doesn't distract me enough to pull away from Casper. But the blinding white pain that suddenly washes over me makes my whole body slack. He holds me to keep me from falling.

"Megan," he cries.

The pain swallows me. Burning, searing throbbing. I take short, shallow breaths.

"Hold on, Megan!" His voice is muffled by the pierce ringing in my ears. My eyes are heavy, and my body is numbing. I can still hear his voice and I cling onto it with everything I have. "I need help. Please. She's...shot!"

His words jumble in my mind as my eyes close. Slowly, slowly, I hear no other sounds.

This is how I die in this lifetime. Murder. Now Casper will have to live out his entire life without me.

We will be reborn again. We will find each other. We will end this. We must find a way to end the war. End Vincent. We will find a way to live.

PLAYLIST

Lost In Paradise – Evanescence

Heartlines – Florence + the Machine

Nursery Rhyme of Innocence and Experience – Natalie Merchant

Invented – Jimmy Eat World

Imaginary – Evanescence

Shake It Out (acoustic) – Florence + the Machine

When You Find Me – Joshua Radin

Joga – Bjork

Not In Love – Crystal Castles feat. Robert Smith

Snow White Queen – Evanescence

Song Beneath The Song – Maria Taylor

My Slow World – Baron Bane

The Ocean – Tegan & Sara

Stay – Rihanna feat. Mikky Ekko

My Heart Is Broken – Evanescence

Carrigan Richards is the author of *Pieces of Me* and the *Elemental Enchanters Series*. She graduated from Kennesaw State University with a degree in English. She lives near Atlanta with her dog.

www.carriganrichards.com

Social: @authorcarriganrichards